Single
White Failure

GJH Sibson

Clink
Street

Published by Clink Street Publishing 2021

Copyright © 2021

First edition.

ISBN:
978-1-913962-51-7 - paperback
978-1-913962-52-4 - ebook

Introduction

This book was first written in the early Noughties and published in 2005. Some of the references may seem out of date already - online dating was in its infancy, there was barely any social media. And no one was swiping right. And yet, the dance was still the same. Read and enjoy - I'm just glad that a lot of the crap that happened to me only happened offline.

GJHS 2021

Praise for Single White Failure

"A terrific debut - we have all been there!"
Toby Young, The Spectator

"If you've lost your faith in men, he may just restore it."
The Sunday Times

"You may be my perfect man."
Vanessa Feltz, BBC Radio 2

"My favourite writer on dating!"
Samantha Brett, Sydney Morning Herald

"I can't remember the last book that made me laugh so much. Buy two copies - one to keep, and the other to lend to your friends."
Amazon Reader

For Neddy 1

&

Neddy 2

Acknowledgments

Strictly speaking, I'm not sure that anyone should be *thanked* for helping with this book – it would be like thanking your girlfriend for bringing home a virulent strain of gonorrhoea. It only seemed funny after the event.

But in the good spirit of *Acknowledgements* sections, there are a number of people I would like to thank for their support, understanding and listening to me for hours on end, boring them with ideas and unfunny jokes.

My Mum and Dad, for everything; Hayley, for her unbelievable support, intelligence and inspiration; Pop, for being the original storyteller; Matt, Ed, Will H. and Stockers, for being there during the early days; Rosie, for reading the first drafts and kindly laughing; Oscar, F. Scott and George Mac. F; to the Durham crowd – *non nobis solum*.

Contents

1

Closure

There are days that change your life. Leaving someone you love is no exception. Perhaps it is one of the biggest, and hardest, things that you can ever commit to. Committing to someone at the outset is easy, deciding to leave them is harder. Sometimes you just have to do it. My life is about to change, this is the story, prepare yourself.

I'm late home from work. I didn't need to be, I'm supposed to be at the theatre with my girlfriend Jessica. Right now, I should be getting lost around Covent Garden, looking for the Donmar Warehouse. Jessica should be sinking into an ever-deeper mood, moaning about her feet (women in China are protesting against having their feet bound in a similar fashion) and rebuking me for my lack of planning – for forgetting the address. Instead, I'm walking home slowly, taking my time, making sure I'll be an hour late. Why? Because tonight is the night. I still love her, and it is the hardest thing I have ever had to do. But the relationship has been sour for over a year. I told her I had to work late because I thought it would create one of those arguments that has pitted our lives for the past twelve months. I thought it would be easier to end it if there was a huge scene, lots of name calling and the usual nasty remarks. Bollocks would I be so lucky.

With a certain amount of fear, and my lunch threatening to launch an assault on my gullet, I slowly slide my key into the front door. It takes several attempts, my hand is trembling like an alcoholic's reaching for a tinny.

Finally, the door gives in. The flat is as quiet as a vacuum. Where is she? Like Jason tracking down the Gorgon, I pick my way through the hall, peering into each of the rooms. I hear a soft hissing from the lounge. As I peer around the door, I see MTV is on mute. In front of the box, Jessica is sitting cross-legged, her straightening irons discarded on her lap. She is absorbed by 50 Cent, silently beatboxing with his homies.

'Hi,' I say.

She turns around and gives me a loving, understanding smile.

'Hi, baby. I'm so sorry you had to stay late.'

Eh? Am I in the right flat? I smile, planting myself down on the sofa. She sits next to me. I can't look at her, I feel ill. She looks beautiful, in her dressing gown and all made-up. She tells me that she has even prepared a meal, as we can no longer make the theatre. God, I feel awful.

But this isn't normal – she must have read my mind. She is being totally reasonable. I don't remember the last time things were like this. My intricate plan of staging a huge row has backfired. Jessica is always doing that, being one step ahead. 'It's no good, be strong,' I tell myself – 'you have to leave her!'

For the past six months, I have been trying to make this relationship work. But at every turn, Jessica makes me feel worse about myself. Last Valentine's Day, I decided to give her a painting, one that I'd done myself. Painting is one of my hobbies and, whilst I'm no great master, I'm usually pretty pleased with my efforts. And I thought it would be romantic and personal.

I spent a couple of months sketching, priming and painting. The subject was an abstract nude, a woman half-crouched with her back to the world, tasteful and sincere, bright colours and sweeping strokes that took in Mother Nature's curves. A week before the hallowed day, Jessica brought up the subject of presents. It had been an expensive Christmas and she thought it would be a nice alternative to make each other something.

'It's funny you should suggest that,' I said, 'because I've been working on something for you for a while.'

'What is it?' she demanded. 'Is it a painting?'

'Well, er, yes,' I said, taken aback. The tone in her voice was one of a 17-year-old princess who's just been bought a Beamer by her doting father for passing her driving test, but it's in silver rather than pink. I could tell that a tantrum was about to come on.

'You said,' she's emphatic, her voice rising, 'that you were doing me a painting anyway. I want something else too. Where's the thought in giving me a painting you were already going to give me?'

'Okay, sorry.'

Pathetic, I know. Admittedly, I had mentioned the painting idea some time before, in passing. And that was why I thought it'd make a nice Valentine's gift. Obviously not.

I felt awful at the time, like I'd disappointed her. I was sure the painting had been a good idea, thoughtful and romantic. But I'd begun to doubt it. In the end, she convinced me I was in the wrong. I made her something else, and apologised.

I know now that I had been an idiot. I should have got out back then, when I still had some self-respect. But Jessica had this amazing, malevolent power of making me feel as if I was constantly wronging her, she riddled me with guilt.

That's why tonight would be the hardest thing that I have ever done. And I love her so much. It might sound strange that I love her, but also that I have to leave her. Many relationships end because of an infidelity, but there are reasons far worse than that. The mental hurt that one partner can inflict on the other, the guilt and self-loathing, it can be unbearable. To have them throw all those thoughtful gestures back at you, for reasons that you can't even begin to understand, there's little else worse. It's taken me so long to build up the strength to do this; weeks, months even. This time of anguish and self-doubt can't continue. I'm just going to have to take the traditional stance of laying it out in the open, clearly, once and for all.

'Jessica.' I never call her Jessica. Usually, it's 'darling' or 'sweetheart'. She can see I'm looking solemn. My stomach somersaults. I'm telling myself, 'Don't back out now, be a man you can do it.' But look at those puppy dog eyes.

'I don't, what I mean is, I think, well the thing is.' Good one Max, that's telling her.

'Oh my God you're leaving me,' she screams. The bottom lip is trembling, the eyes are welling, and that's just me. She's starting to cry.

'You can't leave me like this!'

Her indignant tone takes me back to my university finals. On the day of my penultimate exam, my mum had collapsed with a stroke – her second in four months. I frantically tried to get hold of my dad, keep in touch with the hospital staff and track down my classics tutor. I really needed Jessica to be there with me. She was at a Spa in Hampshire with her mother. I had called her immediately.

'Oh, that's awful,' she said.

'I know, and I can't get through on my dad's mobile. I wish you were here.'

'I'm sure she'll be fine.' She didn't get the hint.

'I've told my tutor, I'm postponing the exam. Darling, it'd be great if you could come back and help, I really need you.'

'Come back, oh no, I can't,' she said. 'I have a Reiki appointment at five tonight, and mum and I still have another day here.'

I had hoped she would be there for me. That she'd have dropped everything and caught the next train back. But no. It's at such times that you realise all those pillow promises are made of straw.

Is the crying an act or does she mean it? Perhaps she does love me and will miss me. No, think back to the all the things she's done – the countless times you've been there for her, all those romantic gestures never returned and, what's more, the hordes of cash you've spent on her in return for moaning and poodle sitting. Yes, she has a poodle, which since day one has been the bane of my life. This damn dog means more to her than me, which has done wonders for my masculinity.

'Yes, I'm sorry,' I'm perspiring profusely, 'it's not working out, I can't handle you, the poodle or your mum any longer.'

As well as the effing dog, her mum has also invaded our once 'idyllic' life together. It sounds unbelievable, but over the past eighteen months they have shared a room and, at times, a bed. You would have thought that after two failed marriages and that much alimony, she could have afforded somewhere more spacious than the right-hand side of her daughter's bed. But who am I kidding, I knew all along it was just a ploy to control Jessica's life. They tried to tell me it was normal but I wasn't convinced – and I'm from Norfolk!

I spend the next ten minutes trying to put into words why I have to leave her. It's not long enough. I don't want to blame her, but I want to be honest as well. She's crying a lot, I feel worse. My head feels as if it's been dunked in a bucket of ice water. My senses are dulled, I can't breathe or hear properly. I notice that the look in her eyes has changed. From the initial shock, she's now growing mad, mad about the fact that I might, conceivably, have the audacity to leave her – 'no one has ever... left... *ME*.'

I'm expecting a slap. It's not like it would be the first time. It's happened before. A misdemeanour would often result in the nearest projectile coming my way. This time it's my Thrills album – she wouldn't throw one of her own. I can't remember clearly now, but I could have sworn that she passed over the nearest CDs until she got her hands on one of mine.

Her usual routine kicks in, it was only a matter of time. She tries to make me feel insecure, that I can't live without her. She's the only one who cares for me, apparently. She'll kill herself if I leave, she'll get in the car this instant and drive herself into a wall!

Suddenly, her mother returns – this is my cue to leave before she grows more psychotic and the poodle savages me.

I hastily leave the flat, abandoning Jessica in a mixed state of disbelief, anger and tears. I'm shaking like a child. As always, she has reduced me to a quivering idiot. I feel like I need to laugh, ecstatically. Not because I'm happy, I just don't know what else to do. Nervous energy. My ears are still pounding, and I have pins and needles in my extremities.

I feel awful, her tears are fresh on my own cheeks. Suddenly, I feel very alone, frightened; I have given up my partner. The person that I have been with for the last three years, the person I love, is no longer there.

'Have I done the right thing?' I ask myself. The street starts spinning. I know that the die is cast, there's no going back and now I've done it, I'm not sure it was the right thing to do.

I stop at the corner of the street to dry-heave. Nothing happens. I rest my arm on the iron railings, my head is pounding. Perhaps it was me being unreasonable. She was right, I should have given her the painting and made something else, it wasn't much to ask for. How could I have been so thoughtless. And when my mum had the stroke, Jessica had been on a break with her mum. And when I told her I wanted to try triathlon, the smirk she wore told me as plain as day, she had no faith in me whatsoever. I guess she was right. Oh my God, I've made a terrible mistake.

But why do I always feel awful around her? That can't be normal. Your partner is supposed to make you feel better, not worse. I don't think I was being unreasonable – all my friends said I wasn't.

The street is still spinning. I wretch again. Still nothing.

I have a good, long walk through Battersea Park and over Chelsea Bridge. In my head, I replay all the major conflicts we have endured over the past eighteen months, after the honeymoon period had passed. As I begin to think with a newly acquired clarity, I feel satisfied that on each occasion, I was being completely reasonable, but that I always backed down.

The wave of sadness slowly begins to ebb away. Resolving each of our arguments in my head reaffirms my decision.

I begin to feel good – the rotten relationship has been purged. It is like a weight has been lifted off of my shoulders. I am conscious that I can be me again; this old life, from a time before Jessica, the person I used to know has shaken off this other subservient Max, a man with no will of his own. The pain hasn't subsided, I'm conscious that it might not for some time. But I am certain that what I have done is best for me. I start to feel excited, liberated and optimistic. Sort of.

I call up my friend Edward and ask him if he can get to the Bluebird in half an hour. For a drink. I need to talk.

After another thirty minutes of scratching the pavement on Beaufort Street, I edge towards the café on the King's Road. It's a clear evening, the hazy glow of the patio heaters creates a shimmer like Chelsea's in the Mojave Desert. I cross the busy road and, hands in pockets, I stand looking into the café that I come to so often. Tonight, I'm a million miles away. Like James Stewart in *that* Christmas film, I feel like a voyeur, looking in on a happy and beautiful world, people meeting one another, holding hands over tables and exchanging kisses. No one seems to be noticing me. I'm half-expecting George Bailey to stare back at me from the reflection in the window. The last time I was here, Jessica and I had been celebrating her graduation. The melancholy peaks and I fear I've left my *wonderful life* behind.

2

Like the blind men of Indostan describing an elephant

'I know it was tough buddy, but from what you told us, it was definitely for the best,' says Ed as he greets me.

He and Raj, another old friend from uni, were already there when I'd arrived. They'd made the shrewd decision to order three bottles of wine in anticipation. I can always rely upon them, even though I haven't been the best friend over the past few months. I have neglected them, Jessica thought they were a bad influence on me. And they have put up with more than their fair share of my moaning. They know they're in store for some more!

When they spotted me skulk into the café, they both stood up and took it in turns to give me a manly bear hug, accompanied by several compassionate pats on the back. Everyone's looking. I pull up a pew and, like a disgruntled teenager, I plonk myself down. Neither of them says anything for a moment, they're looking hard at me, wearing understanding looks on their faces. This is blokeish support at its best. I start telling them what happened; they're both quiet, listening intently. Ed's doing the nodding, Raj has got the glass-filling covered. All of a sudden, Raj's mobile interrupts my ripping yarn – it's his mum, she's checking I'm ok. He's embarrassed and breaks into Urdu. Ed's hand is still on my shoulder, he realises it's been there a moment too long and self-consciously removes it. They're doing a grand job, and only occasionally putting their foot in it with comments like, 'We knew she was a cow from the start' – not necessarily what I want to hear, but the intention is there. If I'm being honest, it makes me chuckle, and I need a laugh.

Ed's dispensing his usual sincere advice. He's not trying to convince me, he can see I had come to terms with the decision months ago. Ed is an old school friend and a barrister, working in commercial law. When Jessica wasn't there for me after my mum's stroke, Ed had told his clerk to assign the case he was working on to a colleague. He got on the first train to my parents' place. Ed's a bright chap too. Previous tenants in his prestigious set include one Prime Minister, two Lord Chancellors and a top TV presenter. He has always loved his job and revelled in an attention for detail; an academic, professional attention to detail rather than an artistic or creative one. He's the type of guy who'll need his wife to coordinate his wardrobe or decide on a colour scheme for their house. Ed wouldn't have a clue.

There's something 'bread and butter' about Ed. He earns a good packet, but to him, materialism is frivolity. I'm forever being slated about the amount of clothes I buy. Occasionally, he'll splash out on something big, like his precious SLK. God knows what that is, I only know one car from the next by what colour it is. Ed's collectables are his family and friends. Traditionally, he's the sort of chap who'd settle down with the first girl he really likes, and he would have a more successful marriage than the rest of us lumped together. But fate had a different role for him – Lady London wasn't about to let him get away that easy.

'Ed's right,' Raj confirms. 'And now, for the first time, we are all single together'.

I hadn't thought about it like that. I wanted to feel like something good might come out of this rotten day, and I couldn't help but smile as Raj said this. It has to be a good thing, being single together. It should herald the beginning of a new age. God knows, I needed to believe it.

Women form the centre of most men's lives. I know they do mine. We are on a perpetual quest to find a mate, from our early adolescence to the day we get hitched, sometimes even beyond then. For you and me, it's a journey, a voyage of discovery. It's not easy understanding these creatures of riddles, although we all try. Our free time is spent on the hunt, be it partying at the weekends or while holidaying in the Balearics. The sole aim is to find a woman.

'For the first time in our lives we will be actually dating,' Raj points out.

Raj is right, I've never actually *dated* before. It sounds silly, at my age, not to have dated. I met my first girlfriend at school. And I was introduced to Jessica by a friend at university. It was all pretty organic. But I had never actively gone out with the single purpose of chatting up girls in the hope that one might lead to a first date, and from there to subsequent dates and finally ending up with a new girlfriend. I was shit scared.

'We'll be dating woman who are looking for the same thing as us,' Raj continued, 'London women; smart, attractive, successful, and… independent.'

'What about love?' Ed asks.

Raj looks at Ed and frowns, he almost rebukes him. 'Well, that can come later. We don't all need to be in search of love right now. London is to be enjoyed, love is for after London.'

I think back to when I was younger. 'Guys I'm so out of practice, it was easy before, now how am I ever going to convince one of these professional-type women to go out with *me*.'

When you're in your teens, relationships are terribly serious, innocent affairs. They have a thoroughly attractive, simplistic air about them. You know you love the other person, you spend every day in and out of each other's pockets. I know I loved my first girlfriend very much and she still means a lot to me, even though we were never right for one another. The weekends would be spent together, as part of a big group of friends, drinking crap super-strength cider around camp fires on the beach and philosophising on life. The summers were long, the winters were cosy. You think that this state of bliss is never going to end. Then one day you go off to university, and it does. For no other reason than you grow up and the inevitable happens – you become totally different people.

University had been a blast, it was a three year social event with a £10,000 cover charge. Many of my friends who met at college did go on to marry one another but most of us just wanted to party, after all a relationship only overcomplicated an easy life. You realise now how love was free flowing and easy going back then. And yes, to a certain extent, sex plays a big part of student life. Halls of residence with thin walls and roomies at it like Duracell bunnies. Drunken nights that led to you pulling some swamp donkey in a dingy club as you dance away to Chesney Hawkes. But let's not pretend that was dating.

In the back of our minds, we knew for the most part that we were destined for London. Bright lights, big city, bounty of women. We used to think that London would be our time; a cosmopolitan city full of gorgeous girls from around the globe.

'He's right,' says Ed, 'women don't need us, apart from sex, they don't need a man anymore.'

'Even that can be bought in various sizes from Ann Summers,' Raj chips in. 'We have time enough to settle down, everyone in this town is working hard and outside of work hours they just want to have a good time. It's as simple as that.'

As adolescent guys we had seen older family friends and male relatives make the journey to London. We saw them lead the man-about-town life and we wanted to buy into that lifestyle. We also heard our friends' older sisters brag of their decadent lives – it was right out of the Marquis de Sade. It was everywhere you turned, our generation were liberated and we wanted to be on the receiving end of it. After all, what is the point of slogging your guts out in the office if you can't enjoy the fruits of your labour? Buying the sportscar, having the swish pad, going to the great clubs, romancing the pretty girls. Being the would-be playboy is every young guy's dream. For a man, his mid-twenties is one of the pinnacles of his life, independence with means and, in our case, in one of the world's most exciting cities. And now we could enjoy this together, as young single men.

'Guys this is our time. We're in a liberated London, with independent women.'

'What's your point Raj?' I don't get it, I still feel like I'll be forever in love-Siberia. This isn't the time to be thinking about approaching random women in bars.

'London women have everything they want. They're like us; ambitious, carefree and independent. We're different to other generations, they're be looking for the same things in a relationship as us. It'll be somewhere between a one-night stand and a serious monogamous relationship.'

'Really?' Will it be that simple?' I wasn't convinced.

'It's dating on our terms, on mutual terms,' Ed sums up.

Was Ed right? I had never given it a moment's thought before. Why should I; I had lived within the security blanket of a loving relationship, albeit the love felt like it was flowing in one direction only. I had never before given a thought to the city's thriving singleton community.

'Of course Ed's right,' Raj booms.

Raj is certain about everything, there's never a grey area. He's as charming as Ed but they're as different as you can get. Raj charms through his sheer cheek and humour. You simply can't help but like the guy, even with his Huggy Bear wardrobe.

Raj's parents had moved over to England from Kashmir in the 60s. They can't be faulted for the way in which they have brought up their family. They have nurtured a respectful family, and Raj is typical of a first generation Brit – culturally aware, progressive in his thinking, but Mummy Khan still retains the power to put the kibosh on any of his major decisions, particularly those involving potential daughters-in-law – 'Yasmin, what are you talking about, have you seen the size of her mother, what about Reena?'

There's no doubt in my mind, that one day, he will be a successful and wealthy entrepreneur. At the moment he is excelling in his job as an advertising agent at Saatchi's. Champagne binges and vacuous models, that's an average day for Raj. He plays along with it, for the sake of his career, but it's not really his scene. He is a threat to no one and gets on with people of all walks and all ages. Everybody wants to know Raj.

He was the only one of us to have had a serious relationship during our university days. But after an amicable separation and with oodles of cash Raj was already looking forward to investing some considerable wedge in the London Muffdaq.

'Yeah you're right. There's nothing for me to be worried about.'

I guess that the idea of dating for the first time in three years would have most people reaching for their poison of choice. It had been years since I had had to approach a girl and sell myself – in the marketing way, I mean.

'Sure, we can understand that,' Raj carries on, 'but you gotta pick yourself up, brush yourself down and give it a go.' I suppose he has a point.

'I think that what Raj is trying to say,' Ed wades in, Raj rolls his eyes, 'is that there's nothing to fear. We're in London now. Everyone's an equal. You only have to watch TV shows, read magazines or modern literature.'

'He means chicklit, like *Bridget Jones* or the *Sex in the City* girls,' Raj pipes up helpfully, as if I didn't understand.

'Yes, yes, I know that.'

'You're a newly single guy,' he ignores me and carries on, 'some women out there will be looking for a PH.' Ed and I look blank. 'A Potential Husband,' Raj sighs like a primary school teacher at the end of their patience. 'But the majority of women in this city don't have the time or the inclination. We get in the way of their busy lives, like they do in ours. That's just how London is. There will be plenty of girls out there looking for a very casual relationship, even no strings attached sex, if that's what you're up for.'

He has a point. It is what we are led to believe. Kate Moss, Bridget, Carrie, Samantha. These are the types of women that guys of our generation see as the role models for the women of our generation. What reason did we have to disbelieve this image of the newly reborn swinging London. Where sex has become something to be enjoyed for its own sake. Where men can use women and women can use men. And what about that promise of the playboy lifestyle?

We are the freshers in this hedonistic European capital, envied by all countries of the world; even the Americans are rediscovering its awesome electrifying presence. Wasn't it Samuel Johnson who said that once you were tired of London you were tired of life itself?

Raj was right, this couldn't be a more exciting time to be single. There is no need to fear the dating world, of becoming a citizen of Singleton. We are all constantly teetering on the edge of an abyss and each time you meet someone you like, you have to make that leap of faith. What the hell else can you do, never date again? I suppose the main difference back then was that we were more positive, less cynical, excited and naive. A terrible combination.

3

The prick teaser

I was blissfully unaware of my own naivety when, for the first time in my life as an adult, I re-entered the dating scene. If I knew then what I know now, I'd have turned on my heels and run for the nearest monastery. Raj and Ed and me. Three single guys in London. Three silly buggers – ready to go over the top.

A couple of weeks have passed since I severed myself from the person whom I thought was my soulmate. I have been lost during the evenings. To stop myself moping about I have been out on the beers with the guys most nights. At no point have I questioned my decision, but it still feels like a part of me is missing.

A few weeks ago I moved into my new apartment in Angel, near Islington. It's convenient because it's slap bang in the centre of the City. On my walk into work I get to savour all those great things that make London the city it is; red double-deckers, fresh coffee from the Italian deli under my flat, cheap posters advertising bands you've never heard of slapped over the entire façade of dilapidated shops, and small grocers selling vegetables from around the world, the names of which you can't pronounce (the shops or the produce).

It's a Saturday morning, I have just been out to secure my daily intake of coffee from said Italian bistro. They always see me looking in a state. Thankfully, this morning, I don't have the remnants of a spicy Americano pizza in my hair, which on a good day looks slightly unkempt. I pay a fortune for that look; a slightly ruffled, chopped brown mess. My hairdresser assures me it looks great, everyone else seems to think I've just been dragged through the proverbial hawthorn backwards. Are there hawthorns in London? Ed actually winced when I first told him that I paid forty-five quid for the pleasure.

Today it looks particularly untidy. Frankly, I couldn't be arsed. I usually go through this ritual every morning, ruffling with the help of a large blob of *moulding mud*. This morning I am the survivor of a particularly messy evening the night before. It was my flat-warming. I gathered as many of my friends as I could muster at the last minute. Ed and Raj were there, of course. It was my first party without Jessica. It seemed strange, people were asking after her, and hadn't realised that we weren't together any more. They all said it was for the best, once I had put them on the right track. I'm not sure if they meant it, or if they were just trying to make me feel better. Isn't it funny how people always want to know who finished it?

One of the people who made it to the party was Pippa. I knew her from university as well, although she had been on a different course. She had packed in her office job to promote nightclubs in the West End. She's a great girl, a social butterfly of the wildest colours. This girl organises *the* best parties, and most importantly they are wall to wall with prime totty. She was thrilled to find out I was single again. Not like that. I could never sleep with Pippa, it wouldn't seem normal. She is a very attractive girl, but I have known her far too long. It would be like sleeping with your sister. Any opportunity she gets she loves to play matchmaker. Last night she told me about a party she is throwing next weekend to launch a new nightclub. Apparently there will be photos in some society magazine the following week (the type that no one buys), there will be cocktails and nibbles, and one of those annoying goodie bags at the end of the night for those that stay to the bitter end – the type that looks like an expensive carrier bag from a boutique but which contains only useless trinkets produced by famous brands. A Gucci lollipop or a Mont Blanc tin opener.

'Don't worry Max, there will be lots of lovely single girls, all around our age and professionals,' she smiles mischievously, 'attractive, intelligent and you'll have your pick, I'll see to that darling. Besides have I ever let you down before?'

So this will be my first chance to have a bite at the adult dating cherry. And she's right, she has a flawless track record in this department. Pippa has organised some awesome parties in the past and she had always come up trumps with the goods. Only then I had been attached. It had always been a case of *look but don't touch*. But now, as Stiffler would say, "the lock is off the cock, man."

I had told the boys about it immediately. We all agreed that this would be a perfect opportunity to score.

Ed can hardly contain his excitement, 'Guys, picking up at this kind of party is always easier than in a club because you have an implied authentication stamped on your forehead, *you're a friend of my friend, you must be ok.'*

'Poor girls, they won't know what's hit them. I can smell it already,' Raj says.

'Smell what?' I enquire.

'Ass!' Raj explains, as if the answer was obvious all along.

'You really are an idiot sometimes,' Ed laughs.

If these girls are anything like Pippa, this is going to be a belter of a party. Why should I have any reason to think that things would be different now. Oh, how naive I am.

The party has a masquerade theme and is taking place in a vaulted cellar off Sloane Square. Whilst Raj had been at work for the launch of some expensive French fragrance or other, Ed and I have spent the day searching for a mask that I could wear. In true Ed fashion he already had his mask organised. Of course, he had. Naturally, Ed owns a genuine Venetian mask, decorated in gold leaf that his parents had brought back from Venice, as a souvenir.

'What did you say it was called again?' I ask looking at the birdlike mask with its colossal 'beak'.

'Il Dottore.'

'Jesus, it's got a bloody big nose, is that to overcompensate for something else?'

He ignores me.

I couldn't find anything as impressive. Most of the things we came across were covered in feathers and were pink, not quite the image I had in mind. Eventually we found a plain white mask in a toy shop in Covent Garden. Perfect. It was a Friday the 13th type thing that covers the whole of the face. I hit upon the ingenious idea of painting the mask, so I grabbed a children's pack of poster paints as well. Later that day I painted it in blues and reds to resemble a Maori tribal mask. Not only did it look a semi-professional effort, I thought it would give off a good vibe to the girls; original, manly and yet creative. With the rest of me top to toe in black, I now look like a cross between the Milk Tray man and a serial killer.

We arrive at the club, brimming with high expectations. My hair has reassumed its carefully ruffled appearance. I have to admit that Ed's mask does look like the dogs you-know-whats. Ed's large frame suits the cloak that he has opted to wear with his black trousers and shirt. He's gone the whole hog with the Venetian theme. With his hair slicked down though, I can't help but think he reminds me of the *Phantom of the Opera*.

We are the first there. Trying to act chilled, we prop ourselves up at the bar and start on the G&Ts. After all we'll need to loosen up a little by the time the droves of stunners arrive. If the women are as good as Pippa has made out, we'll have to be talking the talk with the best of them. God, I haven't done this in so long. I am seriously out of practice, I haven't actually chatted a girl up in years, literally.

There's some movement by the entrance to the bar. It looks like a couple of girls have arrived; no man would be wearing a mask like that. Or rather no straight man would be wearing a mask like that – not even Raj.

'Darling, I'm so glad you've come.'

It's Pippa. She is looking as lovely as always, tonight in a black cocktail dress and resplendent in an ostrich feather bower. Like Ed, she has opted for an authentic Venetian mask, rather than the Bob Ross paint-by-numbers job. Ed tells me that her mask is known as a Principessa, apparently because it is inspired by Cinderella.

'You must be Ed,' she says to him, smiling. 'I have some lovely girls coming for you this evening, you boys are going to have so much fun!'

That mischievous glint in her eye tells me everything I need to know. Through our masks we give each other an approving glance.

It's not long before the first of the women start to arrive. Pippa is right, there are some fit looking girls. Although you can't exactly be sure. The downside with the masked theme is that you don't know what the girls actually look like. You have to go on her figure, I suppose. Briefly, a horrible image pops into my head; that one of these seemingly delectable creatures whips off her Venetian mask to reveal Richard Blackwood sneering back at me licentiously. And they say adverts don't affect our subconscious.

'Ed, what happens if we spend ages chatting a girl up, putting in the ground work, and then she turns out to be a bit of a hound?'

He thinks for a minute, and then says, 'Well, pull her anyway, and when you get back to hers, ask her to keep the mask on.'

The girls have all made a tremendous effort, with lovely dresses and an array of fanciful masks. I feel shabby in my homemade job. All of a sudden there are mutterings from the other side of the bar. The mutterings become giggles. Someone must have arrived. Sure enough, moments later a new addition to the party is cutting a swathe through the bar. The person is wearing a brightly coloured papier-mâché mask that looks like a clown, with a very long red nose. Two round helium balloons, both gold, are tied to the back of his belt (it's clearly a guy) and are caused to hover a foot or so above his head. He is heading towards us.

'Hey, what's happening knob-jockeys?'

We should have known it would be Raj.

'Ha, what on earth are you wearing?' Ed inquires, justifiably.

'It's a Latino carnival mask,' Raj begins to explain. 'I thought the long nose would infer length in other, more important areas.'

Raj looks up at Ed, 'See you had the same idea, mate, but I guess you're making an ironic statement.'

Raj starts laughing but Ed just acts aloof, drawing himself up as if to rise above the quip. I can tell Raj is smiling cheekily, just like his Venetian mask; its large red lips are shaped into a perpetual mischievous grin.

'Same with the balloons,' he points upwards, as if we hadn't noticed, 'subliminal messaging.'

'Yes, very subtle,' I laugh.

Having furnished the latecomer with a whiskey and coke, we stand in semi-silence, just scoping out the joint. We perform the ritual that all men go through they enter a bar or club or, for that matter, anywhere – the Rating Ritual. It's an automatic procedure I've performed since puberty, when I stopped screaming "yuck" at the television each time I saw a couple kiss. I'm like an automaton, a sleazy Robocop. And when you're part of a group you all do it at the same time, in silence. There is an unspoken understanding that we all have to complete this ritual before the evening can continue. The odd nod or wink is permitted, to draw your fellow Neanderthals' attention to an especially hot target. Other than that there is no talking, no discussion. This is something we have to do for ourselves. Once the first round has been bought, and we're steadily sinking our first bottle of beer, only then will we compare notes.

Now my eyes flit from one girl to the next. The rating begins. Yes. No. No. Definitely not. Ten pinter. Body yes, face no. Face yes, body no. Respectfully doable. No. Dear God, no. Eminently doable. And so it continues.

After a few minutes of this we enter the conflab stage of the ritual. After much weighing up a consensus is reached and we agree to head for a group of girls standing on their own, by the far side of the bar. The four girls are all holding masks to their eyes, the types on sticks that provide just enough mystery to the bearer. Their masks are an elegant tease, which reveal enough of their pretty faces to let you know they are attractive.

'Hi, we thought we'd come over and mingle, my name's Max and this is…' Before I can complete the introductions, the girl on the left chips in, 'Hi Max I'm Mandy, and this is Claire, Sarah and Zoë.'ë

Okay, wait a goddamnpickinminute. This is not normal. The party has only just started. And this is the first group of girls we have approached and they haven't told us to get lost, or given us the collective cold shoulder. Where are the incredulous looks that say 'Er hel-lo, as if we'd be interested in you.' In fact, unless I'm mistaken, they seem keen to chat. Incredible. This is a good start and far better going than I remember. Perhaps this will be easier than I expected.

'Hi, this is my friend Edward.'

They all gape at the nose, and smile sweetly. In unison they say 'Hi' to Ed, like competitors harmonising for a girl band audition.

'So what do you do?' Mandy asks.

And there it is; a question that I would grow to hear and recognise for what it truly is – a part of a girl's own Rating Ritual. There's a silence that always follows this most loaded of questions, which is so incredibly uncomfortable and embarrassing. Even now their eyes are wide open and they are leaning ever more slightly forward, in anticipation of our answer. I could swear that they are chanting under their breath 'Let it be good; doctor, lawyer, banker, millionaire.' Later, I would learn that the answer to this question can, but not necessarily, change your fate for the entire evening. But at this early stage in my new dating life I didn't think anything of it. In the future I would see this curveball coming a mile off. I answer honestly and innocently.

'Well I'm in PR,' I say.

'And I'm a barrister,' Ed adds.

Like spectators on Wimbledon's centre court, the girls shift their focus from me to Ed and finally rest upon the ridiculously dressed Raj.

'Yeah, and I'm Ron Jeremy's body-double,' Raj blurts.

The girls don't laugh. I don't think they had even noticed him, which isn't easy. They are almost startled by the enormity of his mask's nose. Their eyes, now wide open with intrigue, move from his face to the two floating golden globes, bobbing arrogantly above his head. The mask smiles back at them.

'Seriously though, I'm in advertising, I work at Saatchi's,' Raj decides to tell the truth, he must have spotted the loaded question too. At hearing our professions there had been a sudden release, you could almost hear their whoops of joy. It was a sort of climax, a euphoria at the promise of a man with cash. Once they regained their composure and the initial excitement had passed, we moved onto other important topics like where do we live, have we bought or do we rent, do we have life assurance?

Before we knew it, the three of us had separated and were holding court with our own little harem of attentive listeners. This can't be right, they are giggling in the right places at our inane jokes and surprisingly, my own group of three masked beauties genuinely seem interested in my story of how I fucked up my interview with Max Clifford. The next thing you know, they'll be joining me in playing 'Bohemian Rhapsody' on air guitar or offering to sort my *FHM* back catalogue by the Dewey Decimal system. Something is up. This has never happened before, that's for sure. I actually think that these very attractive girls are all really keen. I look over to Ed, who is sweet talking his own posse of lovelies. He looks up and, tipping his bottle of Bud in my direction, acknowledges our initial success. I look towards Raj. He is lost in play with two blonde girls and his balloons.

It is at this point that a girl to my left grabs my arm.

'Hi honey, how ya doin'?' she says.

Her voice is like a lullaby. I can't quite place her accent, it is clearly antipodean, but I never know the difference between the Kiwis and the Aussies. She is a tall, deep-tanned girl with an abundance of tight blonde curls cascading around her shoulders.

'Hi, I'm having a great time, thanks. How about you?'

'S'alright. I like your mask by the way.' Her lips curl upwards at the corner. 'It is supposed to be a Maori war mask, isn't it?'

'Er, yes, precisely,' I say bluffing. 'How did you know that?'

'Well I grew up with the Maoris,' she says, smiling again, this time to reveal a row of perfect white teeth.

Shit, are Maoris from Australia or New Zealand? It's like that popular factoid; are polar bears from the Arctic and penguins from the Antarctic, or vice versa? I can never bloody remember. Wait, A for Aborigine and A for Australia, that means Maoris are from New Zealand. She's a Kiwi.

'So how long have you been over from New Zealand?' I ask, as if the possibility that she is an Aussie had never entered my mind for a nanosecond.

'Wow, I'm impressed, most people think I'm from Australia.'

'Huh, well, how could they?!'

And we both share a contemptuous laugh at those ignoramuses.

'Sorry, my name's Max.'

'Hi Max, I'm Leticia,' she says.

We lean in and exchange kisses, her skin is so very soft. As we move apart, Leticia places her hands behind her head and undoes the black satin ribbon of her powder pink mask. The mask is like something Zorro might have worn, although not in pink, of course. She draws the mask from her face to expose a dainty nose and high cheekbones. Her blue eyes flash with passion.

This is the first time that this has happened to me. That a girl has approached me. *She* is the one that grabbed *my* arm. She came over here expressly to talk to me. She is attracted to me. Ed and Raj were right, we're equals. We all want the same thing, London women are the way forward.

'So Max, are you single or attached?' and then she pauses, her gaze intensifies, 'or attached and looking?'

Bloody hell, this girl doesn't mince her words. So, I proceed to tell her about my recent release, sorry I mean the tragedy of my recent break up with Jessica. Then we get onto the age thing. She's surprised that I'm only 26. I didn't realise then that age could be such an issue. As a 26-year-old guy no one will look at you twice if you're seen out arm-in-arm with an 18-year-old girl or a 40-year-old woman. But, it seems, the same thing cannot be said to apply to a woman in her mid-thirties upwards who is seeing a man ten years her junior. Other people judge her in a way that the man is never judged. I reckoned this girl is somewhere around my own age. I tell her that I have recently turned 26.

'Oh, so what star sign does that make you?' she asks.

Okay, I know what you're thinking, that should have been alarm bell number one, cue for me to make that mad dash to my Benedictine Brothers. But for some reason I choose to ignore it.

'I'm a Scorpio,' I answer.

'A Scorpio, eh?' she shouts out, enthusiastically.

Leticia reels off all the qualities, and some of the flaws, pertaining to male Scorpios. It's all the usual claptrap, but I'm enjoying it. I always think that talking about someone's star sign is like palm reading at high school. It's an excuse to flirt with the other person outrageously while maintaining the pretence of an interesting discussion. As she comes to the end of her list, she says mischievously, 'And, as you'll probably know, Scorpio is the sexual sign of the Zodiac.' She pauses for a second, considering me, 'Do you like sex?'

Holy crap where did that come from? I just about manage to keep down my swig of beer that I had been drinking coolly as she paddled her astrological mumbo jumbo.

'Well, yes, I er, like it as much as the next guy.'

Okay, so I need to improve my chat. In fairness, I wasn't expecting a glamazon from down under to take me by the scruff of my neck and out ante me in the flirting stakes.

'C'mon Max, are you good in bed?' She's showing me no mercy.

Even I can see by now that this girl is clearly 'up for it'. The thing is, it's fazing me slightly to have a woman like Leticia talking to me in such a direct manner. Isn't this my job, to try it on with the dodgy questions? There is a marked difference, however, when a girl flirts with a guy like this, the lines employed cease to be sleazy and pervy. In fact, they have a newly found air of acceptability about them.

I am not used to women being so direct, but this is nothing, she is just getting warmed up. I'm trying to act cool, as if I've been asked these questions by even more attractive women a hundred times before.

'Well I guess you'd have to ask the women I've been with for the answer, I couldn't say.'

I don't think I'm succeeding. I thought that being coy would be the best tack to take. If I'm being honest, I'm probably hoping to avoid further uncomfortable questioning and bumble my way along to a cheeky snog. Somehow I don't think that Leticia will let me off that easy.

'Bollocks,' she screams out. 'You must know if you're good or not?'

There's no point in putting up a fight with a chick like this. There's nothing for it but to be as frank in this as her. And I suppose that she has a point, I must have some notion of my sexual prowess, or the lack thereof. So, I tell her that I think I am pretty damn good. And what about her? What a surprise, she loves sex.

'Max...' her eyes look up at me seductively, she's playing erotically with rim of her glass.

Dear God, it's like something out of a cheesy Channel 5 soft porn film.

'What kind of thing do you like doing in bed?' she grins cheekily as she polishes off her question and devours the olive in her martini.

I don't believe someone I have known for all of five minutes has ever asked me that before. I know what the answer is, but it feels a little uncomfortable coming out with it. After all, what is acceptable to some people isn't to others. Will she judge me? I decide to couch my reply in non-committal phraseology.

'Well, I think it's important to be confident, find out what each other likes and most importantly, to be totally relaxed and utterly uninhibited.'

A good answer I thought. But it is clearly not sufficient for Leticia. She laughs, and I can't help thinking that it's partially *at me*. I feel about as composed as a 15-year-old who's just caught a glimpse of a girl's boob for the first time.

'I agree,' she says, 'that's all good, but tell me what you would do to me.'

Jesus. The only time a girl has asked me that is in the heat of the moment when things start getting a little *dirty*. And then it's in the confines of my bedroom (or hers) rather than in a bustling bar. Each time I go to answer I stop, worrying again, what is acceptable, what isn't. Do I mention positions, places, touching, kissing, penetrating? Fuck. I keep it quite romantic, and throw in the odd evocative word like mouth, lick, penetrate and taste. I try and repaint the Hollywood lovemaking scene. She's groaning and murmuring as I tell her. It's kind of getting me going, I have to stop myself before I go too far and introduce vegetables and whisks into my list. For the first time, it seems to satisfy her.

Now it's her turn.

'I like to use all different types of sensations, hot...' there's a pause as she sips her drink and allows one of the ice cubes to flow between those luscious lips and loll around on her tongue, '... and cold!'

All of a sudden she loses control of the ice cube, which, having a mind of its own, escapes her ample mouth. It dribbles down her chin like a small glacier before dropping to the floor. We pretend it hasn't happened. Trying to regain her cool composure the little hussy returns to her sexual fantasies. The words she uses are considerably more explicit than mine. Phrases like 'on my knees' and 'taking you all in' seem to crop up at regular intervals.

'Ultimately, I like to take control, and do every position possible.'

When you are making a move on a girl, or as in this case when she is about to devour *you*, there is nothing quite as annoying as when her single friend(s) interrupts your pathetic flirting. Where a girl is out on the pull with a friend who is attached or has, herself, been unsuccessful in pulling, that friend is the antithesis of the guy's wingman. If I'm out with Raj and he is about to score with a girl by the bar, but I have had no luck of my own, I will still do everything in my power to make his journey to the honeypot as slick as possible. Sometimes, if they come as a pair, this will require me to take one for the team. This is a particularly unpleasant task if the subject of my friend's lasciviousness has a moose for a mate who is acting a gooseberry. To help him out you are obliged to crack on to the minging friend. Another time springs to mind, my old friend Dirty Dave saw me getting it on with a girl on the dancefloor of a club in Marbella. Knowing that I had no local currency of my own, my brother-in-arms brushed past me and shoved a wad of euros into my sweaty palm, enough for a taxi ride back to her hotel. Women don't seem to operate like that. Unless the girl's friend has scored herself, the jolly green demon possesses miss singleton and *she* will do everything in her power to derail your attempts to get into her best friend's knickers.

A girl has suddenly interrupted our salacious banter and half-wedged herself between Leticia and myself. With her back to me, and ignoring my very existence, the girl says, 'Leticia, I think I'm heading off now.'

It's the unsuccessful best friend.

'Oh great,' I'm thinking. 'We get this far, being as erotic as hell, and now she's going to sod off.'

'Are you coming with me?' the thoughtful bint asks Leticia, continuing to ignore my presence.

Leticia's gaze hasn't left mine since her friend appeared. I know that I'm probably looking downright despondent at the thought of her going home. A man may like to think of himself as the predator, and on the whole it's true, but when a woman knows what she wants then nothing will stand in her way. Not that I'm complaining, of course.

'Am I leaving now?' my little minx asks me.

Without any pretence of politeness the friend finally reels round and scowls at me. It's as if she's saying 'How dare you speak to my friend, she can do ten times better than you, you little sex obsessed shit!' I look from Leticia to the unimpressed mate, and back to Leticia, who is still smiling mischievously. I'm sure she's wanting me to say 'No, you're not going yet, I want you to stay.' But I can't. I'm not sure why exactly. The friend has now replaced the scowl with a look of sheer contempt, her hands are on her hips. I imagine her calling out, like an audience member on the *Ricki Lake* show, 'Girlfriend, ya shud leave him!' Leticia gets bored waiting for me to answer, I think she can sense the animosity in the air. In the end she answers for me, 'No, I'm not leaving yet, he's coming home with me.'

And at that point the rest of the evening is set in motion, without any consultation with myself. I feel like a commodity; a sex object in a futuristic 70s sci-fi, where gender roles have been reversed and the world is run by Amazonian cyborgs. I have been selected by this particular punter for her evening's entertainment. How refreshing.

The girlfriend storms out, rolling her eyes as she strides past Leticia, who simply laughs it off. I sink my beer and decide to regain some of the masculine ground that I surrendered earlier. After all, as a guy I need to feel as if I played at least some part in picking her up. If not for my benefit then for Ed and Raj. I grab Leticia's hand, 'Come on, let's go to your place.' I can see she wasn't expecting it, but was far from protesting. I wink at Ed as I leave the bar.

Luckily there are a wealth of cabs loitering around the exit to the club. Having hailed one, we huddle up on the back seat. I love London cabs. I don't mean the shitty unlicensed minicabs, with their dodgy air fresheners and plastic faux-leather foam-backed seats. The London Hackney cab, a.k.a. the *black cab,* is one of the world's few remaining forms of luxury travel. We don't respect it or savour it nearly enough. It is the Orient Express of the public highway.

As we sink back and get comfy, I realise that something is up. The sexy little harlot that I dragged out of the bar has started to cuddle and pet me affectionately. You might be thinking, 'What's wrong with that?' And I'll tell you. This behaviour, this form of affection doesn't seem to be the epitome of her carnal offerings in the club. Shouldn't she be leaning back into the corner of the cab, making eyes at me seductively but refusing my touch? Or perhaps ravishing my neck with kisses and whispering dirty promises, nibbling at my ear as she goes. Shouldn't she have at least undone my flies by now?

We eventually pull up at her predictable Victorian terrace somewhere in Fulham. I pay the cabbie. After we enter her flat I pass by the bedroom, and I think to myself, 'Aye, aye there'll be fun and games to be had in there in a matter of minutes.'

'Cup of tea?' she asks merrily, returning to her lullaby-like voice.

Sorry, did I hear right, a cup of tea? Unless I'm mistaken, I haven't come round to visit an elderly relative. 'Don't be so bloody harsh Max,' I think to myself. She probably just wants to feel relaxed, light up some candles, get in the mood. I shouldn't be so mercenary, I guess. I sit down, politely and recline on the sofa, kick off my shoes and make myself at home.

'Milk?' she asks.

'Er, yes milk's fine, thanks.'

I can't help thinking 'Milk, no bloody sugar and you naked on this coffee table will do just fine.' All of her talk back at the bar has got me all wound up. I'm starting to feel really horny and I want to dispense with all the crap and start acting out some of our earlier conversations. Bring on the hot and the cold.

Fifteen minutes later I'm sitting there clasping a Harry Potter mug and poring over her family photo album. Aunty Beryl from Waikokopu and her strange breed of Shih Tzu couldn't have been further from my mind. But I continue to feign an interest, spurred on only by the fact that each page I turn is a page closer to the fornicating we had discussed at length an hour earlier. Alas, I hadn't realised that this was just volume one of eight of her antipodean life history. Another hour passes, she's rabbiting away next to me. Each picture has a story to accompany it. As I'm almost ready to fall asleep, she leans across and starts to nibble at my ear once again. It's like an instant pick me up. Am I about to be rewarded for my incontrovertible enthusiasm for her mind-numbing mementos? She gets up and slinks off to the bedroom. 'This is it!' I'm thinking. It's 3 am but the fun's about to start. I jump up and run through the lounge towards the bedroom, hopping as I pull off one sock and then the other. I'm stripped down to my boxers before you can shout 'Kiwis do it down under.' I dive onto her enormous bed and am swallowed up by the sea of fluffy cushions. I get under the sheets and wait for her. The toilet flushes, I hear the bathroom light-pull go and the door click shut. The hall light is turned off. There she is, standing in the door way, lit by the bedside lamp. She's wearing French knickers and a pretty little silk camisole. At last. She slinks in and wriggles under the sheets. She resumes her nibbling. It's annoying the hell out of me but I'm now so up for it that she could be doing a Mike Tyson and chew the ear clean off and I wouldn't care.

'Goodnight.'

Goodnight. What the fuck do you mean 'goodnight'? Goodnight and a kiss on the cheek. What happened to re-enacting the *Karma Sutra*, the hot and the cold, that ravenous insatiable sexual appetite she had bragged about just hours earlier.

'I'm sorry I don't go all the way on the first night, the man never comes back.'

4

Shameless

I'm a man. I'm in control, right? I mean, I have been led to believe that I am the dominant branch of the species. Since the days I played with Action Man, to being weaned, during my early adult life, on *Baywatch* and *Commando*. Anthropologists have studied primitive man, man of the jungle and man of the deserts. It is widely accepted that man is the predator, the hunter gatherer; he is *primus inter pares*. Zoologists have witnessed similar patterns in the animal kingdom. Take the lion for example, when *he* wants some action, he just grabs the lioness by the mane and hops on. The same kind of virility and prowess is evidenced with studs, roosters and bulls alike. In the human world I'm the same, aren't I? Am I bollocks.

The fact that it is actually women who are the superior really hit home one evening, when I was out with my mate Abbie. She works just around the corner from me, near Soho. One of her colleagues is leaving London, for a spell in the company's New York office. The girl's leaving drinks are being held at a bar called Blend, in Covent Garden. I'm running late. As I was about to leave, my boss had asked me to give him an update on a client's advert. I hate it when I get caught like that, just as I'm sneaking out the office at the end of a busy week. Now the rain is whipping around me, like a small whirlwind, as I rush along the stone streets of Covent Garden. Through the blur of the rain, I can make out the vibrant glows of small neon lights, advertising the bar. Rushing for shelter, and the warmth and vibe of the bar, I hurl myself through the entrance, the doorman holding the door open for me, like a matador pulling back his cloak to let the bull pass. Standing on the threshold, the wet now a dim and distant history, I brush myself down. Reminiscent of an Irish wolfhound, coming in from the wet, I shake the rain from my coat. Panting slightly, from my short burst of exercise, I regain my composure and, for the first time, glance around the interior of the bar.

This West End bar has been taken over by the bunch of city types, lawyers and insurance brokers, kitted out in their Lewin's shirts and Tyrwhitt's ties, the odd Hermès accessory stands out but that aside there is nothing exceptional. That is apart from the vision of beauty who locked into my gaze the moment I walked in. The bar itself is at the far end of the room. Between me and the bar are a sea of early drinkers that could resemble a city trading floor. This particular girl is sat at one of a series of high-level bar tables, like an oasis amongst the swathes of pinstripes. Her eyes still haven't left mine. She smiles and turns to her male drinking companion, laughing. I'm not sure she's not laughing at me, or telling him some strange chap is checking her out. Next thing I know, my day dreaming is broken by Abbie waving at me from the other side of the bar.

I buy her a Cosmopolitan, the inept barman is having trouble lighting the zest of the orange peel. It's funny, I think that is one of life's myths. I have never seen a barman do that properly. They always screw it up. After having about four attempts, they acknowledge the serious loss of cool points and just squeeze the unobliging rind, before throwing it into the cocktail, accepting defeat. You know, I reckon a barman who could do that, first time off, would never be short of sex, he'd have the chicks lining up. Christ, if he can light the zest of an orange, making a woman climax would be a cinch by comparison.

I get myself a Carib. Luckily, the barman has less trouble inserting the wedge of lime than with his citrus pyrotechnics. I waste no time in getting the lowdown on the attractive girl from Abbie.

'So who is that lovely looking girl?'

'What girl?' she says.

Although why she had to ask I don't know, I would have thought it was pretty clear. Sure, there were one or two lookers, but none as stunningly attractive as this particular girl.

'The one by the bar, at the table with the chap,' I say as if it's obvious.

She looks in the direction of my none too subtle nods. A look of realisation and mirth breaks across her face.

'Oh you don't have a chance!' she exclaims with great enthusiasm. 'That's Isabel,' she unhelpfully explains.

'Right, and who is *Isabel?*' I probe further, not put asunder by my flatmate's lack of confidence in my abilities.

'She's a big earner in the corporate department of the firm. Every man has tried it on with her, from senior partner down to the photocopy lads. She has none of it.'

Okay, so it's not looking great. But, there it is again, she's looking in my direction. She's smiling at me, not breaking her gaze. You know when someone is making it obvious that they are interested. You know a flirt when you see one. Don't you?

'But Abbie, I swear she is flirting with me. She keeps giving me the eye!' I try and convince her.

'Are you sure?' she feels the need to question me. Probably rightly so.

'Yes, I'm telling you, from the moment I walked in, she keeps staring at me. Why don't you introduce us?'

I put the proposal to her. She doesn't look too happy about it.

'This is a work do, it's not entirely appropriate,' she tries to wriggle out of it.

'Well according to you, I have no chance anyway, so we can just have a civilised chat.'

She wants to argue back, but she sees my point.

'Come on then!'

We make our way through the crowds at the bar. The woman in question, Isabel, has seen us making our way through the punters. She's still looking at me, but with a little surprise in her eyes, as if she has just spotted the office twunt coming over to tell her his latest whacky joke. She keeps leaning across to whisper at the bloke she is seated next to, her eyes never leaving mine. We get nearer. A few feet away and the guy next to her gets up from his seat and walks in the other direction, not even acknowledging us, as we approach.

'Hi Isabel, thought I'd come over and say hi.'

'Hi, how's things?' she asks Abbie, refusing to acknowledge me.

'Pretty tired, been a busy week. Oh, by the way, this is my friend Max.'

Abbie makes the introduction in exemplary fashion. Isabel looks from Abbie, to me. She looks even more beautiful up close. Straight dark blonde hair down to her shoulders, and large liquid eyes. Blue pools that send you swimming. A face like a doll's and a very toned, athletic figure, bronzed from a recent tropical holiday, no doubt. Abbie had already told me that she is 31, but you would swear she isn't a day over 25. Her skin is perfect.

'Hi, pleased to meet you,' she shakes my hand.

I feel like we're at a board meeting, rather than having a bevvy in a bar. The cheekiness, and the openness, that had been in her eyes, moments before, has disappeared. She's civil, but she seems utterly indifferent. There's no flirtation in those eyes. 'Is it the same girl?' I think to myself, but a quick look around tells me she doesn't have a friendlier twin tucked away somewhere.

As soon as the introduction has been dispensed with, Isabel turns her attention to Abbie.

'Abbie, didn't you say you were seeing some chap who is in the army?' she asks her.

She is right, too. Abbie has been dating some lieutenant in the Black Watch for the last few weeks. He is up at his regiment's HQ at the moment, waiting for the all clear to head out to the Gulf. There is a rumour that the Black Watch will be heading to the southern city of Basra, in Iraq, which they will help to secure. Just so the Americans can head north and make a dog's dinner of taking Baghdad, probably killing a load of Brits along the way. Still I suppose there will be more Military Crosses for our boys pulling dying comrades from burning trucks who came under friendly fire, it's not all bad news.

'Yes, he's just waiting for orders to head to Iraq,' she informs the Ice Maiden.

'I thought so,' Isabel says. 'My partner left for there today, flew to southern Iraq.'

'Oh, I didn't realise,' Abbie turns her gaze on me.

'Yes, he's a major in the Royal Welsh,' she thoughtfully elaborates.

'Ah, the good old Royal Welsh,' I think to myself, I'm sure my grandfather fought with them in the Second World War. Wait-a-fucking-minute! Her *partner*? As in a boyfriend, lover, significant-other-half? I look at Abbie, she gives me that predictable *I told you so* look. She's amused by my total surprise. And yet, I was sure she had been flirting with me, the little minx.

'Yes, we've been together nine years,' she continues, as if to twist the knife deeper. 'I am so worried for him, particularly as we hope to get married, when he returns in six months.'

Well, that does it. I am happy to hold up my hands when I'm wrong. I must have totally misread her signals. But I was convinced. After all, why would you stare at someone in such a way, unless you were interested. Perhaps she never thought I would actually come over and talk to her. Who knows? All I do know is that you go through a great deal from the age of 22 to 31, and if you manage to stay with someone for that long, it has to be something special. And so, I put any thoughts of cracking onto this girl well out of my mind. The annoying thing is, having just been introduced, I now have to stand here and listen to these two lovesick puppies drone on about their other halves.

'Oh they're so brave' or 'It is so difficult being a forces "wife", isn't it Abbie? – Oh yes, it is Isabel.'

And they carry on like this for some fifteen minutes. I feel like I am in a Rudyard Kipling book, or in a production of *The Four Feathers*. Not only do I feel miffed at losing out on this woman, the pair of them are also doing a damned good job of making me feel utterly inadequate. Forget *small penis* jokes. Just compare your average office working bloke to one of Her Majesty's soldiers, and an officer at that, and it will make him feel about 'this small' – envisage your thumb and forefinger half an inch apart. And, of course, once we had agreed (well they agreed and I nodded when prompted) how brave they are, we moved onto the compelling subject of their regimental uniforms. Okay move the forefinger so it is now only a quarter inch from your thumb. They both start giggling uncontrollably like schoolgirls. They are all a fluster over camouflage gear and *cam* paint. Then there's the civvies uniform and, of course, the *pièce de résistance*, the officer's dress uniform. This is the part of the officer's wardrobe which is reserved for formal occasions – navy trousers, red stripes, fitted coats, sabre at the side etc., etc. As you can probably appreciate, I am completely excluded from this conversation. I look around the bar, to see if there are any other girls that I like the look of. Preferably ones that won't be liable to talk about Sean Bean and varieties of military dress.

It's at this moment, lost in boredom and concentration (I'm trying to peel the label off my beer bottle without tearing it) that I am shocked for a second time. Isabel and Abbie have been talking about the history of Isabel's relationship with the Major. The fact that over nine years they have had their ups and downs, the odd break up here and there but they always get back together. Apparently she knows that he is the one for her, she will marry him. She has told him that they have to get engaged when he returns from Iraq. The label is half-off, no significant tears as yet. While not being a serious participant to this conversation, I have been catching the odd snippets. And then Isabel drops the bombshell, 'But he won't be back for six months, and while he's away I have every intention of playing around, and having some fun.'

She says it coolly, as if it's what we expected her to say. It really is not the logical conclusion to the preceding conversation. I can't believe I heard her correctly, it's such a bolt out the blue that I involuntarily tear the beer label in two, half is in my hand and the other half remains stuck firmly to the bottle. Just as well I hadn't been taking a swig, otherwise the two girls would have been covered in a spray of warm Mexican lager. Abbie is as stunned as I am, we look at each other in utter disbelief. So I was right, she had been flirting with me. Abbie's disbelief turns to a stifled laugh. She raises her eyebrows at me, and mischievously gives me a wink, 'I think I'm going to go the little girl's room.' And with that she turns on her heels, leaving the Major's missus and me together, alone.

Isabel is still smiling at Abbie's back, as she melts into the throng. Up to this point Isabel hasn't paid me any real attention. I feel nervous. What on earth am I going to talk to her about? As it happens, I don't have to struggle thinking for a topic for long.

'Thank God for that,' Isabel says with a sigh, as soon as Abbie is out of earshot. She turns on her bar stool to face me properly for the first time. Instantly, the flirty girl I spotted when I arrived at the bar has returned. I can see the desire in her eye, the infidelity.

'I wondered how long it would be until she left the two of us alone!'

And all of a sudden the hunter has become the hunted. I can't believe I am hearing this right. Does this girl have no shame whatsoever? I babble something incoherent, finishing with a pathetic light-hearted chuckle, as if in agreement.

'You were flirting with me, across the room, from the moment you walked in, weren't you?' the merciless hussy says.

Clearly, she isn't going to make this easy for me. I tell her that, yes, I spotted her almost immediately. And that I thought she was reciprocating in the flirting antics. At this she laughs, and says that she was.

'I think it's important that when you fancy someone, you let them know. Life's too short not to act on these things.'

I mutter something to the effect that I agree completely, hence why I came over and introduced myself.

'But you have a boyfriend, well more than that by the sounds of things, a fiancée,' I allude to the barrier that prevents us acting on this flirting.

'Yes, I do, but as I just said, I have six months while he's not here, and I want to have some fun.'

Now call me old fashioned, but you just don't cheat on your other half, whom you have been with for nearly a decade. Especially when the poor bastard has been sent to war that day. He's risking his life for Queen and country, he may well die. And the thing that is keeping him warm at night, keeping him sane as he sits holed-up in some godforsaken place, with a bunch of goatherds for company, is the very thing that is offering to 'open sesame' for the first random bloke she meets in a bar, the very day of his departure. If I'm being honest, the image of the Major in his dress uniform had been annoying me a few moments earlier, but now I feel quite gutted for the bloke. Granted, not quite gutted enough to pass off any invitation from his girlfriend to sample her lip gloss flavour of choice, but there is a tinge of guilt nevertheless.

'You know, you really are my type. You are everything that I go for in a man, and it's rare that you click like we did, the moment you walked in. I know you felt it too!'

Clearly, she's not feeling even the remotest twinge of guilt. And she is right. Of course she is, she's not the type of lass who is ever wrong, and if she is, you keep *shtum*.

Blow me if she doesn't lean up from her perch and, placing one hand on my cheek, envelopes my lips with hers. Her wet tongue convinces my lips to open, it darts into my mouth and makes contact with mine. It's a brief kiss, but a good one. As she pulls away, I look towards the other side of the bar to see Abbie shaking her head in humorous disgust. The rest of her work colleagues are looking on in disbelief; Isabel has gone from Miss Perfect to Miss Perfidious.

The crowd give up on the bar and drag us along to the place next door, which has a dancefloor. Isabel won't let me out of her grasp, not that there is anywhere else I would sooner be. I still feel slightly guilty. But I try and repress it. I have been telling myself, 'It's her boyfriend, I owe this guy nothing, it's her choice, she's the one who owes him the loyalty, not me.' It still feels wrong.

In the club we form a group with Abbie and some of her workmates to dance to some bump n' grind tunes. Both my hands are planted firmly on Isabel's *derrière*. Her buttocks, like two badgers in a sack, jaunt along to the music. Intermittently one of us leans in for a snog. It's not remotely romantic. As I position myself for one of my bouts of tonsil hockey, she pulls my ear towards her lips. She whispers, 'You know, I'm very good at Yoga?'

I say that I don't. Then I add that I'm not very supple.

'Don't worry,' she retorts. 'I'm flexible enough for the both of us.'

The crazy bint then unhooks her arms from around my neck and, bending backwards at her waist, goes into what I believe yoga enthusiasts colloquially call the 'crab.' Her hands are behind her head, she is on all fours, but upside down, if you see what I mean? And then, with impressive control, she comes out of the *crab*. She returns to an upright position, before jumping up in the air, opening her legs, in a scissor-like movement, and lands on the floor in a splits. Now that, in itself, is quite a skill. But it's not the type of thing you want to see your woman do in a popular London nightspot to S Club 7's 'Reach'. Sorry, someone else's woman. Nevertheless.

I'm not an especially self-conscious guy, on the whole. However, this is one of those moments, when you want a chasm the size of the Grand Canyon to open up and swallow you. But I should know by now that nothing ever swallows on request. After dancing with Isabel, I can now empathise with the poor girl you see in a club whose drunk boyfriend thinks he can break dance or body pop to Van Morrison.

Whilst I am doing the *Timberlake* with the unfaithful extra to the contortionist act at the Moscow State Circus, Ed is having an equally bizarre encounter with a girl who promised so much. He had decided that bars were no longer his scene. Bars and clubs are good to frequent with your buddies but they aren't the place to find a girl. Well, obviously, you can find a girl in your average city watering hole but there is a high probability of picking up a bunny boiler. It's a bit like playing Russian roulette with a barrel full of slugs. I mean, how do you know if she's a crisp crunchy Golden Delicious or the rotter in the apple cart. Ed believed that where he had been going wrong was with his impulsiveness. Stopping girls in the street, at the supermarket or in a bar was no longer the solution. He doesn't know anything about them, their history. He would need to check out the filly's pedigree in future before making any commitment. And so it was that Ed found himself introduced to Louise, a friend of a friend of a friend. She is an educated girl whose charm had taken her to places that her peers only dreamt of through the storyboards in *Heat*. She had poise, elegance and sophistication tattooed on her left buttock. They had met over dinner, placed carefully next to each other by their attached friends. Ed had been instantly attracted to this statuesque girl with phoenix red hair. She is as manly as a woman can be whilst retaining an utmost feminine quality. Her voice is constantly tuned in the right key.

On their first meeting everything had seemed… delightful. But, after several months of single life in London, Ed had now grown to exercise caution. It is when things appear so good that you need to be at your most vigilant. Like the old Japanese proverb, as soon as the garden has reached perfection, a mighty wind blows in the seeds of weeds and the blossom falls from the trees. When you are least expecting it, beauty has been replaced with ugliness.

Seeing their mission near accomplished, the other dinner guests had bored of the pair's incessant chattering, like a pair of woodpeckers hammering away at the usual subjects that one talks about at dinner parties. The extraordinary thing is that this girl agrees with everything that Ed says, she is even finishing his sentences for him. It's not unusual for people to agree, but in Ed's case it is rarer to find a kindred ideologist in a woman. He verges somewhat on the English stoic; back to basics conservatism and family values ideals that are so wonderfully British of the 1950s but lost in today's world, not to mention in the City. Louise, however, seemed all for it. Acting the gentleman, his *faux* bastard persona now fully in remission, Ed had thanked Louise for a stimulating evening and asked if he could take her to the opera the following Tuesday, preceded by dinner at the Caprice. Ed might be tighter than your average Mallard's rusty nail hole but when a girl arrives on the scene his frugal disposition withers away.

I am still in the club with Isabel, who is bending over to show me the crab for the umpteenth time, I find myself apologising to the other punters who had been expecting to dance rather than being a member of the audience at a freakshow. I feel like Tom Cruise taking Dustin Hoffman out on the town. If only I was about to slink into one of those plush red seats at the Royal Opera House, with the curtain about to come up on *La Cenerentola*. That lucky bastard Ed is bound to be having a much better night than me – nice nosh and a normal girl, and I have always been partial to a bit of Rossini. Little did I know the surprise that was awaiting Edward as he was herded into the slaughter house, led by the carrot dangling in front of his Bottomesque nose.

Ed met Louise at Covent Garden tube station around six. As one of the most popular places to meet for an evening out in London, it also has to be one of the best places to conduct that addictive sport of 'people watching'. It is the premier social muster station in the capital, drawing all kinds of colourful characters. If I arrange to meet someone at Covent Garden, I never mind getting there early, to gaze upon the other people, lost in their own worlds. You see them searching for that familiar face amongst the endless tide of tourists, lovers, would-be lovers and entertainers pouring out through the barriers. Like meerkats on the African plains, they stand precariously on their tiptoes, to peer over shoulders and through the coppice of bodies. When they finally spot the subject of their rendezvous, they fall out of their pensive trance and, usually wearing a large smile, they wade through the swelling crowd. During the preceding few minutes you have been second guessing who will be paired with whom.

The rain has stopped but the streets are still glistening. The cobble stones look as if they have been highly polished. There's a man in his forties to Ed's left. He's rolling up and down on his heels. He's quite a tall man, he looks educated. The man's aftershave wafts upwind, overpowering those near him, of which, Ed is one. The man's head shifts, furtively, from left to right. A girl with short blonde hair and black roots stands between them. She's sort of slouching, her hands thrust deep into her jean pockets. On the other side of Ed there is a young woman, in her early twenties. Her long dark hair is well conditioned, she looks like she should be in a Timotei advert. Her freshly applied rouge is set off by her alabaster skin. Topiarised eyebrows, sparkling teeth, expectation and nervousness in her eyes. She's done up to the nines, black trousers and long black coat. She's clutching a fake LV handbag, with both hands, in front of her. Ed's head swings to the left, the tall man has started forward, with a jerk. He's spotted the subject of his meeting. She's a woman in her late twenties, also well-educated looking. A professional of something-or-other. She looks stunning, that's not to say that she is beautiful, but she has made the most of herself, and looks good for it. She's wearing a very short dress, fishnet tights and black FMBs. He grabs her and snogs her.

'A man would never kiss his wife like that,' Ed thinks to himself, 'he's definitely having an affair.'

Sure enough, pulling away, the man gives another surreptitious glance around the crowd. With his hand at the base of her back he gently guides his companion through the crowd and in the direction of their destination. As he disappears, and Ed's attention returns to looking for his own date, he notices the attractive girl to his right fidgeting. She's leaning forward slightly. No, yes, perhaps. She's chewing her lip.

'Don't do that,' he thinks, 'you'll get lipstick all over your teeth.'

Yes, definitely, she's spotted him, or her. She staggers uncertainly forward, still clutching her bag in the same fashion, as if it provides her with some security. A guy of the same age has seen her and is walking towards her, his eyes looking everywhere but at her, until they are up close. He goes to kiss her on the right cheek, she shows him her left and they almost lock lips. They look uncomfortable, yet brimming with excitement all the same. They laugh and correct themselves, and finally manage to exchange kisses. He stands aback , slightly, he's clearly paying her a compliment. Those pallid cheeks appear to be flushed with a little more colour. They must be on a first date.

'Hello, Edward.'

The voice comes out of nowhere. Startled he spins around to see Louise standing at his left. He hopes that she wasn't standing there long, thinking he was perving at some girl. Which, in fairness, would be a justified conclusion, normally. But it just so happened to be innocent, on this occasion. He pulls his attention away from the couple, snaps out of his reverie and remembers why he is at Covent Garden.

'Louise, hi, sorry I was lost in my own world,' Ed stammers.

'Yes, so I can see.'

She glances over his shoulder at the young girl, inviting him to explain himself. Ed follows her glance.

'Oh yes, ha ha,' he laughs nervously. 'Was just people watching, so interesting.'

'Of course,' she snaps back, smiling mischievously.

Hesitantly, but not without enthusiasm, Ed embraces his date and plants a kiss on each cheek. Greeting Louise he must have looked like the girl with the white cheeks, meeting her date, just a few moments ago. Although he needn't have been so concerned about what Louise thought. He really could have dropped any gentlemanly courtesies and snogged her there and then. But of course he didn't know that then. If he had known what she was really like, he would have been likely to commandeer one of the herd of rickshaws gathering outside the tube exit and pedal himself all the way back to the King's Road. Instead the perilous rickshaw ride would wait for later.

With their arms locked it is difficult to see who is leading whom to the restaurant. They pause by a man dressed as Charlie Chaplin. The only difference in appearance to the real McCoy is the fact he is sprayed silver, from head to toe. Each time a small child places money in the bowler hat he proffers, he pats them on the head.

'Surely this should be illegal,' Ed thinks to himself.

There are numerous other street entertainers, but never enough to satisfy the hordes of Italian and South American tourists that gather around them in awe. A fire-eater, a bearded lady and a contortionist (come to think of it my disco dance partner would have been right at home). The happy couple arrive at the illuminated entrance to the Caprice. The autumnal evening is left outside, in preference for the cosy interior of the Michelin starred restaurant. Ed might not be able to answer the *maitre d'* in French but Louise doesn't notice, she is too engrossed in the celebrity soap stars seated at the table next to theirs.

Over the starter, they talk about what has happened in their lives during the past week and how amusing it had been to be set up by their friends. Part of the way through the main course (confit of Gressingham duck for him and broiled sea bream for her) they run out of fresh topics, and so revisit those they had discussed at their first meeting. A relaxation sweeps over them, as they bask happily in the one's total and utter agreement with the other. And that's how they stay until coffee makes its way to their table, accompanied by a selection of handmade chocolates. Then the chat dries up. A slightly awkward silence dawns. Not that type of silence that is comfortable and to be enjoyed, where you feel so at ease in each other's company. Not that silence where your fingers find hers, through the debris of napkin rings, discarded baguette and half empty bottle of sparkling Italian mineral water. Those treasured moments gazing stupidly, in an almost bovine kind of way, into each other's eyes. No, this silence is uncomfortable, where you fumble for something to say. And so they devour the chocolates and swig back the scolding coffee.

Ed sighs with delight as the bill arrives, it signals the end of the first part of the date. The uncomfortable silence aside, he decides that the date is going okay, so far. Now he can parade her on his arm as they make the short walk to the Royal Opera House. Once the opera begins there'll be no more awkward silences. Everyone will be silent. No pressure. He knows that this has been a pest, which always plagues his first dates and that from this point on, things always usually go more smoothly.

Obediently they follow the usher from the oyster bar, in the high-ceilinged regency reception, where they had been drinking Veuve Clicquot. He leads them through the warren of hallways, lit subtly by antique French chandeliers, which give off a dull glow. They emerge into the great opera hall, at the summit of the circle and look down at the base camp that is the stalls. Having convinced two old birds in their pearls and clutching theatre binoculars to move out the way, Ed and Louise ease themselves into the scarlet carpet seats. Louise fidgets, making sure her dress isn't creased. After a couple of minutes of rearranging, flattening and tugging at her outfit, she pulls out the programme, for which Ed had forked out a small fortune. They feel obliged to pick their way pathologically through the list of players. They read out to each other irrelevant details on the biographies of singers they have never heard of. Sparingly the lights dim and they are plunged into an aristocratic darkness. The curtain comes up and a drunken Don Magnifico enters stage left, he is berating his two ugly daughters in Italian verse.

Ed had erroneously expected to watch this operatic fairy-tale in comparative tranquillity and to enjoy the mere presence of the beautiful girl at his side.

'This is it,' Ed thinks, 'I have arrived. I have a job I love, I have a great flat and now I'm sitting in the opera next to a great girl. And, what's more, I'm more stuffed, from some great nosh, than a teddy at the picnic. What more could I ask for?'

And, as if to answer Ed's rhetorical question, Louise suddenly slides her fingers in between his, his hand had been resting invitingly on his knee. Ed is thinking to himself that she must be keen after that little gesture. Now he knows that if he wants to go in for the kill, at the end of the night, he'll be sure that she will respond. Positively, that is. And this happy state of affairs continues well into the second half. A little time before the finale, at the point where Dandini's true identity as the *faux* prince is revealed, it happens. In the middle of Don Ramiro's search for Cinders, Louise slides her slightly moist hand from underneath Ed's clammy fingers. She begins to rub. Yes, rub. To rub slowly and firmly along the top of his leg, working boldly towards his inner thigh. Her unabashed eyes don't leave the stage, not for a moment, not even when Ed whimpered pathetically. And then, as if she is rummaging around for the last biscuit in the barrel, Louise lies the palm of her hand triumphantly on his wedding tackle. Ed lets out another involuntary little whine. She begins to massage his crotch, a bit like she's kneading dough. Ed has now forgotten all about Prince Don-Thingamabob and his search for Whatshername's slipper. Louise coolly takes Ed's hand and drops it into her own lap. What's he supposed to do, start rubbing as well? It would be like the princess trying to find the proverbial pea, through all those clothes. So he decides to just leave it there, looking vulnerable and lifeless. Louise carries on kneading. It is only the drama of the wedding fanfare that saves Ed from climaxing, there and then. Somehow he manages to harness his excitement, if only temporarily.

The players take their final bows, the curtains fall for the last time and the applause subsides. The rubbing has ceased.

'Well, bloody good, I thought,' Ed says, as if nothing's happened.

Louise looks at him, cheekily.

'Good,' she says.

56

Ed has a suspicion that she isn't talking about the opera. They get up and head for the cloakroom, along with the other two thousand members of the auditorium. Nothing is said about the incident as they queue, nor after they have collected their coats and are leaving the Royal Opera House. Ed is feeling a bit self-conscious as it is, and wouldn't know how to talk about it anyway. On occasions like this, silence is better, he decides. Louise, he thinks, must have had a momentary and uncharacteristic urge, brought on by the romantic power of Rossini (which should never be underestimated, in Ed's opinion). He had just been surprised, that was all. He hadn't taken her for that sort of lass, the type who checks out her date's package on the back row of the cinema. But, as it turns out, this is merely the tip of the iceberg.

They round the corner of Covent Garden market, weaving in and out of the great stone columns that support the market's roof. Emerging from behind one of the pillars, Ed catches a glint in Louise's eye. A mischievous glint that he feels he wasn't supposed to see. She starts to slow her pace and reaches for his hand. Her grip intensifies. They almost come to a stop, nearing one of the columns. She turns to face Ed – now reduced to a quivering rabbit in headlights. He knows something's coming, he's just not sure what, exactly. She looks different to how she normally looks. Her whole demeanour has adopted the mischief that Ed had caught a glimpse of in her eyes, just seconds before. For some reason he feels as if the real Louise has just awoken, casting aside the demure Dr Jekyll side of her personality. An overtly sexual Ms Hyde was waiting all the time, lurking under the surface, just waiting to break out. He can feel it. Then suddenly, Ms Piggy throws Kermit up against the sandstone pillar, kissing him in a way that can only be described as *ferocious*. Love bites erupt on his neck and his half-nibbled ear begins to burn. He tries to land a kiss on her, here and there, but she's having none of it. There is no interrupting her feasting. Finally, she feels satisfied, and pulls away, panting and gasping for air, her snake-like eyes alight.

Ed, still in shock, remains with his back to the pillar, his arms enveloped about its girth.

'Mmm, that was fun,' she smiles and licks her vermilion lips.

Ed, concerned that that was just the entrée, quickly pulls himself together.

'Yes, was rather,' he grabs her hand and jauntily pulls her into the open cobbled square.

'Right what shall we do now?' she has become very assertive, Ed notices. It perturbs him. He fishes around for suggestions but finds it difficult to think of something, where he won't be freshly devoured. You might be thinking through all this, 'Why is he complaining – surely this is a good thing, having your date all over you like an E. coli rash?'

And it would be a fair question to ask. But when you find someone that you are really into, like Ed has with Louise, you have a picture in your mind, of what she will be like. And Ed's perfect woman is something like the 'Executive Wife' – the type of partner who will hand out canapés at work soirées, or lift random babies aloft for you to kiss, should you chose to run for parliament. Ed would like to think of her as more virtuous, more traditionally ladylike. It's a case of each to their own – subjective rules of attraction. Ed's perfect woman simply doesn't go around molesting her man in public. It's just not what Ed was expecting.

Louise is looking around her, like a child amidst fairground attractions, deciding which one to go on next. Then she suddenly finds what she is looking for.

'Oh, I know, have you ever taken a ride in one of those rickshaw things?' she asks.

Ed stutters, 'Well, I er, no, it is rather late…'

Because Ed was so into Louise, and because it is clear she isn't the type of girl he thought she was, he just wants to go home. What's the point? To put it simply, he is disappointed and no longer interested. She's just the same as the others. But before he can protest any further, Louise has pulled him in the direction of the nearest vacant cab.

'Great let's have a go then,' she insists.

The driver rings his bell, to acknowledge them, and invites them to take a seat. Louise plonks herself in the semi-sheltered cab and pats the empty part of the seat next to her. It's an order, rather than an inviting pat. Ed's heart is filled with dread, he just wants to call the night to an end. He wants her to be the Louise he thought she was at the start of the night. If he gets in the cab, it's bound to get worse, although he's not sure how. Yet, he has no choice. Somewhat wearily, he steps into the cab and squashes up next to her. The driver is seated on his bicycle, a few inches in front of their knees, with his back to them. He is a Frenchman and is sporting a pencil moustache and artistic goatee. He turns in his bicycle seat, to face them, 'Whair wud yoo like tu go?'

'Drive! I don't care where, just drive!' Louise bellows out the order.

Ed winces. The driver raises his eyebrows in offence.

'Oui, mademoiselle,' he says facetiously.

By now, Ed realises that there is no way out. As Dirty would say on occasions like this, 'Sometimes boys, it's easier to do it, than not do it.' It has sunk in by now that Louise is not quite the girl Ed had thought she was, at first. And, never being one to look a gift whore in the mouth, Ed decides to get the hell on with it.

With a slight jolt, they are thrown back into their seat and the rickshaw starts its journey through the streets of London's West End. It's clear from the start that this will not be the London equivalent to a romantic trip on a Venetian gondola, or sipping Glühwein in the back of a horse-drawn sled in the Tyrol. Oh no, Louise has no interest in kisses and cuddles, this has all the trademarks of a ride on a funfair ghost train through the house of horrors. As soon as M. Le Cycliste gets some momentum going, the carriage rocking around over the cobbles, Louise wastes no time in engulfing Ed. She is kissing him, feverishly, like an overexcited guppy. She pushes him into the corner of the cab, placing all her weight against him. Her perfume is filling his lungs. Her hair is getting caught in the crossfire of their kissing. What can he do but gnaw back at her? And gnaw he does, with all the gusto he can muster.

Ed's kissing is now on the offensive. He pushes her back into her side of the cab. The more forceful he is, the more she seems to groan with pleasure. Stepping up the ante somewhat, Ed moves for the Rigby trademark manoeuvre, known as the 'tit and fumble.' He places his right arm behind her back, and starts to grope her right poont. With his free hand, he begins looking for that *pea* that he thought earlier would have been elusive. But surprisingly, his highly dextrous fingers seem to hit their target immediately, and Louise is sent wild with pleasure. With his left hand working its magic in her crotch, Louise almost relapses into a total submission. She starts to paw at Ed's lap. She's back to her rubbing, which has the obvious effect on Ed. Before he knows it, she's tugging at his flies. Zip. And then they're undone. Louise's petite little hand shoots inside his trousers and grabs a hold of the Rigby crown jewels. Enthusiastically she makes long firm strokes. Understandably, Ed is really into it now, who wouldn't be? Having resolved the fact that she is not the woman he thought she was, he treats her in the only way that is fitting. Any previous hesitancy he had, has long vanished. His right hand reaches inside her low-cut top and frees her right tit from where it was nestling happily, in her bra. Now, cupped lovingly in Ed's palm, in the open air, he squeezes excitedly.

You might think it's a bit risqué. But you ask any self-respecting London cabbie, and he'll keep you entertained for hours with stories of exhibitionist wives and girlfriends giving blossas to their other halves in the back of their Hackney cabs. At least Ed and Louise know that their French driver doesn't have the benefit of a rear-view mirror, to spy on their antics. But it's not the driver they need to worry about.

You know when you're doing a particular thing, and something in the back of your mind tells you that you should pause for a minute and take stock. That something has changed in the scenario, from when you first set out. For example, you're at home and you go out on some useless errand, like the shopping, and return to the house half an hour later. As you walk back through the front door, something instantly tells you that the house is not as you left it. You can't quite put your finger on it, there's no one particular thing. It's a feeling. And then, with a more pathological survey, you notice a teacup placed in a way you don't remember placing it, a door half closed that you think you left open or a dead body lying across your path with a hatchet in its back.

It's this feeling that suddenly washes over Ed, as he sits in the back of the rickshaw, airing Louise's boob. Something has changed, in the regime of things. What's different? And then, to his utter horror, he realises – it's stopped. The rickshaw has come to a halt. His eyes focus, and a new clarity of his surroundings dawns. His mind very quickly assimilates the new state of affairs. The first thing he notices, is their French driver bent over his pedals, spluttering swear words in his native tongue. He is fiddling with the machinations of the bike, the chain lies on the road surface by his feet. Ed looks up, and sees the billboards of several large theatres, the odd massive cinema – the type that holds international premieres. Bright neon lights. Restaurants. Faces. Cameras. Flashes. The penny drops, Ed's heart hits the back of his teeth.

They are in Leicester Square.

The rickshaw has broken down outside the Odeon, London's biggest cinema in the busiest part of the capital. Every night of the year, this square is teeming with tourists and Londoners alike, often gathering to watch celebrities totter up red carpets to peddle their latest blockbuster. Ed had been oblivious to the fact that they must have been sitting there for a couple of minutes, fornicating in the back of the open cab, for all and sundry to see. A crowd has gathered around the rickshaw. A multicultural, multi-aged all-representative mob, many of whom clutch cameras – digital, stills and video. They are all busy pointing, laughing, recording. In shock, Ed looks back at Louise. She hasn't even noticed, she is still lost in her ignorance, as she kisses his neck. With a cry of '*putain!*' the driver signals his success at refitting the chain. Keeping the vehicle stationary, he peddles the wrong way, to make sure the chain is aligned correctly. Ed glances around the ever-growing throng. They are all staring at him, Louise's tit and her hand, which is busy rummaging around in his pants. Open-mouthed Ed looks down at his date, and gives a wry smile, the hilarity of the whole escapade hits home. He fondles her once more and seeks out her mouth, for a deep kiss. The crowd cheers with enthusiasm. Relinquishing her breast momentarily, he turns his attention to the spectators, and gives them a thumbs up. They whoop with delight, endorsing his antics.

'Drive on!'

This public display of affection continues on the tube journey back to Louise's place. Luckily for Ed, Louise's behaviour would not prove to be an empty gesture, like my Australian prick tease. It was a sure sign of things to come, quite literally. A cup of Darjeeling is not the first thing to be offered to Ed, as he staggers into her apartment. The collide in a frenzy of passion, separate and throw themselves back at each other. The pair ricochet from one wall in the hall to the other, like a human pinball. Pictures come off the wall, they trip over shoes, discarded thoughtlessly on the floor. Ed rips off her top, the one boob has since re-joined its partner in the brassier, but not for long. Having undone his shirt, getting frustrated with her buttery fingers scrabbling at the buttons, she pulls it down over the back of his shoulders, finally freeing it from his arms. Ed hops like a child, from one foot to the other, tugging at his socks. Socks are always the worst garments to free yourself of when in a romantic or passionate state of undress, I find. Next they are at each other's trousers. She fumbles with his zipper, and he is struggling to undo her fastener. Finally, both clasps give way, and the pair bend over to free each other from their clothes, colliding heads on their way down. But rather than break their concentration, in order to laugh, as one normally would, they hurl themselves into another tonguing fest. Ed can't get the bra undone, all deftness failing him. She reaches behind her and nimbly separates the straps. She's had more practice. To avoid banging heads again, the remove their own pants. They pause for a minute, to take in each other's naked body, not speaking, not kissing. Then, Louise turns to her right and, with an impatient kick of her feet, the unzipped FMBs are propelled through the air, crash-landing somewhere in the lounge. She jumps up into Ed's arms, and the two fall back into the bedroom.

The first thing that comes into Ed's head in the morning, when he awakes, are the faces of the people who had gathered around the rickshaw.

'The guys have got to hear this one,' he muses.

He chuckles to himself, and his shaking wakes the sleeping woman at his side. After their three hour long, frenzied sex session, they had fallen asleep – ironically, in a romantic embrace, just as Ed might have hoped at the start of the evening. The sex was mind-blowing, that's for sure, but somehow he still feels disappointed. It's an anticlimax – of sorts. He would have been happier with this, and just this. Louise asleep on his chest, cuddling him so he can't leave her.

Now that the fun has passed, he doesn't want to be there. It's confusing. The sex was incredible, but that doesn't mean it was meaningful. It was just sex. And now he wants to leave, he doesn't want to stay, to make idle chit chat until midday. With the other Louise, he would have happily stayed with her all day. She wakes up, kisses his chest.

'Morning, you!' she manages to get the words out of her dry mouth.

'Morning,' Ed says, a little uncomfortably. 'I have to go,' he lies.

'Why? Stay here, have some breakfast,' she suggests.

Ed starts to feel guilty, he now has to lie some more.

'I can't, I'd love to but I have a trial I have to prepare for, it will take all weekend,' he sees the disappointment in her eyes.

'Okay, no problem.' Accepting the rebuff, she says, 'Well, if you want a shower, there's a fresh towel on the side of the bath, and a new toothbrush in the rack.'

Ed nods at her, smiles, and kisses her on the forehead. He can't kiss her on the mouth, it's just too stinky and dry.

'Wait, toothbrush?' he thinks.

Ignoring this strange suggestion, he clambers out of the bed, trying to disrupt her as little as possible. He walks to the threshold of the bedroom door, glances back at Louise, who has already drifted back to sleep. He thinks to himself, of what could have been. And then he heads into the bathroom.

The bathroom is a small and tidy little room, littered with girlie products and laced with that sweet smell that denotes all female washrooms. He looks in the mirror and thinks, 'God, I look like shit.' He casts his eye around the bathroom, picks up a perfume bottle, and cautiously smells it. It smells like Louise, how she smelt that first night. His gaze falls upon the bath and, sure enough, there on the side are a stack of fresh soft white towels. He looks at the rack, next to the mirror. His heart is filled, once again, with a feeling of dread.

As he gazes upon the neat rows of toothbrushes, resplendent in their uniform box-packaging and standing to attention like a platoon on parade, realisation dawns on Ed. Self-realisation that like every other young man in London with a large income and good genes he leads the life of a hunted partridge. That he is a number, one of many to have trodden this particular path. That there had been many before him and that there would be still more to follow. He had loved her that was sure. He could not help but wonder if the woman he would marry would have such a history of lovers. No, *lovers*, he thinks, is too romantic a word. Byron and Shelley have no place in this scenario, *shags* is a more appropriate word. Somewhat despondent and depressed Ed accepts his fate, he takes up one of the toothbrushes and rips off the wrapping.

5

The truth, the whole truth and nothing but the truth

Have you ever seen a child take a biscuit from the cookie jar just before tea, despite having been told expressly not to, as it'll spoil their appetite? At which point, they are inevitably caught by the all-seeing, all-hearing and all-knowing omnipresent mother. The cheeky imp of an infant boldly contrives the most convoluted story to account for the missing cookie and to try to explain the tell-tale crumbs, still clinging obstinately around their chops. They lie. With all credit, the said five-year-old does a good job but Mummy is wise to their tricks, and it's not long before the kid is blubbing and confessing all.

Men are like kids. Not simply with respect to their fascination of gadgets or for watching cartoons, with a view to sincerely deliberating the superior parts of the little mermaid's attributes. They also lie. It is an inane part of our makeup – the deception gene.

Whenever I have a girlfriend, I lie on a daily basis. It's not malicious, I'm not lying to cover up any infidelities. I do it because I believe the deception is a better state of affairs than the truth. I do it to avoid arguments and because I think that if I were her, I'd sooner not know. However often she tells me to tell the truth, whatever the truth might be, I still can't bring myself to do it. An amnesty is usually offered, a promise not to get mad. But we all remember those amnesties from childhood, promises that you won't get a smack if you tell Mummy who drove their Tonka Truck over the bonnet of her car. You confess all and the next thing you know, wallop! And it's the same with your loved one later on in life, save that the anticipated wallop is replaced by the nearest object that lends itself as a projectile (one of a proper shape that a girl is able to throw of course i.e. not ball-shaped). In short, it's often just downright easier to lie. I lie because it makes my life less complicated. It's like one of those easy mazes in a kid's puzzle book – 'show Fido the quickest way to his buried bone.' You don't follow the long squiggle, that would be silly, you take the straight line from the dog to the oversized chicken femur.

More often than not, the girl in question isn't actually bothered about the answer. But it is imperative to her that I am honest at all times. However much she says that though, I can't bring myself to tell her the truth. And she knows that I'm lying, usually. Don't be fooled into thinking that women only get this sixth sense after having children, oh no, they have honed the skill of spotting a fib all their lives.

When I was with Jessica, I would find myself telling a lie most days (or as I liked to call them, 'little porky pies' – it made me feel less guilty, or rather, not guilty at all).

1. Her: 'How many women have you slept with?'
   Me: '4' – I always say 4. It is a good in-between number; not too few to be inexperienced and yet it still makes them feel special, like I'm selective. Am I bollocks.
   Truth: (12)

2. Her: 'Do you fancy my best friend?'
   Me: 'No!' *emphatic*
   Truth: (All I can think about is her in sussies spread-eagled on my bed begging me to let her sister join in)

3. Her: 'Has your ex contacted you recently?'
   Me: 'No darling, of course not.'

Truth: (Yes, in fact I met her for lunch last week, we're just
friends but I know that you hate her and if I had told
you, you'd think something had happened)

4. Her: 'What are you doing tonight?'
   Me: 'Going out with my mates'
Truth: (true)

But – the supplementary question:

Her: 'Can't you go another night? I wanted us to cook spag
bol, drink Lambrini and watch *Bridget Jones*… again.'
Me: 'No I can't, I'd love to but I have to see Edward and
Raj because Raj needs comforting after his new
girlfriend, you know Charlotte, has been diagnosed
with chlamydia and they're waiting for the test results
to see if she can still have children. Also, Edward and
I really have to meet up and go through the business
details of the company we set up last year before the
end of this financial year.'
Truth: (We're getting shitfaced)

Conversely to the male of the species, I have found that
women are usually brutally honest. The truth is not something
to fear. Jessica never had a problem with being upfront. She
was always telling me how much she disapproved of my friends
or if my clothes didn't look right. It has been even worse in the
single world. You pluck up the courage to chat to a girl in a bar,
only to be sneered at and told in a lady-like manner, "Fuck off,
you're too short".

What is even more frightening is how honest and
unabashed a woman can be about what she wants from you
and out of a relationship. We had all been finding it difficult
to see a woman on our terms, or even where our terms were
actually considered. But the women we were dating had been
making their intentions very clear from the start. They weren't

apologetic for what, at times, seem unreal demands to be making; whilst we felt we had to keep our cards close to our chest, like a losing hand in a poker game against Cat Ballou.

My girlfriends tell the truth because that's what they would want to hear, it doesn't matter what I want. Frankly, I don't care if my girlfriend tells the odd porky pie, in fact there are times when I wish she would. I want to be able to believe that she's a virgin when we go to bed together. I don't want to have the type of conversation made famous in the scene between Andie MacDowell and Hugh Grant in *Four Weddings*. I don't want to know that Billy Bob loved to do it up against the wall or that Jimmy's is bigger than mine. If her ex calls one evening, I would prefer it if she made out it was her mum. Guys are like ostriches. Perhaps men aren't so beleaguered by their internal guilt, they don't feel a need to have everything out in the open. My lying makes my life easier at the moment of committing the untruth. Ironically, it usually leads to complications and confrontations when I am inevitably found out.

I have been working at the same media company for the past eighteen months. It was the ideal starter job in London, but it wouldn't be good for my career to stick with this place, so I have secured a job with a bigger company situated in the West End. It will be good to be within walking distance of Covent Garden and the multitude of bars and clubs that help to make this part of town so appealing. If nothing else, I will be able to smile every time I walk through Covent Garden market and picture Ed in the back of his rickshaw, getting jerked off for the world to see.

I only have a couple more days in this job. Presently, I'm in the process of going through the last few files on my desk and nicking all the company's knowhow. I get an email from one of the girls on front desk. Curiously, don't you find there is a tendency to employ blondes with long legs and big tits on reception. Ours is no exception. Her name is Carol, she is 24 and lives in Southend. I've spent the past one and a half years walking past her in the mornings, at lunch and on the way home at night. As soon as I am out of sight, I usually have to wipe the saliva that has been dribbling from the corner of my mouth. Each time, I smile (perhaps a little more enthusiastically than your average smile) and say hi, perhaps I ask her how her day's going, you know the sort of thing. But other than that, we've spoken relatively little.

Her email says that she's sorry to hear I'm leaving, and to make sure I say bye before I go. I'm not actually leaving until Friday, and it's only Tuesday. I give her a call.

'Hey Carol, it's…'

'Hi Max, nice surprise.' I hope she has caller I.D. on her phone.

'Er, yeah. Just wanted to say thanks for the email.'

'Oh no problem, I didn't know you were leaving. Bad boy, you didn't tell me. We should have a drink together before you leave.'

I almost drop the receiver. She just asked me out. Cool.

'Erm, yeah, sounds good. I'm free tomorrow evening, is that good for you?' I ask.

'Perfect, let's go to Jerry's after work.'

Jerry's is the wine bar next to the office. I meet her outside the back entrance around five the next day. She didn't want the other girls on reception to know we are meeting up, they gossip too much, apparently. I am a big proponent of not shitting on your doorstep, but I leave in two days, what can go wrong?

She's donned a very short camel skirt for the occasion and a loose white summer blouse. Black Versace shades perch on the crown of her head, keeping her long blonde hair from falling forward.

Ensconcing ourselves at one of the terrace tables for two, we order a couple of glasses of white wine. This is the first time that we have ever really talked. The conversation is pretty routine, as first date conversations go. It is a date, there was never a pretence that it is a 'goodbye' drink. Then we start to talk about sex (inevitably) and her sex life in particular.

'So do you normally have sex with other women, when you have a girlfriend?' she asks.

'Er, no,' I say, a little shocked, 'Not normally. Why, do you?'

'No, of course not. But I don't mind if my boyfriend does, as long as he lets me know and doesn't do it behind my back. It's only sex after all.'

This would be music to most men's ears. But it goes against the usual rules of nature, and soon my excitement turns to concern. Perhaps that should have been my first warning. What was I saying about Andie MacDowell?

The evening ends on a good note, with a rather pleasant snog and a brief fumble of her mammorious delights. And we arrange to meet up again once I've settled into my new job.

I see her the next morning as I saunter into work, past the front desk. She surreptitiously gives me a little wave. The other girls are bound to know what's going on. Oh well, I'll be gone in two days. I give her a wave and a big smile. As I go up in the lift, I start to feel a little nostalgic about the place. Getting to my glass-partitioned office, I sink into the chair and treat myself to a full 360-degree swizzle, before booting up the computer. I take a chug of my Pret coffee and slam the cup on my desk. Carol's emailed me already, to say thanks for a lovely evening. I start to pen my own response, expressing similar sentiments and how I'm looking forward to another drink with her, some time. I'm two lines in, the phone rings. It's reception.

'Hey you, how's it going? Did you get my email?' It's Carol.

'Ye-es, I was just writing you one back,' I explain.

'Great, well send it, send it!'

I'm not sure what to put in the email now, I just told her it all over the phone. So I briefly repeat myself and send it. She replies almost instantly, saying exactly the same as she said on the phone. How strange.

I have only been working for half an hour before she calls again.

'Hey, how you doing?,' she asks as if it has been days since we last spoke.

'Yeah, still good, how are you?'

'I'm really well, thanks. Just thought I'd let you know that I'm working till 4 pm today,' she thoughtfully explains.

'Great, well I'm going to have to go, I have a lot to get through today.'

'Sure, see ya.'

I hang up. I shake my head and go back to sipping my latte. Full fat, double shot, extra sugar latte.

Dan, from general office, pops his head round the door and gives me my morning's post. Three letters from clients, an industry circular and one piece of internal post. I bin the circular, file the client mail and tear open the internal letter. Holy shit, it's from Carol. It's dated this morning. I read it in utter disbelief. It's a love letter. In parts it is exceptionally complimentary, but the whole tone of the letter is very worrying. These are sentiments that you surely can't hold for someone after one date, but even if you do, you don't tell them. As well as the nice things she says, she also manages to touch on numerous abstract subjects like fidelity, the pill, her future. It's all a bit odd.

The phone rings, it's her again. In a frenzy I press the divert button. An email from her appears, it asks if I have received the letter. I decide to ignore it. What am I going to do, I can't avoid her. If I want to take lunch, I have to walk past her. I'll just have to sit it out until after four.

There are more calls, all of which are diverted through to voicemail. They are coming so frequently now that I have to answer, I have to tell her to stop calling.

'Carol!' I say sharply, as I put the receiver to my ear.

'Hey Max, how are you?'

'Er, yes, fine thanks.'

'Listen I can only be quick, meet me by the lift at four.'

'Carol, why do I need to meet you?'

'Just meet me, I have to give you something.' And then she hangs up. I feel nauseous. I start to think about all the terrible things she might want to give me; a giant teddy holding a red satin heart that says 'I love you snuggle bunny,' a Winnie the Pooh helium balloon, an STD?

It's just before four and I'm fidgeting by the lift shaft. My hands are clammy and I'm rocking on the heels of my feet. The lift counter, the one on the right, is counting up from the ground floor. I'm on the third floor, it's just gone past first. It's stopped, no, it's moving to second. It's left second. Ping. Is it her? Is anyone looking? No, thank God, it's quiet. The silver doors slide open and Carol pops her head around the corner, as if to check the coast is clear. It's like something out of a low budget espionage film from the 1950s, *Matt Helm* perhaps?

She runs up to me, her long legs bounding along like a springbok's. She plants a kiss on my cheek, looks left and then right. She thrusts something into my chest, 'Here, this is for you.' And with that she runs for cover back into the lift, which hasn't even had a chance to close its doors and head back down to reception.

I stand there bewildered. Getting a grip, trawling myself back into reality, I scurry into one of the team meeting rooms. I slide the frosted-glass door to.

'Not another letter,' I plead with myself.

Deciding not to sit down, I rip open the envelope. It looks like another letter, if only it was. Carol has written me a poem. An eight-stanza poem entitled 'My Ego'. I begin to shudder with fear as I read from one line to the next. It talks of me being 'the skin that she wears', 'her reason for living' and that I am 'the destroyer of women's hearts'.

I spend the next two days as if I'm on some covert military operation. I get in early, to avoid seeing her on reception and leave only once her shift has finished. They are two of the longest days of my life. My colleagues think that I've gone mad, that I've become a recluse. I refuse to answer my phone.

I left work on the Friday and I never saw Carol again. But why did I feel as if I had done something wrong? I felt like the bad guy, for what I wanted, even though I believed my 'terms' were reasonable. I felt that Carol had acted utterly unreasonably, but because she was so upfront about her intentions, because she told the truth about what she wanted, it was all ok, however ludicrous it appeared. I didn't feel as if I could be as honest with Carol as she had been with me.

Ultimately, I felt weaker through my deception, or rather my inability to lay my cards on the table. But my girlfriends seemed to gain strength in their relationship by telling the truth. I realised that if they are comfortable telling me that I am the *skin that they wear,* then surely I can tell them that I would sooner have a relaxed relationship, consisting of the occasional dinner and trip to the theatre.

There's not much you can say in opposition to the truth, it's a case of like it or lump it. What if I tried the honest approach? So I did.

The next week I go out with a friend of mine called Chantal. She is a cracking girl with an ethnic mix of Afro-Caribbean and Oriental. It would be fair to describe her as exotically attractive. Chantal is a petite thing with a great figure and, as Ed correctly asserts about Oriental women, she has tits like rocks.

We had been on a few dates, hanging out with friends. One night, we decide to have dinner together, round at her place. It is the first time we've been together alone. Dinner was lovely, I really enjoy her company. But there is that definite feeling in the air that tonight will be the time when things step up a gear or two. Even though each other's intentions are quite clear, both of us pretend it's like any other previous time we have been together.

As we're chatting on the couch, over a glass of shiraz, she starts flirting even more outrageously. The last thing I want is another Ms Right. I want my own strong independent successful woman that I have been promised by society, the sexual revolution, TV, the propaganda glossies. Chantal seems like the kind of girl who could do 'casual' – the kind who wants to party but doesn't expect to be legs akimbo in the delivery room nine months from now, with me holding her hand, telling her to 'breathe'.

Yet, I am still concerned that I could be lured by the promise of a physical relationship, only to feel trapped in something more serious. If that happened, I know I would do a runner, and lose an important friendship in the process. I decide that this has to be the right time to try being honest.

No deception, no promises – no longer a man of straw.

'My God Max, you're such hard work!'

Oh no, she's going to say it, I know she is. It's at times like this that, as a guy, you appear as though you don't know what they're getting at, that you're blind. But it's not that, I know full well what's coming. It's just that I hate tackling these complicated kinds of issues. I stay silent, looking quizzically as if she's slightly deranged.

'I'm just going to come out with it,' she soldiers on, as she realises that I'm not going to say anything.

I'm feeling more uncomfortable by the second.

'Max,' she says, earnestly.

'Yes, Chantal?'

'You know I really like you. And I want to take things further.'

The pretence is over. It's crunch time. I know what I want – I want to take things further too. But is it worth stealing even one kiss, if it will be followed by all the usual aggro. Will she turn out to be cool after all, should we make the relationship a physical one. Will I feel trapped. Will I lose a friend? Oh God, why aren't I at home playing on my Xbox!

Normally, this is where I would agree with whatever the girl says, clasping my hands together with delight and yelping, 'Me too.' Not this time. For a change, I will be totally honest with Chantal. It's not the easiest thing to do, at this very moment, but it is fair on her and she should respect me for being honest with her. If it turns out that she isn't into a casual relationship, then at least she can't claim I was never upfront with her, or that I deceived her. Here we go.

'Chantal, I do like you,' I start, sincerely. 'It's easy to see we're attracted to one another. The only thing is, I don't want to have a serious relationship at the moment, having recently finished one and the fact there's so much going on in my life. I like you, you're a friend and I wouldn't want to hurt you.'

While I'm talking, I notice that she starts to look at me a little indignantly. I think she thought the last bit was arrogant, but it wasn't, at least it wasn't intended to be.

'Max, what do you think you can do to me that will hurt me?'

I have a few ideas of my own. I stop myself, just in time.

She continues, 'If two people like each other, it'd be a shame for them not to act on it.'

I don't say anything, I don't know what to say. I look down at the stem of my wine glass that I'm twiddling between my thumb and forefinger. The small remaining drop of red wine revolves around the inside of the glass, *Christ's tears* drip down the inside.

'Of course, you're right Chantal,' I say finally, 'I also want to go out with you and for us to spend more time together; as something more than friends but less than a couple. You must know that my priorities at the moment lie with my work and my friends.'

There, it wasn't that tough.

'That's fine, I don't especially want a relationship either.'

Something in her voice didn't sound right. It was that last bit, that seemingly innocuous declaration. Chantal was lying. It's the worm wriggling on the line to reel me in. Once I've bitten, she thinks that she will be able to change my mind, that she will change *me*. Normally, she wouldn't have had to lie because, as the man, I would never normally have been honest, I would have lied before she did. I would have falsely accepted her intentions of us heading towards something vaguely serious, only to extract myself from the 'relationship' at some future, not-so-far-off point in time. This was the reverse – Chantal agreeing to a casual affair with a view to turning it into a committed monogamous relationship at some future not-so-far-off point in time.

But I didn't fully realise that then.

I wade in and kiss her, as I had wanted to all evening, and with a guilt-free conscience. I have taken the bait.

The following week, Chantal is going away on a skiing holiday with friends to the Trois Vallées. Things have progressed but everything is as we agreed. The night before she leaves for the Alps, we see each other for dinner and to take in the new version of *The Nutcracker*.

The next morning, I walk her to the tube station. We stand on the platform for the Northern Line. A train is one minute away, according to the display. With a swoosh of cold air it enters the platform.

'Well, have a fantastic time,' I hug her.

'Oh I'm sure I will, it's a shame you can't come along, if we'd been seeing each other earlier you'd be coming!'

'Yes, I suppose so,' I'm not sure what else to say to that. 'I'll call you when you get back then.'

'Okay, bye,' she gives me a kiss and jumps on the train.

Every day that Chantal is away, I receive a text message from the slopes. It's touching base romantic stuff. But it's not even one text a day, it's several texts at all hours, giving me updates of her day.

A week later, she gets back. Her flight arrives at midday. The overhead seatbelt light can only have just been turned off when she sends me a text from the tarmac.

'I'm back,' she announces.

'Okay, good for you,' I think to myself. I reply, 'Gr8 hope u had a good time ☺ x.'

Twenty minutes later my phone beeps at me again, 'So wot r u up 2?'

It's a Sunday but I'm working. She knows that one of my filming projects at work has taken off, I told her this during our text-fest earlier in the week. I reply anyway, 'I am waiting 4 a friend to call – we r doing the film thing I told u about – I am waiting for his call – otherwise we could have gone for coffee later.'

I'm sending so many bloody text messages my thumbs are more blistered than a leper with a Gameboy. I thought that my message was clear. That I am busy right now, but that we'll meet up another time. Bugger me, if she doesn't write back with, 'What number does he have 4 u? – home or mobile? U could come out with me and he could still call u.'

?

This is neurotic. She is driving me insane, and it's exactly the thing that I wanted to avoid. I don't want someone questioning everything I do. My wife will be able to do that. It will be her God-given right as mother to my children, but not someone I have snogged once or twice.

She had expected to see me the day she got home. None of my reasons as to why I couldn't see her seemed to be acceptable.

The next day at work I receive the email I was fearing, 'Hey, how's it going, really peed off at this end…'

I know where this is going. I can't ignore it, so I play along with it in the hope that we might reach the inevitable all the quicker. I do that aggravating guy thing of pretending that I don't know what she is getting at and that I haven't remotely sensed she might be annoyed.

The next email arrives in my in box, 'Yeah just lots of crap but I don't want to bother you with my whining while you're busy at work!!?!?!?'

'Don't worry, go on,' I type back.

Ping, the next email arrives, 'Well if you insist (1) I may get the sack (2) I think you have gone AWOL on me (3) a close family friend is dying (4) I have twisted my neck and it hurts.'

I come in second above the dying age-old family friend, a guy you've dated for a week, you have got to be kidding me.

Eventually, she abandons the texting and emailing, and calls me.

'So what am I, a girl you can call up whenever you need sex or to have a pretty woman on your arm?'

Of course she isn't, she is my friend above anything else. We haven't even slept together yet. This is what I had wanted to avoid all along. Imagine if we had slept together. I wanted us to enjoy each other's company without the commitment of a serious relationship.

77

'Chantal, I told you where my priorities have to lie at the moment. I am not looking for a serious relationship.' I hear her sigh on the other end of the receiver, as I pause before continuing, 'Clearly, you weren't being honest with me when you said that you weren't either. I feel you have deceived me, I have been used.'

Okay, so I added the last bit. The truth is, I didn't want to make her feel worse, as she was clearly upset, but she was starting to blame me for what had happened. Normally, that blame would be justified because through non-malicious deceit, I would have painted a false picture of promises that I never intended to fulfil, by the things I said or didn't say. But not this time. This was me reminding her of what we had agreed and that she should respect my honesty.

I realised that she had no comeback whatsoever, and so did she. I hadn't been a so-called bastard. Chantal had decided to take the plunge, knowing all the facts. Any deception had been on her own part against herself. I think that's what might have made it worse. Perhaps it's a comforting thought that a guy is a lying bastard, a woman can apportion blame for her own mistakes.

If there's an inkling that the guy wants 'fun' but nothing more, and yet he smooches his way into her *La Perla* undies, when it all goes Pete Tong, the man can be blamed as a love rat for tricking her into bed. But if the man says, 'Honey, we can knock bones but we won't be doing this with a view to becoming serious,' then it's there in black and white. You're giving the woman the choice, with full and frank disclosure – take it or leave it. If either party wants more and it's not reciprocated then you can't blame the other person for your own change of heart when those feelings aren't returned.

For the first time ever, I feel totally empowered. There is no self-doubt, no guilt (some men, like Dirty Dave, couldn't give a monkey's either way, but some do). I could hold my head high, I'm not a bastard. This is pro-choice. If someone exercises their prerogative to change their mind, it's not right to make the other person feel bad if they don't want to follow suit.

Honesty, I discovered, is the best policy.

6

A little less conversation

Holly 07811444097: 'Yes I'm fine – if u just wanted us 2 b a physical thing I wish u had been honest about it in the 1st place – that's all'

If language is the dress of thought, then conversation must be the glue that holds a relationship together.

Text messages are a wonderful thing. They allow you to regulate your social relationships without any personal interaction whatsoever. You can pick up people in bars without hardly talking to them. You can have sex with them without uttering more than a few sweet nothings and, thereafter, the whole relationship can be conducted with the press of a few buttons. It's no wonder that, in an increasingly hectic life, people are relying on the text message. The result is that relationships suffer; people are losing the ability to talk to each other.

'Hi Max.' It's Ed, phoning from what sounds like a busy street.

'Ed, mate, how's things?'

'Shit!'

'How come?'

'You know that girl I was seeing – the one from Coffee Republic?'

I remember her, a small girl with red hair, 'Yeah, Julia right?'

'Yes, well the cow just dumped me.'

'No way, I'm sorry mate.'

'But that's not the worst bit, do you want to know how she dumped me?' he asks.

'Go on.'

'By fucking text message.' I just about manage to stifle a laugh, 'She said "I can't c u any more".'

'I'm sorry, buddy. She was cute too.'

'But she couldn't even be bothered to write the words out in full!'

Typical Ed. He finds it a greater affront that she has corrupted the English language than the fact that she has dumped him.

You have to ask yourself though, why couldn't she have made one quick call? I thought it was just guys that were cowards in this department. It's not an enviable task, dumping someone, but it is important to do it properly. It's important to the dumpee and the dumper. No one wants to be kicked into touch but you do want to hear it, from a living person, not that the first you know about it is from the beep emitted by your Nokia.

It made me realise how relationships are also a vehicle for self-development. Going through the tough times is just as important as enjoying the good ones. We all need to learn from our experiences, it's what makes us who we are. If we rely on the easy way out all the time, instead of facing the hard crap, we're just going to make it difficult for ourselves in the future. What will happen when we are with someone who does matter? It's a case of not sparing the rod for the good of the child. Picture it, ten years from now, you and your future partner are having an argument, perhaps you have money problems or they're having an affair – are you telling me that you're going to sort out your problems by sitting in different rooms of the house texting each other? The reconciliatory electronic appendage. Is it possible to sum up all your feelings, beliefs, emotions, anger in a one-line text of mangled English shite? So how are you going to know how to say the right thing?

That's what Holly's text message made me think. Clearly, she had issues to discuss. I could appreciate that there was some anger lingering behind her message, and hurt and dismay, perhaps even a little desire. But there is so much more surrounding this one-line text than the simple content of the message. How could we talk about all her concerns? We couldn't. If I had lacked understanding, then by not talking about it, I couldn't learn from my mistakes. Likewise, she could not learn from her own misgivings, maybe that she had misread my feelings or that she had, at least, shut her eyes to them. Perhaps, if we had talked about it, we would be better prepared for the next time we meet someone.

Later that night, Ed, Raj and I meet at one of our regular haunts for a few beers. Milk & Honey is a private member's club in Soho. The club's entrance is a blacked-out fire door on Poland Street. If someone hasn't taken you there, you would never know it existed, it's like something out of the Prohibition era. It's not a pretentious bar, you pay a small annual fee for the privilege of drinking until the wee hours without being shoved like you're constantly in a rugby scrum.

This evening it's fairly quiet. A few women have gathered at the other end of the bar for what sounds like closing-the-deal drinks. The vaulted stone ceiling and soft red lighting gives the bar a warm and friendly feel. Ed has just bought a round.

'Why is it that flaws in men's characteristics are to be admonished,' he says suddenly, 'or where possible eradicated, while flaws in the female of the species are tolerated, nay embraced, even encouraged?'

We squeeze our limes and push the wedges down the necks of our beer bottles. We take a few gulps, pondering Ed's last comment.

'Flaws are flaws,' he continues, before one of us can reply, 'they shouldn't be encouraged, try to overcome them.'

'Yeah, you could be right,' I take another sip of my Corona. 'Jessica told me six months after we broke up that she had been a difficult bitch – her words, not mine – because she loved me so much, because she didn't want to lose me, because she was *insecure*.'

'Oh well, that's ok then,' Raj laughs.

'It's a bit like a wifebeater slapping his wife around. It's his problem, and he can't use love and the insecurity of losing his partner as an excuse for such unacceptable behaviour,' says Ed.

'Mate, it's a bit of an extreme example, but I know what you mean.'

'The same goes for "that time of the month",' says Raj. 'How the hell does a hormone imbalance justify treating your nearest and dearest like crap!?'

Likewise, I have tried as hard as I can to accept the side effects of this monthly phenomenon, but my understanding and tolerance is never reciprocated when I have my own hard times. On the rare occasions that I'm stressed at work, or having a hard time in life generally, *that* is no excuse for short temper, apparently.

'Yeah, and it doesn't even stop there,' says Raj. 'As well as putting up with a miserable troll for one week out of every four, I am supposed to appreciate everything that goes with it; the fem-products, the adverts, the women talking about it. And yet, I go to scratch my nuts once or delve into my pants to rearrange the family jewels and I invite a volley of abuse. Suddenly, I am a disgusting bloke. You try having a ten-inch salami and a pair of plums dangling between your legs and tell me it's not a little uncomfortable from time to time. Sorry guys, I'm starting to rant, it's just been bugging me.'

'No, you're completely right,' Ed agrees. 'Those bloody Tampax adverts are completely misleading. The women in those ads are all happy and smiling. They're running around in tight white hot-pants on a beach playing Frisbee. None of my girlfriends have been like that when they've "had the painters in" – it's greasy hair, wearing old trackie bottoms and a constant scowl that says "come anywhere near my breasts, even mention the act of sex or say anything that might upset me and I will cut off your balls".'

'And girls can't even throw a Frisbee,' laughs Raj.

Allegedly, we live in an age of equality. The behaviour of men in the pre-fifties had been criticised heavily by women, and I suppose by many men as well, let's say society in general. It was agreed that women should no longer be beholden to their husbands – this was the twentieth century. Society was tired of men taking women for granted, with some having a wife at home while boffing their secretary on the side, knowing the financially dependent wife would never leave him. Prior to marriage, the guys would try it on with the women; a guy who succeeded was a stud but a woman who played along was a tramp. With the sexual revolution came free love and from that a form of sexual equality where the women wouldn't be stigmatised by going out on the pull. The guys were supposed to take on board some of the traits that women naturally nurtured, like the desire for commitment, respect, consideration, openness and discussion. It seems ironic that the qualities which feminism tried to curb in men have become the norm for society at large; infidelity, personal drive and ambition at any cost, placing work above the family, materialism and envy.

'We talk about love and emotion and commitment,' says Ed.

'Sure we do.'

'So why are we always criticised for only thinking about sex. I've had monogamous relationships.'

'The difference is,' I begin, 'as men, we can distinguish between love and sex.'

'True,' says Ed, 'there's not necessarily emotion involved when we have sex. It seems women find it hard to do that, even though they're told they can, by all the girlie propaganda.'

'Girlie propaganda?' says Raj, quizzically.

'*Cosmo.*'

'Ah.'

'They don't seem to be able to handle this sexual freedom, the type of sexual freedom that us men enjoy and yet that is exactly what they are told to pursue,' says Ed. 'That's why Holly sent you that text.'

It's true. When I see a girl that I find attractive, and I want to sleep with her then I can do so without feeling any guilt for the lack of strong emotional feelings towards her. Obviously, if I am going out with a girl I love then I'll have sex with her, but it's quite different. I realise that it's also possible to come across a girl who I find physically attractive but who I don't want to date (sometimes good looks aren't even a prerequisite, but let's leave Dirty out of this for a moment). It's a natural desire. And If you both want to enjoy a purely sexual relationship, then you should be able to do so without any self-deception, guilt or other sentiments imposed upon you by the shackles of emotion. Isn't that what we've all been told.

The point is that for men there is a big difference between love and sex. The former will incorporate the latter, but the latter can be enjoyed for its own sake. Morally, it may be wrong, but this explains why in television shows the guy who has had the extramarital affair speaks those immortal lines, 'Darling, it didn't mean anything.' A man will often have an affair because he is tempted by simple shallow reasons, i.e. the temptress is cute. A woman is more likely to have an affair because of deep rooted problems in her marriage; the fact she doesn't feel like she is respected by her hubby, that she is taken for granted, that he doesn't appreciate her or acknowledge her worth etc. It might not be right, and I am in no way condoning affairs, in fact I hate them, but the man isn't lying, he's being totally honest.

'You think that's it then,' says Raj, 'that women find it difficult to distinguish between love and sex, which they rarely see as being mutually exclusive – the two are the same thing, they come hand in hand.'

'Yes, of course.' says Ed, 'Nice idiom by the way.'

'Thanks.'

'Think about it,' I say, 'you see a woman you're attracted to, do you have to love her to sleep with her? No, of course not.'

'So what does it matter if women don't choose to distinguish between love and sex?' Raj asks.

'Nothing,' I answer, 'in fact, I think it's cool. The problem arises when girls don't think that they are in bonds with their emotions. When they believe that they can have sex on a regular basis with someone and not become emotionally attached to them. That's why Holly was pissed off, she had been playing it like a man, but all the time suppressing her true feelings.'

'Man, women always over complicate relationships,' Raj concludes.

Guys aren't just shallow sex obsessed predators but we are more simple in our relationships and possibly more honest with ourselves. It's not just sexual relationships, it's any relationship. The amount of girls that I've met recently who, at some point, have said to me, 'You know, I have more male friends than I do female friends.'

I think I'm going to laugh or cry the next time I hear a girl say that to me. It's almost as annoying as being handed a copy of *Ms London* every day as I come out of the tube. I always see the same Oriental guy distributing the magazine, I want to roll it up and continuously beat him round the head with it, while screaming, 'Do I look like part of the fucking readership!'

The 'male friends' quote invokes a similar reaction in me. What never ceases to amaze me is how they say it, as if they're special. I think they believe all other girls hang around in giggling groups painting each other's nails, while she chills with the guys, sinking those Buds, watching the game. It's bullshit. Not every girl can have more male friends than female friends or they would never hang out with each other. Besides, it's not natural. I bet that if you asked her guy friends if she was their best mate that they would look back at you with blank, vacant expressions. It reminds me of the line from that Oscar Wilde play, that between men and women there is no such thing as friendship; there is love, lust and passion but never friendship. Women have lots of platonic male friends, whereas men just know women they haven't shagged yet.

I sat in the park the other day, during my lunch break. The text from Holly had been playing on my mind. I was thinking about it while partaking in one of my favourite sports – people watching. Next to me were sat a group of three guys who had been joined by one uber-foxy barrister type. One of the men was chatting with the foxy girl in deep, earnest conversation. Meanwhile, the other two chatted bollocks, as guys tend to do together. Our friend here was clearly lending an ear, perhaps being a shoulder to cry on, listening attentively to her problems. After 40 minutes of tutting in the right places, nodding with empathy and clasping her hand in support, the girl thanked him for being there for her. She quickly said goodbye to the other two men and headed back across the lawn. She probably went away from that conversation thinking what a great friend she had in the avid listener. The poor girl didn't realise that he was just working up to the right moment to launch an assault into her undies. As soon as she was out of earshot, the guy leans across to his friends and informs them that it's just a matter of time until she is screaming his name in a moment of ecstasy. They congratulate him on his most excellent efforts and slap him on the back in good fraternal spirit.

Perhaps women do know this, that we can't be trusted. Perhaps this explains the recent craze for women having a token gay friend. Fag hags. But I don't understand this either. It seems as insane to me as them all having a majority of guy friends and no female friends. If you told me that there was a craze for guys having a token lesbian friend, now that I could understand. Buy one, get one free. But with women it's not sexual, it's supposed to be that the gay man understands the woman's issues, he knows where she's coming from. I appreciate that the stereotypical gay man is more into the home, into fashion, that he likes shopping etc. but there's more to it than that, it is this supposed empathy, an unspoken understanding. They are peas in the proverbial pod. But a gay man has more in common with the heterosexual man when it comes to procuring sex, than he does with a woman.

The gay man has one flaw in this revolutionary concept – he is a man. (Guys stay with me here, I have a point I promise.) You watch the behaviour of gay men in a gay club, they are the same as heterosexual men (preferences aside). They are also very predatory, confident, open and, above all, uncomplicated.

There are obviously some differences in the hetero/homo world. A gay man walking into a straight bar must despair. For starters, there is the obvious fact that no one can dance.

Particularly us blokes, who for the most part have the hip grinding skills of David Brent. For some reason, it's not cool to relax and have fun. You can't do your own thing and let everyone else do theirs. Instead, the blokes stand around holding their pint glasses to their chests and try to look menacing. Eventually, after ten pints and some serious coaxing from various women, we start to dance. I say dance, rather we move like mental patients, devoid of any rhythm. Rather than trying to dance properly, we dance stupidly, probably because we think it's funny. But if we are being honest it's because we don't like to look stupid by trying to do something properly and failing miserably. Also, because all other blokes are in the same boat, we know that we have support from fellow soulless males. It's only because we're embarrassed, and we think that, this way, we can maintain our machismo. Having gone through that phase, we finally start to dance seriously, but still badly, as we know it's the only chance we have of scoring. And there's only one thing worse than everyone watching us dance like our dads – going home alone.

The thing is, it's all down to the hunt and the failure of the hunt. The desire to score, and the fear of losing out to another pint-holding skinhead with all the rhythm of a Peruvian sloth. This is undoubtedly one of the reasons for the greater amount of aggression in a straight bar. That and, of course, the sexual tension. The tension between the hunter and the hunted.

The atmosphere in a straight bar can be so serious and intense, there's a frenzy to score. It's not a case of letting yourself go and having a good time. If you start to do your own thing, for example dancing like you're in the Rio Carnival, everyone would take the piss.

Rather than getting down to the tunes and enjoying themselves, everyone seems to be in deep conversation. Usually it's about mundane crap, and all with one end in mind – a shag. Everyone knows it. Both the man and the woman. It's a game of deception. They should be out having a good time, but instead they choose to stand around immersed in serious diatribe. You spend literally hours selling yourself to the other person. The chat up. And, of course, they're not being honest with themselves, or each other. The man feels obliged to put in the groundwork. The woman convinces herself that if he does this, then he is genuinely interested in her. They both want to go home with each other. Rather than acknowledging this fact, and hooking up from the start, they feel the need to go through this mating ritual of discussing life history, their job and holiday plans. Finally, three hours and five caipirinhas later, just before the club closes, they drunkenly snog and inevitably wake up together the next day.

But it's not like that in a gay club. The punters at Heaven or The Village can be themselves. They have fun, do what they want to do, dance, don't criticise and don't make trouble. The big difference is that there's no sexual tension to spoil the night.

There is one convention that exists in gay society that shows how all men are the same, gay, bi or hetero. If one gay guy sees another bloke in the club that he fancies, and the second guy acknowledges his eyeing up, they hook up for some sex. Possibly even there and then, vacant cubicles permitting. Nothing more, nothing less. And afterwards there are no demands. What a great friggin' idea. Gay society has uncomplicated the sexual relationship. Because it's involving another man they have been able to dispense with all the emotional crap and accept that you can have sex for sex's sake. There's no need to stand chatting about your last Christmas shopping trip to New York or feigning an interest in the trading of convertible bonds. Make the approach. Put your cards on the table. And *giddy-up*.

Needless to say, love can happen as well. You can meet a long-term partner at one of these places. But they accept the fact that this is not always the aim for a Friday night. You can also be attracted to someone and just want to give them a thoroughly good seeing to. No need to feel guilty about it.

Now why can't we incorporate that into heterosexual life? Think how awesome it would be if you saw a guy or a girl in a club, you were both attracted to each other, on a base level, and wanted to have sex. I think back to my Kiwi prick tease, for example. We could have had the whole full and frank disclosure of sexual interests, gone back to hers, left the family photo albums firmly in the bookcase and shagged like rabbits. We could have got up the next morning, had a civil cuppa and gone on our way. You know what? I would have been much more likely to give her a call and meet up again if I hadn't had to deal with all that rubbish, all the hypocrisy. Kiwi girl didn't want to sleep with me because she thought I wouldn't come back. The irony is that I didn't go back to her because she refused after making all her 'promises'. She played these stupid games, she wasn't being honest with either of us.

Raj was briefly seeing a girl who told him, after having completed three dates, that she felt she could have sex with him. Apparently, she had exercised enough restraint by holding out over the three dates even though she had wanted to sleep with him on the first night. This is sexual intercourse. If you can't look at it as 'fun' and that it is always something meaningful, then it's a serious matter and holding out for one or two dates is meaningless.

We are adults and we are allowed to enjoy sex for sex's sake, aren't we? Isn't that what the sexual revolution was about?

This great discovery by homosexual society is no discovery at all, they are merely doing what comes naturally, to excuse the pun. They're guys. It would never work in the heterosexual dating scene exactly because women *are* still restricted in their sexual exploits by their emotions. The guilt that, deep down somewhere, they shouldn't really be enjoying sex. And, of course, they are still restricted by that magic number, the one that represents the total number of guys that it is acceptable to have slept with by the time they get married.

This is the fundamental difference between men and women – the number of acceptable premarital sexual partners. Women have a maximum, men have a minimum.

Once again, this explains the angry text message from Holly. I had known Holly for years and always fancied her. Holly's sex life had deteriorated over the past year. More to the point, there wasn't any. She wanted to have a purely sexual relationship with a friend, with me. She knew I liked her, respected her, she was my friend. But you see, that wasn't enough, she had to be able to think, at least, that I sort of loved her. Perhaps she did have such strong feelings towards me, even though they could never have been taken to their natural conclusion. It was not enough that we were attracted to each other sexually and that we could allow ourselves to enjoy the sex together.

It happened one time, as we neared the point of no return in the bedroom, that she suddenly confessed her deeper feelings towards me. This was a bit of a blow. I know you're thinking that I should have reciprocated in such sentiments and finished the job in hand, but I couldn't bring myself to do it, she was my friend after all.

It was after this night that the obsessive and neurotic text messages started. I told her that I was happy to have sex with her and be friends, but that I couldn't go out with her. Besides, she was engaged to be married that following summer. A guy called James who she had met at a university hockey reunion. They had been living together for nearly a year now.

7

Staying single is the solution

My efforts to find an intelligent, attractive and, most importantly, sane woman had started to plummet to desperation point. In fact, it is nowhere near desperation; desperation is lurking around the corner. It's the new year, and it's always said that the new year is the perfect excuse to try something new. That was Jones's argument anyway. Jones is a girl I work with; a tall lass with auburn hair. She only likes to be known by her surname, I think it's because she loathes her given name, Daisy. Over the Christmas break, a friend of hers had told her about a singles night, which aimed itself at successful city types, the supposed beautiful people. If she got in there now, she might even have a date by the time February 14th arrives.

Over the past few months, singles nights had become the preferred party night. Everywhere you turn, there are adverts for this or that singles gathering. Billboards, the sides of buses, men and women's magazines or on the tube, even in flyers with your sandwiches. The X million single people in London had been identified as a consumer market. Most of this group have a high disposable income and spend the majority of their free time looking for a partner; why not help them on their way and relieve them of some that cash in the process? No longer are the classifieds and the ads for singles parties confined to the back of the *Metro*. A new bread of singletons is being born – the 'I'm Single and I'm Proud'! It seems that these party nights are as much 'coming-out' parties as they are an evening designed to help you find Mr/Ms Right. It's *single pride*.

But a part of me could not totally sever my prejudice towards such events that had built up over the years and which society told me were 'sad'. I could picture it already; 30-something *rah* girls in pink pashminas pulling up in their Z3s on the hunt for sperm donors. And then there would be the male of the species, if you can call them that. The men who think they're guaranteed a pull, men like the computer science graduates in drip dry shirts or spivvy law clerks with ties knotted so fat they defy belief. But Jones had been single now for the longest time she could ever remember (about six weeks), she clearly needed the proverbial 'some', and hearing her go on about it just reminded me of my own futile position. In fact, I had decided that our office had become like a carbon copy of the *'Gimme, gimme, gimme'* apartment in the cringingly hilarious sitcom of the same name. The only difference being that Jones isn't a fat repulsive ginga and, despite my recent propensity for baking cookies, I am not gay. So in the hope of finding Jones a man, I am game.

Following Jones's instructions, the first thing I have to do is go onto the Single No More website and sign up for one of their events. Single No More is the name of the organiser and, as you will see, it is totally misbranded. I hate signing up for things on the net. There are endless drop-down boxes to select from, boxes to tick and private details to enter. The first hurdle, in this instance, is the selection of a username. When you sign up for one of their events, this is the name that will appear on the guest list, the idea being that other guests can check out each other's profiles online. Luckily, I realise that you have to be careful in what you plump for, otherwise I could instantly label myself a twunt, along with 'Mr10incher' and 'Mad4itMan'. I check out the girls who have signed up. Many of their names are just as bad, with women in their 30s calling themselves 'discochick' or 'legal bird'. It just makes them sound too calculating, trying to perpetuate the myth of their youth, like they think it's the kind of image guys will find attractive. It's really not what men want to hear, well Mr Drip-dry might not care and the ones in it for a quick bit of how's-your-father won't give a toss but, trust me, the rest of us just cringe.

And when I thought I had racked my brains hard enough, searching for some cool and witty name that you think the other sex will find so alluring they're dropping their knickers at the mere thought of you, the bastards ask you the mother of all questions – 'Tell us one funny thing about yourself.' My mum used to dress me in skirts when I was four. Well that's funny but not exactly what my date, pull or potential future girlfriend will want to hear. The thing is, something that is funny to someone know me will, by its very nature, be embarrassing. It's also unlikely to be the kind of thing that you would normally say when trying to endear yourself to a member of the opposite sex. And, of course, if you put nothing then you will be condemned as being boring. So now I have to reveal some innermost secret to a website, which will be used to sum me up, used to rate me against all the barristers' clerks and IT geeks. I have to be able to think of something better than 'I designed Lara Croft's breasts'. Perhaps I could put that I used to live on a Caribbean island. Women always want to go to paradise – if I can't manage it in the bedroom I could take them on holiday. It would, at the very least, provide a good conversation topic, wouldn't it? I could also let them think it's like my second home (which, in a way, it is) and that if they date me they will get to go there. It had worked before. But no, I decide to put that I used to live in a castle. It's not as glamorous as it sounds, it was part of my college at university. This would also go on to explain my username, 'Castleman', which I had thought was fairly innocuous and yet supplied an essential element of mystery. It would also make the women think I had oodles of cash (pathetic, I know). I should have stuck to the Caribbean idea.

London is drenched in the typical January weather; wet and cold and windy. People are rushing from one shop to another, or from various modes of transport to the shelter of their destination. A woman who passes us is berating her boyfriend for not covering her with a sufficient portion of the umbrella;

apparently her hair is getting 'fucking wet, and then it'll be all wispy,' and she won't want 'that cow Andrea' seeing her like that, because 'Andrea will be looking immaculate like she always bloody is.'

The event is being held in a bar, just off Piccadilly, called the Sugar Reef. If it wasn't raining, the huge neon billboards would look like casino lights against a Vegas sky. Jones seems to have high expectations, while I have very little. I still can't get the prejudices out of my mind.

'Max, for God's sake, it *will* be good fun, besides you have to try everything at least once.'

I snigger.

'Except that,' she looks at me like an older sister might look at her disgusting little brother who just farted, 'I'm never trying that.'

Working together, we have got to know each other's sense of humour too well and our jokes are probably too crude for our own good.

'But, isn't it a bit, well, sad?' I ask, returning to the subject of our impending night of schmoozing with other singletons.

'No, it's not sad, that's just your prejudice. You think it's sad, because society said it was sad. Now it's *chic*.'

'I never thought I'd resort to this,' I mutter to myself.

'Stop being such a bore!'

'Have you told anyone you're going?' I ask.

'No, of course not, don't be bloody stupid. Have you?'

'No.'

The bar is underground and, unhelpfully, it is dimly lit. But without a shadow of a doubt there are Jamie and Kevin the legal clerks, with their mates Ian, Geoff and 'Mad-for-it' Mikey the computer programmers. Oh well, I guess it might be easier for me to score in this place.

As we enter the bar, the organisers check us in. They tick off our usernames from the endless list of participants. I try to mutter 'Castleman' several times, hoping that the gathering queue don't hear. But the guy with the clipboard is either deaf or he is enjoying watching me squirm with embarrassment. In the end I shout out CASTLEMAN, to a barrage of sniggers. Then a couple of organisers, who are all wearing Single No More t-shirts, lead us through to another room. They line us up and, in turn, place us in front of a white wall, as if we are about to face a Mexican firing squad. It's almost as bad, they take a Polaroid photo of me.

'Take this photo,' the girl with the camera says, 'and place it on the big wall in the main bar under the little sticker that has your username on it.' I look at her quizzically. 'What's your name?'

'Max'

'No, your username?'

'You don't want to know,' and I snatch the Polaroid before she can probe me further.

As I get into the bar, I see Jones looking for her spot on the girls' side of the wall. I go to the part of the wall designated 'C' and quickly find the small space reserved for 'Castleman'. All the participants have been given business cards with our username and Single No More email address printed on them.

'It's simple Max,' Jones explains, to my utter disbelief, 'if you see a picture of a girl you like, you put your card in the plastic wallet dangling under their photo. They will, hopefully, do the same to you. Enjoy.'

My God, this really is like something out of *Logan's Run*.

We agree to split up and survey the photos for potential matches.

It's a matter of minutes before Jones is instantly targeted by one of the techy nerds in green chinos, faded black cotton roll neck and olive green jacket. The foppy blond haired chap introduces himself as the Rt. Hon. James Johnson. Apparently, Jones is privileged as she is only the third person he has ever told of his title. He meant in his life but I have a feeling it might be in the course of the evening – he has clearly read Toby Young's book one time too many. Foolishly, I decide to leave her with the pretend-peer and grab a drink at the bar.

Within seconds the *cougars* have spotted their prey, out in the open, alone and vulnerable, ready to bring down. 'Cougar' is the name us young bucks at university had given to older women who feast on the flesh of adolescent males. Not quite the MILF that is Stiffler's mum, rather something less appealing – the mutton dressed as lamb species. *Saga-louts.* And, most worrying of all, you have little chance of fending off an attack.

In this instance, there are three of them. The pack have me encircled, there is no way out, I have to make conversation.

''Ello, you're a bit of a cutey ain'chya!' says the one on my right with peroxide highlights and four-inch nail extensions. ''Ere, anyone eva told'ya you look like Jewd Law'ah?' the old hag adds.

'Well, er, I suppose, perhaps once or twice…'

I suddenly realise one of them is holding my arse. Oh God, she's seeing if I am ripe for the picking. They just don't give a shit, these cougars, they have no shame. They just stand there, mojitos in hand, sipping stupidly with that inane 'So what ya gonna do now love?' look on their gormless faces.

'So wot's ya username?' asks the one with the chunky Tiffany's Heart Tag necklace and matching bracelet (she probably has a fucking Tiffany's coil fitted).

This could be my opportunity to bore them stupid with stories of my college days. 'That'll send them packing,' I think.

'Castleman,' I say, with pride.

Their fake tan faces cringe to the point of resembling sun-dried tomatoes. The harpy in the middle screeches, 'Oh, yaw vat arrogant wanka wot said 'ee lived in a castle!'

With a sneer and a look of utter disgust, it was decided that I am not to their liking. Wrong kind of meat. And, as soon as the pack had descended, it dispersed. They return to prowling. But wait a minute, even though I'm repulsed by these old dolly birds, I am concerned that they have turned me down. That they had thought my username and 'funny fact' were shit. If they think that, then the attractive younger girls are bound to think I am a stuck-up twunt. Bollocks.

Still, seeing Jones fight off Lord Lucan on the other side of the bar makes me chuckle and spurs me on to make the most of the evening. I saunter over to a blonde girl and her voluptuous Asian friend.

'Hi, my names, er… Castleman.'

They start giggling. 'Yes, yes *I'm* the arse who said he lived in a castle.' And yes, that noise you can hear is me crashing and burning. They stifle their laughs.

'Really, er… great name,' the blonde girl says sarcastically.

'I know, I can see now that it was a crap choice. So what are your usernames?'

'I'm Wondergirl69,' says the blonde.

'And I'm ExoticPrincess,' the Asian girl says smiling sweetly.

I am about to laugh but I have a feeling that they won't see any funny side to their names as I can with my own useless attempt. I nod enthusiastically instead.

Within a few minutes we've forgotten about the hilarities of the introductions and we're getting along admirably.

'Actually,' ExoticPrincess says suddenly, 'I spotted you as soon as you came in, were we at med school together?'

'Ding dong,' says the Leslie Philips in my head. Is that a line, or is she being genuine?

'I don't think so, I studied history and now I work in PR,' I tell her. She shrugs it off. 'But, I do feel as if I recognise you from somewhere,' I lie.

As it transpires, we do live near each other in Angel. Perhaps she had seen me on the tube and misplaced my face.

'So ExoticPrincess, what's your real name?' I ask.

'It's Lakshmi.'

'Nice name!'

Next thing I know, there's a hand on my arm. Lakshmi seems really nice, I feel refreshed. We talk for a while about travel, food and city life.

'So what do you do, Lakshmi?'

'As I said, I went to med school in Bombay and London. I qualified as a paediatrician. Part of my job involves voluntary work out in India and Africa. I'm the director of a charity, which promotes understanding on childbirth and infant mortality.'

Now I am incredibly impressed. Attractive, intelligent and caring. What every man is looking for in a girlfriend. She also comes across as being really level-headed; but there must be something wrong with her, why else is she at a singles event? Oh yeah, so am I.

Lakshmi does seem like the sort of girl I could take to a cocktail party and leave her from the start to mingle on her own. And you know what, at the end of the evening everyone would be enthralled by this eastern delight, even the other women. She might just past the ultimate girl test.

Tasting success, I get her number and arrange to meet her for a drink at a restaurant near where we live. There is this great Thai place on the high street that would be the perfect venue. I am always quite conscious that the first date should be pretty laidback, a kind of 'get to know each other' chat, to see if you both actually get on.

About half an hour before we are supposed to meet, I get a call from Lakshmi asking if we should have dinner together as well? Bugger. It's not really what I had in mind. Although she seems lovely, I just feel that dinner is a bit too much for the first date. It's a commitment to a long, and often expensive, evening. And at this stage, I still don't know if we will really hit it off. Dinner should be reserved for date number two. The perfect thing with coffee, or drinks, is that if you really hit it off you can always move on to dinner or call the night to a close, think about stuff and have dinner next time.

'Actually, I had a big working lunch, sorry I'm really not hungry,' I lie.

Perhaps I should have realised at that point that she may be a little keen but, I suppose, the idea of having found a potentially boringly 'normal' woman in London was making me light-headed. I may even be able to have sex again without feeling like a male praying mantis.

A few minutes later I arrive at the Blue Elephant, (despite its name I promise you it's not a gay biker bar). In the evenings there is often live music to serenade the guests. Tonight there's a throwback to the seventies playing his Fender.

Lakshmi is already sat at the bar, sipping a vibrant fruit daiquiri. She looks radiant. Having exchanged kisses, a rather overindulgent three times, we snatch up our drinks and she leads the way over to a solitary sofa opposite the bar. It looks like it's intended for punters waiting for a table but it serves our needs, I guess. The restaurant is full of families and young couples tucking into their chow meins.

During the next couple of hours, we cover all the topics under the sun; ostensibly, all is going very well. We're not necessarily agreeing on everything but Lakshmi has something to say about every issue, which I really like. an opinion and is able to argue her point with conviction. Good, so far. On things like culture and travel we appear to have the same interests and philosophies. This is too good to be true. And it is.

I really need to learn to listen to my first instincts. This illusion is about to shatter around me. The first thing that alludes me to her total insanity comes about when we broach the subject of politics. I managed to spot quite early on that Lakshmi could be a little socialist to say the least, you know, somewhere to the left of Chairman Mao. Sure enough, it transpires that she's redder than a post box in the Kremlin. Generally I don't care what political views a person holds, whether they are communist, fascist or any shade in between if they are able to support their views with considered reason and are open to constructive criticism. The most important thing is that people listen to the beliefs of others and defend their right to hold such beliefs, however morally repugnant they may seem. She finishes her political diatribe on Third World debt and asks, 'So where would you place yourself politically?'

'Generally, to the right of centre, with some beliefs being socialist and some further to the right, it depends on the issue.'

I saw her move back sharply into the corner of the settee as soon as the words 'right of centre' left my mouth. Her mouth is still wide open in surprise, or is it disgust? Not that I should, but I feel like launching into an apology for my beliefs. I try to make it better, 'Uh, my friends, though, are of all schools of thought; some are socialist, some are Marxist anti-capitalists and the odd one is even a raging commie but, I suppose, on the whole they tend to be Toryish.' She's still in shock. I feel as if I have just confessed to dabbling in sadomasochism or that I have a particularly virulent strain of a highly contagious disease. I suppose some people would say that being a Tory these days equates to the same thing, but nonetheless. The little strumpet leans back, the knitted furrows on her brow show her genuine concern, and bugger me if she doesn't say, 'I don't think I can tell my friends that I'm dating a Tory.' Whatthefuck? We're having coffee. Who says we're dating, I think I have a say in this, that's why we're having coffee. Christ, we haven't even exchanged bodily fluids yet. I feel like an expensive Gucci handbag that she's thinking of buying but she has just realised that the clasp doesn't go with her evening dress.

'I thought you were teasing me,' she says.

'Er, no. That is my political stance, as I say it does depend on the issue.'

'No, I can see you weren't joking now.'

I feel like saying, 'These are my personal beliefs that you're deriding you intolerant bint!' But I can't. She then has the audacity to proclaim, 'Let's forget about it all now, shall we?'

Am I supposed to be grateful? And with that I watch her positively shake her head, clearing her moral conscience, and force a smile back onto that pretty face. I would swear she's thinking, 'No get a grip Lakshmi, he's got a good job, an environmental activist trustafarian would be better, but you've looked already and can't find one.'

I think I decided at this stage that my little Bolshevik was a Kremlin short of a Red Square. As a man, it's often difficult to be ruthlessly frank as women can be. I would like get up and walk out at that moment but it would be contrary to my upbringing and my social conditioning. A social gravity keeps my bum firmly planted to the sofa. I'll just have to sit it out to the bitter end of the date. Nob.

Over the past couple of hours, the would-be Hank Marvin has been dazzling us with his renditions of 'Blue Hotel' and 'Walking in Memphis'. He strikes the opening chord of 'Ain't No Sunshine', and Lakshmi positively whoops with excitement.

'Ooh I love this song, let's dance.'

?

Oh-My-God. Is that the sound of my bowels dissolving. Honey, if you haven't noticed we are in a Goddamnmotherfucking family Thai eatery not Bar Mamba on the Charing Cross Road. I never mind being the first on the dancefloor but this is a Thai restaurant. Everyone else is seated. It's Hank Marvin. It's a THAI FUCKING RESTAURANT.

So I get up and dance. Well, I couldn't refuse, could I? Bar the melodies of the music man, a hush falls over the restaurant. All the other guests are thinking to themselves, 'What are those two idiots doing?' That is except for one old bat who has gone soppy eyed and clearly thinks that this is the most romantic gesture she has seen since her husband asked her to feel his one-eyed trouser-snake on the back seat of his Triumph Herald in '65.

There I am, slow dancing in that last-dance-of-the-night teenage disco style, hoping and begging that none of my neighbours walk past the glass window that runs full length of the restaurant; the window I am dancing in front of. Hank thinks that this is great, he has never been able to muster an applause for his labours up til now, let alone have two people strut their stuff. This is like a mosh pit to this man and he's playing to the crowd. So the bastard plays the song three times over, extending my agony. And then it happens, she moves in for the kill. It's that moment when you know what's coming and there is nothing you can do to stop it. I feel her head rise slightly off my chest, her dancing slows and she looks up with those sultry eyes, inviting me to make a move. I grin inanely. And when I don't lean in to snog her, she mistakes my lack of enthusiasm for shyness. Before I know it, her tongue is prising open my clammed up lips. The only thing running through my mind is, 'What the hell's that smell?' I realise that she had obviously made herself up when she disappeared to the loo a few moments before suggesting the vertical desire of the horizontal pleasure. She reeks of powder – it's her foundation makeup. She must have plastered the stuff on. It's making me choke, I just want to get out of there. Eventually Hank strums his final riff and lets us take our seats.

All has now changed. In the course of that one dance I have become hers. Whereas previously we had been sitting opposite one another, she is now on top of me. The mad cow is twirling my hair and playing ring-o'ring-a-poses on the palm of my hand. The rest of the diners are still staring in disbelief. I think the staff are worried that I am about to bend her over one of their plaster Thai deity's and give her a thoroughly good tupping.

Bugger me if she doesn't ask for another dance. This is taking the piss, I have to leave.

'You know Max, I think you'll really like my parents,' she says out of the blue.

'Your who, sorry, what?'

'You're Christian, aren't you?' It's as if she's thinking out loud rather than asking me a question directly. But I answer anyway.

'Erm, yes, I suppose so.'

'Mmm'

'What do you mean, "Mmm"?'

'What do you think about people who convert to a different faith to get married?'

'Well…'

'Isn't that a cute baby over there, Max!'

You've never seen a grown man force down a fruit daiquiri so quickly. I drag the waiter over to the table and demand the bill. 'Hunter my son, it's time to make your apologies and effect your getaway,' I tell myself.

'Lakshmi, I didn't realise what time it is.'

'Why, what time is it?' she asks.

'Wow, it's 8.30 already,' I say, wearing that 'doesn't time fly when you're having fun' expression.

'Oh,' she says, sadly. Despite everything, I feel guilty about my deception when I see that she doesn't want me to go. I feel like a bastard.

'Yeah, I have to get some work done before tomorrow. God, I hate these corporate slave drivers.'

Of course, yes, you poor thing. These massive conglomerates and leech-like multinationals shouldn't make such demands of their workers!'

'Er, yeah. Quite right. I'm so sorry I have to go. But, let's do it again some time.'

'Okay, what about tomorrow?' she says.

'Tomorrow?' I'm getting up from the couch, my jacket is already over my shoulders. I tug it frantically into place.

'Yes, tomorrow,' she persists.

'Yeah, could be good. So long as I don't have any sudden meetings, you know those bastards.'

'Of course,' she says earnestly.

Two minutes later and I am marching at double time down the high street, back to the security of my bachelor pad. I left Lakshmi standing by our table in the restaurant.

That was the last I saw of Lakshmi, I didn't return her calls. She is the type of girl that would grasp onto any contact whatsoever, however negative it is. I could have called her to say she was mad, intolerant and that funnily enough it would never work out between us, so 'see you later'. And you know what, she would only hear the words 'see' 'you' and 'later'. The next thing you know, she would be at my front door with a warm rabbit pie she had just baked. No thanks.

I decide that singles bars and dating websites are things to be consigned to the bottom of the trunk, as far as tools at the disposable of the discerning single man are concerned. Of course, that assumes that you're discerning. If only Raj had learnt from my errors. But then again, when you're wondering where the next one's coming from you will turn to desperate measures, and no man should ever be criticised for treading this dark path, just give him a little sympathy. And so when Raj tries a new tactic of his own to ensnare a woman, his experience makes my run in with Lakshmi look like we'd be giving Brad n' Jennifer a run for their money as couple of the year.

8

M.I.L.F.

There is nothing that attracts a woman to a man more than when the latter is dressed in a pukka suit – whether it's a trendy Ermenegildo Zegna or a classic Saville Row affair with pin stripes and double vents. During our student days we had successfully put this theory to the test. We had taken our suits out of their natural surroundings and introduced them to the clubbing scene. We went to the cheesiest nightclub in Newcastle, suited up, and hit the dancefloor. The results were astounding. The women flocked, and, crooks in hand, we herded them in. We stood out, we looked ridiculous – ridiculous but dapper. They were intrigued as to why we had come out on a student night in our smarts. The thing is, a suit delivers all kinds of connotations, among others, a pride in self-grooming, a certain maturity and that self-confidence to be what you are. But most importantly, it speaks success and cash, and lots of it. This effect is never more acute than when the suit is taken out of its natural habitat. Back then it was such a master pulling technique that we replicated it time and time again following in the footsteps of the Rat Pack and the Flaming Ferraris. Well, perhaps more like a well-dressed version of the *Young Ones*, but it seemed to do the trick.

One Thursday evening in April Raj decides to take this arcane philosophy to another level. The sports jacket. That sartorial holy grail.

'Max, I need to attract a different type of woman.'

'What sort of type?' I ask.

'The more mature woman – the type who knows what she wants and isn't afraid to go get it,' he explains.

'Ah, a M.I.L.F.!'

'Mother-I'd-Like-to-Fuck – got it in one, buddy. And the sports jacket will be just the thing to allure her. Wait there, I'll show you.'

His jacket of choice is a good Harris tweed, *sans* leather elbow patches and with a bold red check.

'Mate, it's going to look the mutt's nuts,' he assures me.

'Right,' I remain unconvinced.

'Man, I'm telling you, no one else is going to be wearing one of these.'

'No, I'm sure you're right.'

Raj is a cool guy and, as I've already said, he is renowned for his sharp dress sense. He can pull most things off but it's fair to say that he is not your archetypal Hackett customer. You would be forgiven for thinking that Raj is more west coast 'Cali' than Middlesbrough born and bred. If he was any more chilled he'd make your average surfer dude seem positively edgy. His usual attire consists of skateboard baggies with the crotch dangling somewhere around your midcalf with a PFD (personal flotation device) as a belt and a t-shirt depicting the Goo Goo Dolls. You might think, this isn't your regular convivial boulevardier, the sort one would expect to see donning a tweed jacket to stroll down Jermyn Street, and you would be right. But Raj had grown bored of frumpy girls in their mid-twenties, with their Moto hipsters, overhanging beer-gut and builder's bum, accommodating cheese wire g-strings that cut into the middle of their back-cleavage. The same girls who come with two oversized suitcases of emotional baggage – they're so full, they had to sit on them to squeeze in the last bit of 'fucked-upness'.

'Dude,' he starts, 'the girls I've gone out with recently have all lacked the confidence to live out their fantasies, one didn't even want to do it doggie-style, because she thought that I didn't love her if I wasn't looking into her eyes as I shagged her.'

'Dirty had that happen once,' I say.

'What did he do?'

'He did her from behind anyway, and as she was about to climax, shoved his work-pass photo in front of her face.'

'Nice,' he says. 'But seriously, I think the older woman, a woman in her mid-thirties, will have come out the other side of this dating hell. She will have put it all behind her and embraced who she is. Women of that age are so damn sexy.'

Sane men will go to extreme lengths to get laid.

Raj, now tooled up for the evening ahead of him, plumps for a night of partying at the West End club, Attica. Ed and I tag along on his sharking expedition, as his wingmen. Following on from my recent escapades, I am more than happy to sit the hunt out, on this occasion, and instead help my *compadres* get lucky. The idea of pulling another random of unknown pedigree isn't appealing, it has to be said.

The first task of the evening is to get past the clipboard nazis who are barring our way to the pleasuredome. Two colossuses, of what appear to be Sardinian origin, flank the entrance to the club. Loitering between them is the obligatory dolly bird, or should I say Keeper of the List. The list is the scroll that contains the names of the chosen few, the lucky ones who may descend the steps into the decadence and debauchery that passes itself off as an exclusive London club. Brimming with confidence, finger on the charm trigger, I saunter up to the hag on the door. Like all Keepers of the List, she's a poison dwarf. A scrawny late-thirties has-been. Her hair has been chemically treated one time too many. Those freshly polished boots are straight from Gestapo supplies. She's wearing the latest catwalk design, which frankly would hang better on a goat. The quintessential *faux*-fur lined full-length coat is draped across her bony shoulders. Her beady eyes look me up and down as I, the *lesserling*, approach the starry gate to the den of iniquity.

'Hello, how are you?' Okay, so I'm trying to be nice – even I know when a bit of toadying doesn't go amiss. Don't act like you wouldn't do the same, this woman is the only thing stopping us getting to London's prime ladies.

'Name?' Her purple painted talons drum the clipboard.

'My name's Max…' A pathetic submissive voice emits itself from my mouth, the voice of a grovelling desperado.

'Who are you with?,' Frau Ziegenbok demands.

'I'm with a party organised by Pippa Makepeace.'

Yes, I know, it sounds like she should be a Bond girl but I swear that's her name. As the hag gazes down the list of the chosen darlings I tell her that there are three of us.

'Any girls?' she asks continuing to not look up.

'Sorry, what do you mean?'

'You know what girls are don't you?' Finally she looks up at me facetiously, 'You know those things you have come here to molest this evening?' I smile, laugh nervously, smile some more but she's having none of it.

'Well, are there any girls in your group?'

'In the club, yes, but it's just us three at the moment.'

'In that case, please queue in the men's queue.'

'No, there are girls but they're inside already!' I plead some more.

'Men's queue!' She's growing impatient. She wants as little chat as possible, if I push it any more I'm liable to be refused entry, she knows that she's got me by the balls. One of the Sardinian brutes starts to move me towards the long line of equally peeved looking blokes.

How does this work anyway? The men's queue, what the fuck is that? We have to wait until more girls go in, what do they think we are, salivating predators waiting to feast on the vulnerable meat of womankind? Oh yes, point taken. Still, it doesn't quite seem to make sense, if you can only get in by having your name on the list, which ours are, then you already know the ratio of men to women before the night begins. But I know it just isn't worth trying to point out this particular piece of logic to our friend the *Fraulein*, especially as it seems her twin has borrowed the brain cell for the night. We take our place at the back of the queue. It starts to rain.

After an hour or so, the gook on the left, the one without a frontal lobe, lifts the crimson rope that straddles the dark hole to untold pleasures. The three of us muddle past, shifting from one foot to the other as if we're part of a chain gang linked by invisible shackles. The bouncer claps his eyes on Raj and his sports jacket. He can't help but release a chuckle.

'Nice jacket,' he mutters in a thick accent.

'Cheers dude,' Raj slaps the guy on the back and invites him to pull his finger. I don't believe the bouncer is *au fait* with American teenage culture. We move Raj on, before the doorman accepts his offer, only to have Raj let one rip.

Descending into the darkness, the first thing that I become aware of is the fusion of expensive sickly perfume and sweat. Then, like ripples through the air, the pulses from the bass speaker hit my face like gentle admonishing slaps. My ears pop. Lastly, I feel the heat. It's as if I am entering the engine room of a ship, or sneaking into the boiler room at school when I was 11.

At the bar, we part with half our life savings in exchange for some partially cold Coronas. They must have just restocked the fridges with beers, how annoying. We scope out the joint and, without thinking, start to perform the Rating Ritual. The bar girl spots the tweed jacket. I can see that she's confused by it, but also intrigued, in a good way.

'I like your jacket, looks cool,' she smiles at Raj.

'Cheers,' he says, coolly.

Its effects have started already. Encircling the bar there's a dancefloor surrounded by mirrors. On our left there are a series of booths where you can order champagne and seduce the vixen of your choosing. Two It-girls, Chelsea *Deb*-types, walk past and stare at Raj. Normally they would be too self-absorbed to notice *any* guy. The fact that they look at all is approval enough.

'Hey guys, check out the girl on the couch!'

Raj breaks the obligatory silence, he must have spotted something pretty special. He points to a temptress in one of the booths who is sitting alone, sipping Moët from a flute. The bottle, half drunk, protrudes phallic-like from the cooler bucket. As we all stand there gawking, she looks up. She doesn't see the rest of us, her eyes have clapped on the Asian Hugh Heffner in the musty sports jacket at my side. This is Austin Powers magnetism at its best.

Raj puts down his beer and, likes he's stepping off a yacht, saunters through the throng of sweaty dancers. He approaches the woman, who's wearing a short skirt that reveals her long toned pins.

'Hello, I wondered if you'd come over,' the woman peers up from her drink. Her voice is brimming with confidence and it is more bubbly than the champers she's knocking back. This beautiful stranger is older than the average Attica punter, probably twice the age of the pair of It-girls. She must be in her mid to late thirties. She is sultry and relaxed, relaxed with her own femininity, relaxed because of her years of experience. Her movements, from the beating of her eyelids to the sipping of her champers, are slow, paced and effectual. She has had a hundred lovers, but none of them have robbed her of a modicum of her elegance or scarred her beauty.

'I noticed you across the room, you look good,' her voice is silky.

Raj just nods. Smooth.

'Why don't you join me for a drink,' her tongue glides over her ice-white teeth. 'Come, sit next to me,' she pats the luscious lip red sofa.

'There's nothing I'd like more,' Raj ensconces himself at her side.

He's finding it hard not to take his eyes off those long, slender legs. She's wearing a black strappy top with a plunging neckline that reveals magnificent pendulous orbs.

'How thoroughly public spirited of her,' he thinks.

Raj can't believe his luck, he's sure that this woman is up for it big time. And boy is she a woman, definitely no girl, she's 100% all woman... *femme*... *la bella donna*. My friend is not easily fazed, but I think that under normal circumstances even he would acknowledge her overwhelming magnetism. Still, he's playing it very cool, revelling in her attention and her shameless superiority. It must be the jacket.

Before he knows it the last drop of that ambrosia has been supped and there's a mischievous glint in her eye.

'You know, Raj,' she says getting closer, running her fingers through his hair, 'my place isn't that far from here and I have my car parked right outside.'

'Then let's bust a move and split this joint honey!' Raj has always been a one with words.

Meanwhile, Ed and I are rooted to the same spot at the bar, standing open-mouthed, like two chimps at feeding time. We haven't moved since arriving, staring in bewilderment as Raj works his magic. This hot, gorgeous, gift to mankind strides past the bar, dragging our friend by the hand in her wake. As the suave bugger is pulled past us, he flashes us that that knowing look. A theatrical wink and a cheeky grin that the Cheshire Cat would be proud of – thoughtfully sharing his success with his mates, letting us know that he's about to score with the most delectable woman in the club, only to leave us two twits to chat with the vacuous, self-absorbed blondes clutching Prada handbags. Well you have to really, don't you?

Waiting for them outside is a beast of a sportscar, a sleek silver cat. As they pass the other way through the two bouncers, Raj looks back over his shoulder and, inviting a vicious attack, winks in a similar fashion at the doorman who earlier mocked the sacred sports jacket. The doorman snarls. Oblivious to this show of machismo, the dominatrix continues to drag Raj in the direction of her car.

'Wait I don't even know your name,' Raj blurts as he lingers by the passenger door waiting for her to activate the central locking. Raj you friggin' idiot what do you care what her name is.

'Get in the car,' she orders. With a cheeky smile, she slinks round to the driver's side. The interior of the Audi is a predictable black leather, which somehow retains an air of sophistication. Pensively, she caresses the leather wheel before flicking the engine over, which, under her gentle touch, purrs back at her.

'Charlotte, my name's Charlotte.'

She shoots him a playful sideward glance. A slight odour of rubber from the wheelspin lingers outside the club as the TT disappears down Dean Street, taking Raj to a place he never thought he'd go – the clap clinic.

Charlotte's flat is an ultra-sleek, minimalist West End bachelorette pad. She rummages in her Hermès handbag and withdraws a small leather key fob from its depths. For the first time since they left the car there's an awkward silence. When you're travelling back to the girl's place, be it in their sportscar or a cab, you can maintain a pretence that you are there for some reason other than the inevitable conclusion of your journey. But as soon as you get to their front door, there's to be no hiding from the truth. You are about to invade a stranger's personal space, enter the sanctuary of their home. It is stamped with the fingerprints of their personality and filled with the trinkets of their past. Then you will be naked, then you will have sex. And you both know it.

And yet, Raj notices there is something lacking in this success story apartment. Soul. Sure, it looks like it is right out of Conran; there's the Heals furniture, B&O hardware and Jimmy Choo, casually discarded in the hallway, but it is a pretence. So what? What does Raj care, the girl is hot, and willing, which is always a bonus. Charlotte kicks off her heels and disappears into the stainless steel appliance fitted kitchen. More bubbly is cracked open, this time a vintage Bolly. Raj is so excited she could have served up Dr Pepper and he wouldn't care, but it completes the awe she wants to create.

That night, Raj's world was rocked, he trod the path that is a rite of passage for every young man. It might happen just the once but it is to be savoured for life. It is one of the things that as you sit by the fire at 75, resplendent in Argyll blanket, pipe and glass of port you *will* reminisce, with affection, about that one older woman. The successful mature woman. The 35-plus year old. The girl who was netball captain as you were still wetting your pants in junior school, those eight or nine years senior, just enough to create the feeling of unobtainable desire. This time though, she has chosen you.

Raj left the next morning… a King. You had better not have stepped in his way that morning; he felt like he had a dong the size of a German bratwurst and he was liable to pull down his keks and show you just for the goddamn-fucking sake of it.

And things went well for the next few weeks. Charlotte and King Dong dated, doing the usual things a couple do. A bit of dinner, a little restauranting, some art galleries, the odd Sotheby's preview (Raj feigned an interest, it is one of the downsides of shagging the older cultured successful type) and lots of great sex. And he is being driven around Kensington in a TT by a foxy temptress. What could go wrong?

It was after these first few weeks that it happened. Charlotte calls him up and asks him round for a cosy night in. Raj knows what this means, at least, he thinks he does.

Raj stands in the small half-landing between the first and second floors outside the heavy white door to Charlotte's apartment. The period iron lift rattles into action in the stairwell behind him. Raj watches the cage slowly pass the first floor. Inside there's a woman in her forties clutching a small white poodle, shaved in that stupid way people have poodles *coiffured*. The dog is wearing pink Pringle briefs. Fucking poodles.

Charlotte appears at the door of her apartment, wearing little more than a silky dressing gown. Raj is in shock.

'This is a result,' he thinks to himself, 'straight on to the nookie and bypassing any idle chit chat on Pollock over canapés.'

For some strange reason though, tonight she seems like her mind is elsewhere. She leads him silently past the rows of shoes in the hall, through into the wood-floored lounge. Through the Victorian sash window Notting Hill is becoming alive with the hustle and bustle of young couples strolling to other couples' homes for an evening of dinner parties and predictable conversation. As the two of them sit on the sofa, Charlotte might be responding to his kisses and gropes but he can feel that underneath it all she's tense, her hearts not in it.

'Are you ok?' he asks.

Charlotte seems pretty uneasy, her eyes constantly avoiding his.

'Yes I'm fine,' she says. After a pause she adds an unconvincing 'honestly.' Raj, unperturbed, shrugs it off and returns to exploring her tonsils with his tongue, his hand reaching for one of her poonts.

'Well actually,' she starts, reticently, 'there's something I want to ask you.' She leans back out of reach, this time staring him right in the eyes.

An uneasiness wafts over him. 'Sure ask away.' He reaches for his glass of champagne that's resting on her coffee table. The only other thing on the table is a copy of Mario Testino's best works, carefully placed at an angle to make it look like it has been casually thrown down. Raj isn't particularly thirsty, but he feels he needs to do something as he sits uncomfortably, waiting for Charlotte's question.

'Tonight,' she continues, 'I would like us to try something different.'

She sees the blank expression on Raj's face. Very quickly, she blurts, 'Of course, you don't have to.'

She's gone red, a fuchsia flushes her cheeks. The mature independent woman has vanished and, in her place, a shy school girl has appeared.

'Oh bollocks, what the hell can it be?' Raj is thinking to himself, 'I knew this was too good to be true.'

'Sure what kind of thing?' he asks, giving in to intrigue and the ever-powerful, self-destructing hope of fornication. After what seems a heavy pause, she says, 'Well, I'd like to dress up.'

'Phew,' he thinks, 'thank God for that, perhaps it'll be a rubber nurse's outfit.'

'That's ok,' he says, 'lots of people do that, no need to be embarrassed.'

Raj has gone from the rabbit caught in headlights to the reassuring male. Assertive and in control, he puts Charlotte at ease with herself. The schoolgirl in her disappears as quickly as she materialised. She jumps up all excited, 'Excellent, I have the outfit, wait there and I'll put it on.'

She's back to her normal self again. Confident, sexy Charlie is back in full form, and a warm relief washes over Raj. With that she disappears into her dressing room, closing the door almost to. Ever more inquisitive, he leans forward from the sofa, trying to catch a glimpse of naked flesh through the jar. As the door opens, he jumps back into the security of the sofa. Looking up, he nearly chokes on his Bolly. Standing there, legs astride, is Charlotte or what was Charlotte. There's a woman wearing mid-thigh high black leather boots with Perspex platforms, torn fishnets and a lime green PVC miniskirt. Up top she's opted for a purple strappy top, gypsy bangles flap around her wrists and her backcombed hair looks like she's been dragged through a rather vicious hawthorn. The most disturbing thing is the way that she's painted her face; black eye shadow is smudged around her dull, emotionless eyes and a thick coat of vermilion lipstick is globbed on her lips. Raj squints in disbelief. No, it is definitely Charlotte. She looks like the party host who's had a bit to drink and has been crying over an unrequited love. If she was a hooker. The awkward silence returns, a silence like that first night. Another boundary passed, another personal space entered for the first time.

'I'm supposed to be a prostitute!' she declares impatiently.

'No shit,' Raj mutters in disbelief.

'Is it ok, do you like it?'

She's gone from being annoyed to pleading anxiously. Her voice sounds as if it's about to falter. Raj gets a grip on himself, 'Yeah, of course, you look great,' smiling, nodding, trying to look enthusiastic.

'I mean you look downright dirty, sexy,' Raj tries to get into role but all he can think is, 'What the fucking hell do you look like you freak?'

And just when the poor idiot thinks this is as far as this game is going, Charlotte ups the ante.

'Raj, there's something else.'

'Something else?' Now he is worried.

'Yes, I'd like you to drive my car.'

'Okay cool.' That's fine, he can handle that.

'No, no, I want you to drive it tonight, me, down to Kings Cross, drop me off and then return and pick me up. You know, as if you're picking me up as a hooker.'

In a moment Raj is back to being Thumper, mesmerised by the headlights of an oncoming, rather large SUV. What do you say to that? 'Holy-fucking-shit you're bonkers,' is what he'd like to say. But it sort of comes out as 'O-k, if you want.'

'Oh Raj,' she rushes over, kissing him, 'I knew you'd be up for it when you saw me.'

'Ye-ah right. No, I think it's cool, we can do this.'

Good man Raj, you put on a brave face.

As the lovely couple leave the flat, Raj pleads with God that no one spots them. What would his mother say if she saw him?

'Please don't let the woman with the poodle reappear.'

In the bowels of the underground car park Raj ushers his girl into her car as quickly as possible and sets off for Kings Cross.

Just past the train station, outside a rundown jazz shop, Raj slows to a halt. Furtively, he checks that no one is watching them. Without saying a word, she hops out and disappears into the shadows of the doorway. There's graffiti everywhere, rubbish from the kebab shop is piled up to waist height and the street light above the car twitches nervously, flickering on and off. Raj speeds off, conscious of patrolling coppers pulling over this unique curb-crawler. How on Earth could he ever explain himself?

He drives around the block a couple of times, growing ever more concerned about Charlotte. This is far from a safe area of London at the best of times and under normal conditions, let alone when your bird is pretending to be on the game. What if she gets attacked, raped, murdered? He would never be able to forgive himself. He swings the sportscar round and returns to the drop off point.

Thank God, there she is, the silly tart, chewing gum as she stands in the half-light looking like a pro under the lamppost. He crawls the curb at a snail's pace, the electric window wound down.

'Hiya, do you want to get in and we'll go home.'

Clearly roleplaying is a concept wasted on my friend. She ignores him. Raj sighs, he leans across the passenger seat and, in self-disbelief, shouts, 'Yo bitch, you workin' or what?'

That grabs her attention. She smiles.

'Hundred large ones for as much shaggin' as ya can handle, anal's extra.'

Raj is aghast, open-mouthed he stares in disgust at this stranger leaning in through the car window selling her wares. Oh dear Lord, and where did that south London accent materialise from?

'Great,' he says, all other words failing him. He flips the switch to open the door for his *hooker* to get in. Raj checks his mirrors but makes an effort not to catch his own eye, he can't bear to look at himself. The coast is clear. He pulls off at some speed, he has to get away from the scene of the crime. The greater the distance he puts between himself and Kings Cross, the more he will feel cleansed. He can never take the train from there to Newcastle to see his family again. It wouldn't be right. The two of them sit there in silence for the remainder of the drive across London back to Charlotte's pad, with Raj feeling super sensitive and Charlotte a tad self-conscious, no doubt. Sadly his hope of a reprieve is not answered and the roleplay only continues once they get back to the flat.

They face the front door to her flat, once more. They are still feeling awkward, but this time it is for a different reason to that first night. All Raj knows, is that he's glad to be back at the flat and away from public eyes. As soon as the door is shut behind them, Charlotte reels on Raj.

'Now I want you to do me – do me hard, do me fast and do me now.'

A man reaches a certain point where he stops giving a shit and just goes with the flow. I suppose it's an inherent trait that prepares one for marriage. Self-respect, dignity and pride can all fall away at the hands of a woman. The key is to face it stoically and preserve as much of those qualities as you can. Well, it is around now that Raj gives up. He finally bows to her superior will and decides to get in role. He pushes her up against the bedroom wall, her mouth instantly gives way under his (*quel faux pas* – she should know prossies never kiss their clients). He hitches up her lime green number to push aside her knickers. She's not wearing knickers. He drops his own pants and goes at it hammer and tongs. Charlotte is grunting and moaning most enthusiastically. Raj flips her over and starts to bull her from behind. She begins to wail. Her head is banging up against the wall, she's screaming with pleasure, 'Arrgghh yes, give it to me, harder! HARDER!'

Knock, knock. Like a death knoll to their 'lovemaking', a furious rapping is coming from the front door.

'You cannot be serious, who can be calling at this time?' Raj snaps out of his alter ego as a punter.

'Please go and see who it is,' she begs Raj, pushing him back by the shoulders and making him withdraw.

Poor Raj throws a towel around his waist and makes for the front door.

There's a tall skinny guy, probably in his thirties, with glasses and floppy hair standing in the corridor.

'Hi, I'm from next door.'

He looks like shit, but then again it is 2 am. The man shifts from one foot to the other in a bewildered fashion.

'Er, I wondered if you could keep the noise down,' the man says, trying to peer past Raj into the flat.

'Yeah, sorry buddy, I was... well you know how it is right, brother? I'll tell her to keep it down!' He winks.

'Right,' somewhat unsettled, the neighbour stands there in silence looking incomprehensively at the dishevelled young Asian guy in front of him. He sees a tweed sports jacket discarded carelessly on the hall floor, along with other indistinguishable garments of garish colours. He presumes the jacket belongs to the near-naked Asian but somehow can't imagine him wearing it; it seems incongruous.

A few seconds pass, Raj continues to smile smugly with that inane grin that blokes give each other when talking about their conquests. Finally, with nothing more to be said, Raj sheepishly shuts the door in the guy's face. Putting on the safety-chain, he can't help but chuckle to himself at the whole situation. The guy knew Raj had been banging his neighbour senseless. With a smirk on his face he trots back into the bedroom ready to finish off the job, all fired-up from Charlotte's filthy antics.

There she is, sitting in bed, with the covers pulled up around her neck and her knees drawn up to her chin. All images of Charlie the hooker have disappeared, she is no longer in role. Raj is surprised to see her back to her normal self again, and wearing such a guilty look.

'There's something I should tell you.' There's a culpability in her voice.

His heart sinks. What more can there be?

'That guy from next door is my... kinda... boyfriend.'

So there I am, bent over double in a fit of laughter as a genuinely distraught Raj recounts his nightmare to me.

'Bastard, I phoned you for some support,' he says.

Clearly the tables have turned since my Single No More misadventure, which had caused a similar response from an unsympathetic Raj. I had been ribbing the poor guy but I was growing a bit concerned as the story went on.

'Raj, I don't want to tell you this, but, what if this girl doesn't leave the boots and plastic skirt for the bedroom?'

I can hear him wince.

'Oh no, what d'you mean?'

'Well, I've heard about women who have everything; beauty, success and money, but no excitement. So, for their kicks, they become prostitutes by night, for the sheer thrill of it. They don't need the money but they get off on it massively.'

Silence. I can hear him thinking, mulling it over.

'No, she's too classy, too nice (he's trying to convince himself). It was just a roleplay (he thinks some more). But she did know where the hookers were. And she had all the gear. She'd definitely done it before. Shit, you're right what am I gonna do?'

He's my mate, I have to be honest. Trust me, there's nothing that frightens me more than someone stuffing an oversized cotton bud down the end of my todger. But there are times when you have to face the music and take a little pain as the price for all that pleasure.

'Buddy, you should go to the clap clinic.'

'Foockin'ell!' He knew it was coming. 'You're right though. Arhhh shit!'

Raj turns up to the clinic the following day, he had been straight on the phone to them when he had finished talking to me. The building does nothing to ease the anxiety of what any visitor is about to put themselves through. It's an horrendous 1970s single-storey cube. The clinic is like a large bungalow, the only thing missing are the gnomes in the patch of grass leading to the entrance. It has all the design intricacies of a four-year-old's attempt at building a Lego house.

Raj takes a seat in the waiting room. Feeling utterly ashamed of himself, he hopes that no one he knows walks in. This is more embarrassing than going into Boots to buy condoms at 17. At least, back then, you could make out you were just intending to buy toothpaste and when the cashier asked if there was anything else you could cunningly come out with 'Oh yes, I'd better get some johnnies while I'm here.' But not here, why else would you be at the clap clinic than if you thought you had a bad case of the nob rot?

'Mr Khan,' the attendant calls out.

He tries to make out that she's calling for someone else, but everyone else in the room is white. All eyes lie on him. Highly self-consciously, he gets up and ambles through the faded acrylic comfies, avoiding the gaze of the other in-patients.

'Er, Mr Khan,' she calls after him. 'You need the nurse in Room 3.'

Nodding meekly, he shuffles along the beige corridor. The lights hum to themselves. He is begging, praying inside his head that the nurse in Room 3 is some fat old hag. The last thing he needs is some cute busty nurse doing the test, the type of girl who might feasibly feature in one his fantasies. The fantasy where he plays the gynaecologist who romps with two of his nurses and one of his wealthy patients – all at once. He faces the door to Room 3. He takes a deep breath and knocks twice.

'Come in.'

The voice behind the door doesn't sound young, in fact it sounds decidedly middle-aged, with undertones of Nurse Gladys from *Open All Hours*. That's fine, Raj thinks, he can put up with a rotund mother hen type, someone who can put him at his ease during the uncomfortable procedure.

'Ah, you must be Mr Khan, I'm Nurse Calderwell.'

Thank God, she isn't quite as rotund as nurse Gladys but she is short and stocky, that'll do. 'Hi' is all Raj can muster.

After a few seconds he is more relaxed and can't help but release a little chuckle to himself. For some reason he is overcome with bravery, perhaps at the relief of Nurse Calderwell.

'So, I'll drop my keks then?' he says impatiently.

Before the nurse knew it, there's Raj, his skateboard baggies around his ankles and his wedding tackle looking vulnerable.

'Well dear you needn't have taken them down so quickly, but as you have let's get on with it shall we?'

'Yeah, if you don't mind.'

A bit confident considering what's about to happen to him. There's almost some of Ed's stoicism in his voice.

'As you may have been told when you made your appointment, the procedure can be a little uncomfortable,' says the nurse.

At this point, the correct procedure is to break down and blabber like a baby for your mummy but for some strange reason us men have a propensity to put on a false bravado when facing adversity in the company of women – a machismo that inevitably leads to our downfall. This is to be no exception.

'Oh it is good to have a brave patient for a change, most men start to whimper. Perhaps you wouldn't mind our trainee nurse having a go… Claudia.'

Before Raj can protest, a girl appears from behind the blue curtain, the type of partition that all doctor's surgeries are equipped with, for modesty's sake.

Nurse (in training) Claudia, however, is as far from Nurse Gladys as you can imagine. In fact Raj is sure he does recognise her from his favourite fantasy. She is about 5'4, blonde and has something of the Anna Kournikova about her. She might be wearing the starched uniform but you can see the tight bum, pert breasts and tiny waist a mile off. Raj is dumbstruck, shellshocked, buggered. What can he do, protest?

'Now then dear,' says old nurse Calderwell to nurse-in-training Claudia, 'you'll need to get down on your knees like I've shown you before and hold the penis like so.'

Raj shuts his eyes and thinks of his grandma. He starts berating himself, and making oaths that he knows he can never abide by.

'I swear I'll never sleep with a woman again, not until my wedding night, perhaps not even then. Fucking sports jacket!'

He opens his left eye to sneak a peek, and there she is; this vision of 17-year-old beauty, on her knees holding his penis and peering up from those soft blue doe eyes. *Grandmother, grandmother, grandmother.* There's a rush in his loins, the blood pumps through the valves at an uncontrollable rate. Oh no, too late. As he looks down the flag pole raises, the rocket's ready to launch.

With a chuckle she thrusts the cotton bud up.

9

Speed dating

'Hi Max, what are you doing tomorrow night?' It's Abbie, calling from work.

'I was going to chill out at home, why?'

'Forget it, you're coming out with me,' she declares, and I can tell by her tone that she won't take no for an answer. Following my recent spate of late nights, I fancy a couple of evenings relaxing in the comfort of my own home, but I know it's futile putting up a struggle. Perhaps, it could be fun.

'There's a friend of mine having a barbecue at his place up the road, he has some news I think you'll find interesting.'

Abbie forms part of this interesting group of female friends who take it upon themselves to find you a woman as soon as you become single. Abbie is a little less theatrical in her efforts than Pippa. The moment some of them had learnt that I had called it off with Jessica, they were calling me up to arrange blind dates with their friends. It isn't this Jewish mother syndrome that shocked me initially, rather the brutality they employ in their matchmaking. Often they were setting me up with some of their oldest friends. At first, I was expecting all kinds of pep talks about how I should be a gentleman etc. Incredibly it was the total opposite, more often than not they'd say things like, 'All I'm doing is making the initial introduction, what you do with her is up to you.'

As it happens, on this occasion, it isn't a blind date.

'You haven't met this friend of mine before, his name's Gary,' she starts.

'Right.'

'There's a barbecue at his place, you're invited,' she continues. 'He's a TV producer, you'll get on well, I'm sure he'd be entertained by your recent dating horrors.'

The stooge of the party, great.

We turn up to a plush dockside apartment the following evening. A tall guy with dark hair greets us at the door. He's wearing a white Ralph Lauren shirt, tucked into faded blue denims which are slightly on the tight side – far too much on show. This is Gary.

'High Max, come in, grab yourself a beer, we're all on the terrace.'

Gary's a proper Londoner, originally from Blackheath. A Malboro Red hangs from corner of his mouth. He's the type of person who has lots of nervous energy, constantly fidgeting like a Peckham Market salesman. I've got my semi-cold bottle of cheap Belgian beer from the fridge and now I'm standing next to Gary on his terrace, keeping him company as he fails to get the charcoal lit.

'So, Gary, Abbie was telling me that you're a TV producer…'

'That's right, at least, I hope so!' he says burning his fingers rather than igniting the fire-lighter. I give him that vacant-attentive-listener look, willing him to tell all. He gives up on the barbecue.

'Well,' he starts, an excitement has appeared in his voice, 'we do mostly reality television. I work for Lion TV, have you heard of us?'

I haven't.

'Yeah, I think so,' I say.

'Cool, what have you seen?'

'Well, that thing, you know, I think it was on last year, you know…'

Gary isn't helping me out, he's letting me dig myself deeper. The fire-brick he was trying to light lets out a high-pitched whine, as if in sympathy. I take a swig from my beer.

'Right,' he says, clearly not giving a shit about whether I've heard of them or not, 'well, our next project is a look at relationships; marriage, divorce, cohabiting… dating.'

He says the last word with a subtle emphasis, as if it's supposed to mean something to me, like an arcane codeword passed between spies. I look at him vacantly.

Gary starts telling me about his own dating experiences, and his failed marriage. Apparently, it had given him the idea for the TV show.

'The dating episode is proving the hardest to sort out,' he says coyly. 'We're looking at all the different ways people go about dating and finding a date.'

I'm not really listening, I'm too concerned about the lack of half-cooked chicken drumsticks and sausages done to the point of resembling fox turds. I'm starving.

'You ever tried Speed Dating, Max?'

'Hmmm?' I snap out of my daydream about coleslaw and stale bridge rolls.

'Speed Dating? Oh, er, no I haven't. Not sure it's my cup of tea – always thought it sounds like a cross between crazy golf and *Blind Date*.'

'Rubbish,' he smiles, 'you should give it a go… great laugh. We've actually got a Speed Dating event soon, Abbie's coming along, you should too.'

I can't help but think that the Speed Dating concept must have been originally designed by men because all it does is create a contrived environment for something that guys had been doing for years, the Rating Ritual. This sounds to me like a forum for assessing potential bed-mates within the first two minutes of meeting. I mean, what can you actually tell about a stranger in two minutes, in a totally contrived situation? You will only be able to judge the girl (or guy) sitting opposite you on looks. Are they hot, or not?

But how many times have you heard a woman say, 'I didn't find him that attractive when I first met him but he really made me laugh, he's so intelligent, he always has my best interests at heart, we love doing the same things, he's so caring.' The list goes on and on. The one certain thing is that it is virtually impossible to see evidence of these traits in a two-minute interview.

There is, however, ample time to check her form; boobs are big, excellent; short skirt, long legs; fat, definitely a no-no; BOBFOC (Body-Off-Baywatch-Face-Off-Crimewatch), shag once and leave. You get the picture. So this was a place I could go to where the girls would be single and looking, and I would be totally justified in basing my attraction purely on aesthetics, as the girls will probably be doing exactly the same. This sounds like man's territory. Perfect.

'So does that mean you'll help, Max?' Gary asks, turning the sausages on the now flaming barbecue. 'We need friends to come along and make up the numbers.'

Foolishly, I agree to go along to the Speed Dating event. Besides, how bad could it be, a few cameras filming a bunch of twenty-somethings in a bar, right?

'Great,' says Gary. 'So how did you say you know Abbie?' And that was that.

'Hello, Mr Hunter?' It is 9.45 am, I am sitting at my desk at work, trying to figure out how to deflect media attention away from a client who is about to get rear-ended. I am partaking in my daily breakfast of blueberry muffin and strong grande cappuccino.

'Yes, hello how can I help you?'

'My name is Selena, I'm calling from the BBC.' The voice at the end of the phone was firm yet vibrant, betraying hints of south American roots.

'Oh no,' I think to myself, 'the Beeb must have heard about my client already, how's it got out so fast?'

'Look, I'm afraid I really can't comment…' I say firmly.

'Sorry?' Selena says, somewhat bemused. 'I'm a researcher for a new programme on dating,' she explains, 'I was given your details by Gary,' her voice pitches at the end as if she is seeking my confirmation, like annoying LA school kids do in American sitcoms.

The scales fall from my eyes, I suddenly realise what she is getting at – Reality-TV-Gary's Speed Dating extravaganza. But why is she calling me? The fear factor sets in.

'I understand that you are going to the Speed Dating event this Friday and that you have kindly agreed to be filmed by us as part of our new documentary.'

'Well, I er.'

I suppose, strictly speaking, it's true. I had agreed to go and I knew that there would be a camera team milling around. But I thought I was just having a night out with Abbie. The idea of cameras documenting my chatting up potential mates in some perverted anthro-socio study and broadcasting it to the nation is far from appealing. And yet, I could tell that there was more to come, much more. What had this fool Gary signed me up to. Clearly, he had used his friendship with Abbie to fulfil some hidden agenda. I have been set up.

'That's great,' Selena bamboozles on. 'I'm just giving you a call to run over what we'll be doing on the evening itself. As you know the event is being held at the Red Cube in Leicester Square. We're going to take you to another location beforehand, probably a super swish pad in Tower Hill for a pre-Speed Dating interview. This will be your opportunity to tell us what expectations you have from the evening, what dating in London is like in general and if you think alternative dating works, blah blah blah. Then we'll head over to Leicester Square. We'll do a sequence of shots of all the girls taking part, and then you'll be filmed doing your stuff, chatting up the girls for two minutes apiece. Then, when you have gone through all the girls, we'll take you back to the first location and do a post-Speed Dating interview. You'll be able to tell us how you think it went, which girls you liked, whether your expectations were fulfilled and then you'll be told which, if any, of the girls selected you. Hello Mr Hunter?'

Holy shit, first they want to film me giving my 'chat', looking dead cheesy no doubt, and then they'll tell me on national TV if any of the girls found me attractive. What if none of them do? As if reading my mind Selena pipes up, 'I'm sure they'll all pick you,' she finishes the sentence with a sickly showbiz giggle.

And when I think that it can't get any worse, she says, 'Oh, I forgot to mention, we'll do a follow-up piece a week later once you have been on your one-on-one dates with any of your matches.'

This sounds terrible, it really is *reality dating – Blind Date* meets *Big Brother*. And I had been delivered up as the lamb for the slaughter thanks to one of Abbie's so-called friends. Why could I see myself being cast as a new Nasty Nick. Although I was cursing this idiot Gary inside my head, I feel obliged to agree to this hare-brained scheme. I don't want to let Abbie down. On top of that, I can't refuse. It's one of those occasions when you see something terrible unfolding before your eyes but you stand there frozen, not bothering to step out of its path? A simple 'no' would have sufficed, but could I say it? No!

It seems easy now, but try telling a bullish, bombastic researcher 'No.' She's used to dealing with noncommittal members of the public, forcing them into things they really don't want to do. This isn't quite the thing I had in mind, when I first agreed. So much for a random camera crew wandering around taking a few shots. I have suddenly been catapulted into the lead role in a fly-on-the-wall documentary on how to be unsuccessful in dating.

You might think that this could be quite a laugh, but I soon realised that it would be pitted with potential nightmare scenarios, most of which are about to come true. Because I had lacked the guts to tell the researcher that I am no longer game and that I had been misinformed by the organiser, Gary, I find myself in an old man's pub off Leicester Square, shaking like a B-list celeb in rehab. Somewhere along the line I had come up with the ingenious idea of asking Ed and Raj along for support, enticed by the promise of free beer and watching me make an arse of myself. But these are male mates who, in situations like this, prefer only to relish in one's anguish rather than give any support whatsoever.

'Don't worry, buddy,' says Raj facetiously, 'I'm sure they'll all be stunning!'

'Absolutely, and not at all desperate,' Ed adds, smirking.

'Yeah, yeah. Hilarious,' I retaliate. 'Shutthefuckup and drink your free beers.'

'Oh, and we told everyone we know that it'll be on in a couple of weeks,' Raj chokes on his pint in laughter.

'So thoughtful,' it's my turn to be facetious. 'Guys, seriously, I'm going to make such an arse of myself on television that no woman in London will ever want to date me again.' I feel low.

'That's right,' says Ed, 'not even the desperate scavenging cougars will be interested. You will be forced into hiding.' They both laugh again.

'God, I'm going to make Claire Swires look like an amateur.'

Over the next half an hour, one terrible scenario is trumped by the next, and the two gits only pause to swallow vast quantities of bitter. Before we know it, it's time to head across Leicester Square and face the cameras.

They have decided to do my initial interview at the club itself, as if I'm about to go straight into the event. I am sat on a small wooden stall in the basement bar. I can barely see the camera a few feet in front of me because of all the high-powered lighting equipment. The producer is a black shadow, to my right of the cameraman.

'Right, Max,' he says, 'we'll start rolling in just a sec, yeah?'

'Yeah,' I reply, less than enthusiastically.

'I'll ask you a series of questions and please answer them as honestly as you can, it's as simple as that, forget the camera's even here, we're like a couple of friends having a chat, cool?'

'Cool,' he's starting to annoy me already.

'Okay, Bob, and roll camera!' he says to the other shadow. 'Max, how long have you been single?'

'It's been about seven months or so, since my last serious relationship.'

'And counting, eh Max?' he chuckles smugly. Inwardly I want to get up and hit him. 'And how long did that last?'

'About three years.'

'Who finished it?' he snaps back.

'Er, me.'

'Really?'

'Yes, really!' I say, clearly annoyed. 'Do you have to ask that?'

'STOP,' he yells, 'Max, just answer the questions, okay? We don't have much time. Ready Bob, and… roll camera. Max how do you find dating in London?'

'Well, it's different to how I expected, I suppose. People don't really have time to date, as such. It's very intense.'

'Had much luck?'

'Well, er, ha ha, er, I don't know.'

'So you think that Speed Dating will solve London's dating problems, in a world where time is precious?'

'Perhaps, yes, anyway you've got to try everything once, haven't you?' I laugh nervously. I can't see his face, but I can tell he's looking back at me blankly, like I'm a fool.

I return to the upper part of the Red Cube's bar, feeling utterly deflated. And the main part of the event hasn't even happened. I notice that the bar is unusually empty. In the place of the tourists and local party-goers there is camera equipment piled up here and there. A few tables by the bar have been left clear, one of which is occupied by a half-cut Raj and Ed.

I am greeted by an olive-skinned girl in her early twenties who displays all the characteristics of a media studies graduate. She seems fairly efficient, clasping her clipboard and yet she still appears a little meek. Surely this isn't the hard-nosed, no punch-pulling researcher I had spoken to earlier in the week.

'Hi I'm Selena.'

Yep, it's her.

'We spoke on the phone, I'm Max.'

'Ah, hi Max,' she says, 'thank God you're here, we were worried you had decided not to come.' She chuckles, I laugh nervously, and Ed and Raj snigger.

'Why don't you get yourselves a drink from the bar, it's on us, the least we can do,' she smiles sweetly. 'We're just setting up downstairs, when we're done, myself or the producer, Mike, will come up and get you, okay?'

I turn around, Ed and Raj are already at the bar ordering more beers. I can't drink, I don't want to go on camera sozzled. It is likely enough that I'll make a total Muppet of myself as it is, I don't need the help Messrs Daniels and Beams to make it worse.

I sit down with my coke in silence. For some reason my mind goes back to Jessica. I am thinking of her progressively less and less. I never regret my decision, my life is so much better. I am considerably happier. But there are occasions when I think of the few happy times that we shared together. This is one of those times of reflection. I think to myself that if I hadn't left her, I wouldn't be in this damn dingy bar about to make the biggest mistake of my life. I am transported to another place, in a Christmas Carol-like outer body experience. In my mind I am floating outside an Islington apartment, peering in through the window at the cosy interior. Inside there is me in a nice knitted lambs' wool polo neck and cords. A bottle of vino stands half-drunk on the coffee table amongst the remnants of what looks like a delicious pasta concoction. And there she is, a vision of beauty, cuddling up next to me in her Tommy hipster jeans and sloppy American football shirt with that incredible blonde hair tied back off her face. I am watching the TV, laughing, probably at some comedy movie, unaware that she's looking devotedly up at me, as she leans across and plants a kiss on my cheek.

That is where I could be, could have been right now. Instead, I look over at Ed and Raj, on the way to being plastered. They're making small animals out of soggy beermats again. I don't think that I have been nearer to suicide.

Then reality kicks in and I remember that my relationship had never been like that. She was a cow. She'd never just kiss me on the cheek like that. We would have been watching *Eastenders* or the *Hollyoaks* omnibus, and all I would have had was moaning and complaining about the consistency of my ragu, which wasn't to her liking. It would have gone unnoticed that I had slaved over the dinner since getting in from a long day's work.

It is just that annoying habit that we all can have sometimes, of looking back at a period of one's life in a more favourable light than it actually deserves.

'Ah sod it, Raj get me a G&T will you?'

'That's the spirit Hunter!' he says with glee, tanking up the Christian before he faces the lions. It's while Raj is at the bar, ordering my liquid anaesthetic, that I gain the first glimpse of the female participants. They have just started to arrive. I think it was seeing them that made him get me a double. Even Ed and Raj's faces went from laughter to shock as one moose followed another to join the rest of the herd.

'Christ where's Rocky, Bullwinkle !' Raj blurts.

You have never seen a bunch of such unappealing insipid looking girls. This is getting worse by the minute. I think to myself how harsh I'm being but, after all, this is not a show on how to make friends and delve into each other's great personalities. This is brutal honesty. We are all here to see if we can meet someone we are attracted to. And in the *fancying* stakes, it is a serious consideration whether the person sitting opposite me is cute or downright minging.

If I say they are all short and dumpy with greasy hair, I'm being kind. They are dressed like 15-year-old schoolgirls who haven't made the transition from troubled teenager to young woman. It's as if they don't know what looks good on them or what goes with what.

What am I going to do? We sit, dumbfounded. After a few more minutes my two git mates realise it doesn't affect them in the slightest and, actually, it just makes the situation all the more entertaining. I now have to chat up a gaggle of unattractive 16-year-olds.

How can I do this? I am stuck between a rock and a hard place. The cameras will record me chatting up these girls before I am required to give them either the thumbs up or the thumbs down.

'Guys,' I plead, 'there isn't one girl here that I'd like to go on a date with.'

'Don't worry Max,' says Ed, 'I'm sure they're all very nice.'

'You know that's irrelevant. I'm sure they're all very *nice* but I'm supposed to actually fancy one, some, of them. But if I say that on national TV, all the viewers will think that I'm a right arrogant wanker.

'You could just lie,' Raj says, like he's discovered the theory of relativity.

'Yes, but if I pretend to like one or two, this results in several problems; firstly a serious loss of cool points and further ridicule at the hands of the likes of you two. Secondly, I would be acting. I'd have to pull it off first time round or I'd look insincere and appear a wanker all over again.'

TV producers are powerful people, it's so easy for them to edit the film in any light they choose, they are Gods. They can make you look however they want, this is the stuff that Big Brother and all the other fly-on-the-wall docusoaps are made of.

I'm buggered.

There is nothing for it – I have to run.

'Guys, get your coats we're leaving!' I babble desperately.

They are plunged into silence.

'You can't leave, they need you for the show, who else will do it?' Ed says, with an air of genuine sobriety.

'Ed, I don't give a rat's arse, look at those women.' He peers over. 'Do you want to chat them up on TV?' I say.

'But you've already done the pre-date interview thing, you can't leave now.'

'If I'm not in the rest of it, then they won't use the interview part, will they?'

'That's not the point.'

'Mate, this isn't the time for unwavering loyalty, I'm not about to make myself look like a twit on national television for that moron Gary!'

At that moment, from the basement, the producer, Mike, emerges with a pair of sound recorder's headphones around his neck. He comes bounding over towards us.

'Right Max, we're ready for you if you want to come down to the Speed Dating room.' Mike says *Speed Dating* as if he's a gameshow host, the only thing missing are the pistol shot hand gestures. Twunt.

'Yeah sure, we'll just finish our drinks and come straight down.' I stand there smiling, knowing inside that he'd be ranting, raving and cursing my name in about five minutes time. Still smiling, I watch him descend into the basement, or the torture room, whichever way you want to look at it. As soon as his receding foppy mane disappears out of sight, I dart over to my near-pickled mates, 'Right, we have to go now, he wants us down there asap.'

Raj pipes up with the gem, 'The only problem is that my jacket's down there.' He looks over towards the stairs that Producer Mike has just descended.

'Shit,' I say, despairingly. 'Well you're going to have to go down there and get it!'

'What am I gonna say, it'll look a bit suss?'

'I don't know, say you need to make a phone call and your mobile's in your coat,' this is the first helpful thing that Ed has said all night.

As Ed and I put our coats on, we watch a rather sheepish Raj tread carefully down the steps into the makeshift studio. A few moments pass, before he reappears, clutching his Aquascutum three-quarter length.

We saunter over to Raj. Without speaking, we just nod to one another. I throw back the remainder of my G&T, Ed opens his gullet and downs the dregs of his Guinness. Coolly, we breeze out of the bar into an unusually quiet Leicester Square. It's around eight o'clock, and there's a continental warmth in the air. We stand for a moment with our backs to the glass door. We must look as if we've just stepped out for a final fag. None of us actually smoke. I look casually to my left and take a step in the direction of the main square. The three of us walk along the length of the bar's plate glass window, resisting the urge to look back inside. After five or six regular paces, and what seemed like several minutes, we pass the end of the window. Finally, we are out of sight.

'Peg it!'

10

Mr Nice

Why is it that moths are attracted to the flame of a candle? Even when they see another one get its wings burnt, it doesn't seem to teach them a lesson, they still go at that flame. Despite the inevitable, something draws the moth to the golden flickering warmth. Perhaps it's the excitement or the danger, your guess is as good as mine. Maybe the masochistic moth knows it's fatal, but thinks, 'What the heck, my wings need a good singeing.' Women, like these [fragile] moths, can be masochistic in that way too.

I'm sitting outside a pub in Camden Town in the early evening watching such a moth flirt with a nightlight that the waitress has just brought to my table. It has always foxed me how women can be attracted to the bad boy type. The male offspring who is of dubious parentage – the *bastard*. They love the idea of the guy that treats them, well frankly, like shit. And yet, simultaneously, they hate the idea of being used, of being treated like crap. But they're not interested in Mr Nice. Perhaps he appears sexually less endowed or he doesn't provide enough of a challenge. Perhaps, the girl thinks that this time, the flame won't burn her wings, or that deep down, El Git has a heart of gold and that she will be the girl to set it free. However, I'm sure that if she did actually tame the male shrew, the attraction would instantly disappear. Unless, of course, the affair prompted frequent trips to Tiffany's, by way of compensation.

I have an old friend who is the biggest shit to women that I have ever come across. Due to his legendary exploits he is known simply as 'Dirty Dave,' or just plain 'Dirty'. Dirty is a tall guy with a flanker's build and all the arrogance of a drunken rugby player. His hair is a ruffled mop of clipped brown, complete with that public school waxed quiff at the front – you know, Tintin with big balls. He works in advertising and while he's not at all creative, he drinks and lunches all day as if he were born to it. I suppose he was, sort of. He constantly has that dress-down-Friday look about him. When you have a conversation with Dirty, everything is a bit of 'something-action' or there has been a 'schoolboy error'.

Dirty was one of the guys that made up my close circle of mates at uni. He was a year ahead of the rest of us and he played the role of the rebellious prefect at boarding school who took you under his wing and showed you the tricks of survival: how to roll cigarettes, how to smuggle drink into the dorms and how to conceal a blow-up doll about your person while still inflated. He was a good teacher. He's also a good friend and generous in everything he does, even with his women – what's his is yours. Dirty is always single, even if he happens to be attached. And the thing is, most of his women know that this is the case, even the serious ones. Dirty is one of those guys who is firmly of the opinion that if it's the end of the evening and you haven't scored with the cute chick, or the next one down the food chain, then grab the munter. In fact, at the beginning of the evening, why not head for the munter anyway because she'll be standing next to her cute friend who is expecting to get all the attention. According to the Dirty school of thought, Miss Hound of the Baskervilles will be so pleased to have you fawning over her, that you'll be getting your rocks off in no time. After all, man cannot live on gourmet meals alone – occasionally you need a microwave meal for one, or even the odd kebab that you know is nothing more than dog meat. In short, a hole is better than your hand! That's Dirty.

He once went out with a girl whom he himself described as so fat and ugly that he could only have sex with the lights off. He dubbed her *Jabba the Hut t*. Once she questioned the lack of soft lighting during their nocturnal acrobatics and asked if, just for once, they couldn't make love with the light on. Eventually, by way of compromise, Dirty flipped her onto her front, and only then turned the bedside lamp on.

There was another time when he had been shagging one of his lovely lasses for four nights on the trot and somewhat bored he managed to negotiate a night off with the boys. This delightful girl had recently given Dirty a set of keys to her Notting Hill flat. When he staggered in at 3 am, a little worse for wear, there she was, being humped by some random bloke. Dirty, far from being annoyed, hollered a 'good effort' to the chap, doing the wheelbarrow with his girlfriend around the living room floor, and invited him to help himself to a beer in the fridge when he was done. With that he simply closed the door and headed across town to boff some other girl he was seeing on the side. That's Dirty.

Dirty and I have spoken many times about the anomaly of women being attracted to Mr Bastard. During these discussions he usually shakes his head at me in despair, much to my annoyance. He criticises me for promising women too much, maintaining that he's always up front with women, that he promises them nothing other than sex and the odd nice dinner. And they're always more than willing to accept. To Dirty, dating is like prostitution; money is invested by way of dinner and your dividend is received later that night, in the form of good old-fashioned fellatio. Dirty can have sex with a girl one night and fall asleep after he has climaxed only to kick her out the next morning so that he can breakfast in peace. The lucky lady will probably not hear a thing for a week or two and then receive a call out of the blue from Dirty to arrange another romp. Invariably she'll be up for another session. If not, she certainly won't hold a grudge against him. She may moan to her friends, but she certainly won't talk to *him* about how she's feeling.

With me, I make love to them at night, pay attention to their wants and desires, make them breakfast in the morning and bring them freshly ground Jamaican coffee in bed. I've always been a candles-and-petals-man, I'm not a fan of the straight to it shagging. The difference is, if I don't call for 24 hours I'm Satan incarnate. The fact I was probably averting some kind of domestic disaster, helping in the homeless shelter or giving blood is neither here nor there. Granted, none of us are quite *el virtuoso* but, Dirty aside, we aren't necessarily into the four F's (Find 'em, Feel 'em, Fuck 'em, Forget 'em).

On one memorable occasion, Dirty and I were on holiday in Barbados, staying at a family friend's apartment, as we tend to do each year. It's a sort of high-class bloke's holiday. Actually, who am I kidding?! Posh location, agenda always the same, be it Mullins or Magaluf. One particular evening, we went out partying at Harbour Lights, a nightclub by the beach on the outskirts of Bridgetown. It's a tourist pleasure spot, and a major pick up joint on the island. It wasn't long before we hooked up with a couple of English girls. Predictably they were air hostesses, Virgin girls, on the island for a few days layover before flying back to London. It didn't take much convincing to get them back to our amazing sounding gaff.   Now this apartment has to be seen to be believed. It is set into the shallow coral cliff overlooking the narrow strip of marching powder sand and azure sea. Under the lounge a whitewashed terrace with plunge pool has steps that lead down into the water. This place is the perfect pulling pad.

The engine of our yellow Mini Moke cut, and we free-wheeled through the palm trees that surround the condo. *Dukes of Hazzard*-style, we scrambled out to the clicks and screeches of tree frogs and crickets – a Caribbean welcome.

The girls made an ungainly exit, their short skirts really weren't made for being cramped in the back of an open top jeep. Both the girls had dyed blonde hair. To be honest, they looked as stereotypically air-stewardess as you can get. Hair, body, tan, clothes – the whole shebang. Frankly, it was quite a relief, because Dirty and had only been commenting on the flight over that the standard of air hostesses has deteriorated rapidly.

They all seem to be hefty trolls and no amount of foundation will disguise the ugliness. Gone are the busty, aloof model types – the new breed of trolley-dollies can hardly fit down the aisle, you daren't refuse their pack of nibbles on take-off.

Slightly tipsy, with the girls holding onto our arms for support, we staggered up the path to the front door. Dirty, after several attempts, managed to get the key in the lock. As we got in, I headed straight for the fridge to get the Pouilly-Fuissé that we'd left chilling. Unbeknown to me, as I was rinsing the glasses, Dirty was unceremoniously dragging his bird off to the bedroom. I think he must have left his troglodyte's club in the lounge. I returned to the living room to find my girl peering through the white jalousies, out at the moon, whose reflection was flirting with the inky Caribbean sea. Dirty was nowhere to be seen.

'Shall we go down to the terrace for some wine?' I said to her.

As we're leaving, who should fall out of his bedroom but Dirty, stark-bollock naked save for a towel the size of a small flannel, which just covered his essentials.

'Hang on, hold this,' despairingly I passed the bottle and second glass to Ann. We only got chatting to her because Dirty had noticed her name badge – 'Hey, you're a one-woman airline… *Pan Ann* – I always wanted to get my wings with them!'

I wandered over the white tile floor to Dirty, who was stifling a laugh while appearing desperately agitated. He whispered frantically in my ear. Having answered his plea, he winked and slapped me on the back affectionately. I returned to where Ann was standing at the top of the steps to the terrace and pool.

'Is he alright, what did he want?' she asks.

I couldn't think of a good lie that quickly, 'He wanted to know your friend's name.'

See what I mean? Within seconds of getting back to the pad, Dirty was humping her brains out, while I was another two hours before I even got to frenchy Ann. Instead, we talked all kinds of crap under the stars, sipping our rather good Fuissé.

'Look, girls love the bad-boy type, they like being treated like crap. It might be a cliché, but there's some truth in treating 'em mean to keep 'em keen.' Dirty tried to explain the concept of being a bastard to me for the umpteenth time the next day, over flying fish and a cool Banks beer. Apparently, by the time I was uncorking the vino last night, Dirty had already shot his load and was drifting off to sleep. According to Dirty, I promise women what they want from a long-term boyfriend. They get pissed off with me *because* I am attentive, *because* I'm romantic. When things inevitably don't work out they are seriously pissed off. Whereas they never expect anything from him, the *Bastard*. They know what's going to happen.

'You see, they treat you better, the worse you treat them. Mate, they lap it up,' Dirty tried to convince me further.

'So let me get this right, you're telling me that if I treat women like shit, they'll love me for it and come back for more?' I asked in disbelief.

'Precisely,' Dirty said, sipping his rum punch chaser.

'The thing is though, I'm not naturally an arsehole,' I pleaded.

'So learn to be one – give 'em some bastard action, you fucking woman!'

So, in short, I love to cook meals for my woman, I take pride in my personal grooming, and clothes are of the utmost importance to me, I even buy flowers (okay so sometimes they are for me). And, what's more, I have a caring nature, I am a considerate gentleman, I respect women and I am both thoughtful and romantic. And yet, I can't find a woman who has her sights set on anything but waltzing me down the aisle.

I am the ineligible bachelor.

Perhaps there is something in what Dirty was saying, for once. My renaissance man side is clearly a fundamental flaw in my game plan. I think of Ed and Raj who are fellow Mr Nices, in fact all my friends apart from Dirty are decent blokes, and none of them can find a nice girlfriend either.

Ed had been obsessed with a girl for years, from our uni days. He had idolised this girl, worshipped the ground she walked on.

In fairness, Sara was pretty foxy, although perhaps a little full of herself and certainly *'more R than F,'* as my mum would say. I've never known what that means exactly, but in other words she was a promiscuous hussy with style. Ed had been there for this girl when she had had family problems, he had all but done her degree for her, in general he had been her rock during those impressionable and formative years as an undergrad. Of course, I appreciate that this is no reason for her to date Ed but you have to ask yourself, why would you pass up the chance to go out with a man who respects you and has your best interests at heart in favour of strange looking bastards that treat you like dirt (her usual types) – only to complain about how you can't find a nice guy?

Like me, Ed is getting annoyed at hearing female friends talk of their attraction to rough bad boys and how they're not attracted to nice men. I think that a few years of Sara had left him with a bitter taste in his mouth, somewhere between pure tannin and lime pith. Ed had made an assertive choice upon coming to London: he wanted to make a new start. He was fed up of being used, derided for his gentlemanly attitude to women and having his sensitive advances brutally turned down. To put it bluntly, he wanted pussy and he wanted it now. He decided he would become a bastard.

That weekend he went out to get his woman, the first of many that he intended to ensnare with his new tactic. He was out on the prowl, a changed man, he even dressed differently. All traces of relaxed Edward, nice Edward, had disappeared. The Ralph Lauren shirts and smart trousers had been consigned to the back of the wardrobe, in favour of the quintessential *bastard* black. Girls take heed, when you see a guy dressed all in black, it means they want nothing but sex that night, you can liken them to the predatory panther if you will. It's all part of the ceremony, like you're a marine camming up before a mission. It gets the testosterone pumping, you feel good and nothing will stop you getting some action that night.

Bastard Edward makes his entrance at the Café de Paris, with Raj in tow. The air is mixed with old-school hip hop tunes and expensive fragrances. People are dancing and the cocktails are being knocked back like they're going out of fashion. Normally Ed would be sipping on a Long Island Ice Tea himself, chatting with his group of friends and occasionally scoping out the joint for potential women. Potential women he could try it on with, only to crash and burn in great style. Raj notices that Ed is very different tonight, very focused and a little colder than normal, clearly there is something on his mind. They throw back a couple of scotches, Ed's eyes don't leave the gaggle of girls in the centre of the dancefloor. Raj is wisecracking as per usual but his partner in crime is barely listening, nothing will break Ed's concentration. Raj notices Ed's eyes pulse and flicker with interest, some stimulant has caught his attention, and Raj's joke about the nun and the goat goes completely amiss. Instead, he follows Ed's line of sight to where a blonde beauty is dancing.

Without uttering a word, Ed hands him the dregs of his drink and glides towards the blonde. The girl has a great arse, prised nicely into a pair of Diesel hipsters. A real platinum blonde, she gives off that all-American Britney Spears look, before she started dressing like a trailer-tart from Salem. Bastard Ed coolly approaches this fine specimen, swaying to the music just enough to look like he's enjoying himself while oozing the self-confidence of a man who knows what he wants, and is about to take it. Britney (I call her that because I don't think her real name was ever actually determined) gives him a faint smile as he sidles up alongside her. Ed is not known for handling these situations well. He's used to approaching women at legal conventions or at the deep freeze section of his local M&S. On the rare occasions that he does make a play for a girl in a bar or a club he would normally spend the next hour dancing near her, getting closer and closer, risking a little flirt here and a grope there. But not this time. Instead, he peers into her eyes, not smiling, not betraying a single emotion.

'Hey,' he says, a little gruffly.

'Hi,' she says, not especially interested.

He looks at her blonde hair and lets his eyes glide down her neck and between her chest, outrageously admiring her all. He calmly continues to check her out; her arse, her legs and finally he gets to her feet.

'Nice shoes,' he says, eyeing her strappy numbers.

'Thanks,' is all she says.

'*Marni*,' he muses, as if making a mental note.

'Wow, yes,' she's shocked. 'How did you know that?' Now he has her attention. She's smiling.

'Last season, but a classic,' Ed says, as if he's an authority on women's footwear. She's impressed, but then her face flashes with concern.

'Are you gay?'

He takes her by the waist, with his left hand clasping her cheek and he kisses Britney deeply. She doesn't fight back, as previous girls have, no she responds, kissing him back. Ed can feel her quiver in his embraces.

Within the hour they are back at his flat and Ed wastes no time in disrobing her before carrying her through to his bedroom. His shirt discarded, he starts to kiss her, his hands scoping every inch of her. Foreplay is not high on Ed's agenda this evening, he just sets to it, selfishly making himself feel good. But once he gets started, Ed can't help but feel some form of affection for the lovely Britney. Nice Guy Edward starts to feel bad about the way he has seduced this girl, but determined, he gags the imaginary voice of his conscience. He pushes all niceties aside and they embark on a frenzied rutting. It's not long before Mr Nice rears his sanctimonious head. The thing is, Ed might have been successful in getting her home, and of course he wants to be naked with this chick, I mean who wouldn't? But not like this, it's too cold, too detached. He starts to feel more guilty, he can't carry on, he wants to do something for her, he wants to be less selfish. So he goes down on her.

With the pangs of guilt moistly dispensed with, and Britney somewhat satisfied, the two drift off to sleep. Ed wakes up in the morning, with the sun streaming in through his recently restored

Victorian sash windows, and the first thing he claps his eyes on is this vision of nineteen-year-old beauty, nestled into him. This angelic creature has washed away any pretence of a bastard exterior that Ed had conjured up. Her soft skin, those cupid's bow lips, the lovely long lashes and breath like a goat – he can't help but feel endeared towards his conquest. As she stirs, Ed starts to stroke her hair and kiss her softly. He slips out of the bedroom, puts the kettle on and shoves some bread in the toaster. If only Dirty had been there to warn him. It is a sure sign that his bastard façade has truly withered away. The man in the bastard mask is free, Ed is back to his old self and he feels all the better for it.

The news that Ed was getting laid more often than a bet on Grand National day – albeit with the same nag – just made me more angry. Not with Ed, obviously, but with myself. His bad boy image had been short lived but the tactic had had a 100% success rate, even if he had made the mistake of falling for his victim. Shit, if Ed's getting it without complaints, what's holding me back?

Following Ed's success, and taking Dirty's advice, I decide to try it for myself. One Friday night in September, I am at the opening of a new bar in the West End called Opium. Swathes of those very heavy, rich red silks, a den of decadence Singapore-style. Low seating, teak furniture, musk and incense filling your lungs. Fusion beats hang over your head like the thick canopy of a Berber tent. With Dirty Dave over for the weekend, this would be the perfect venue for our first legendary drinking session since Barbados.

As we're sitting in Cambridge Circus, having a catch-up pre-club beer, Dirty declares, 'Max, I invited a friend of mine along this evening.'

'Oh right, what's his name?'

'Actually it's a girl,' he says. 'She's a colleague, well sort of my boss really. She is over from our Paris office on business.'

'Oh bloody hell,' I think. I normally enjoy going out in a mixed group but the most amusing thing about hanging out with Dirty is that the evening is bound to be debauched. That is unlikely to happen with us chaperoning his boss. No matter how much you like to think otherwise, you can never quite act the same way with women around on a sharking trip.

'It's ok, she's a top lass, she's Brazilian originally,' Dirty says quickly, seeing the concern on my face. 'Yes you'll like her, she's curvy, dark skin and great clothes.'

Then I think 'what the hell,' if she's cute perhaps this will be my opportunity to put my plans into effect, to try and be a *bastard*. When better than in the company of the bastard supreme himself.

We finish our beers. Dirty has been regaling me with stories of his latest exploits. I think the most recent conquest was some Polish lass he'd stayed the night with, and when dropping her off in her part of town the next day, she had requested he stop at the end of the road. She insisted she walk the rest of the way down the street to her apartment, as it was likely her husband would be in. Unbelievable.

We meet Maria Jose in a Sloaney wine bar just down the road in Soho, the type of place that serves sickly Chardonnay in goldfish bowl sized glasses. For once, Dirty is right, she is certainly curvy. She walks like she is on the catwalk. This woman oozes sex appeal. In fairness, she could be a Dolce & Gabbana girl, fresh from Milan. Her clothes are indeed complementary, they take her natural beauty to another level. She is wearing a black satin dress, cut at an angle to reveal more thigh on one side than the other. Her ensemble is finished off with elegant black stilettos encrusted tastefully with diamantes. It is modest around her breasts, trust me they don't need to be flagged up – you can see that she has tits the size of ripe cantaloupes. Men neglect their girlfriends just to watch her sway through the punters at the bar. As she comes up close, arm outstretched to shake our hands, we are able to fully appreciate her soft bronzed skin and her silky brown hair, which is lightly curled, and hangs seductively about her shoulders.

'Ah, Maria Jose,' shouts Dirty. He's positively salivating.

'Hi Daveed, it's good to see you,' the south American goddess clasps his hand and kisses him on each cheek.

I think I just came in my pants. Not only is she gorgeous, she has a voice that's so husky it makes Mariella Frostrup sound like a soprano. Those piercing light green eyes turn their focus onto me. I can feel her weighing me up, taking me all in (so to speak).

'You must be Maxxx!' Squelch, damn there it goes again.

Dirty and her are chatting away, catching up on work gossip and the latest instalment of Dirty's work romance. While he's babbling away, Maria Jose occasionally throws a glance in my direction. It may be brief, but it's a penetrating look. Unless I'm mistaken (and I often am) this juanita is interested. We down our drinks and head for Opium.

My party-organiser friend Pippa has sorted us out with the guest list at the club. Because we have a woman in toe, or in Maria Jose's case, leading the way despite not knowing where she is going, it means we are spared the ridicule of standing in the single sad male queue. The witch on the door with the clipboard immediately lets us into the club. Said witch doesn't attempt to make us queue, she sees she has met her match in Maria Jose.

Pippa is there with her usual posse of pashmina wearing, Berkshire-born girlies. Pippa is doing her usual socialite thing, making sure that everyone is okay. She is always flitting from one person to the next, caught in a barrage of luvvie kisses. She is a great girl, and very down to earth, despite this 'club-promoting' façade. But her hangers-on are nothing short of annoying, they are so incredibly pretentious. Having said our hellos to Pippa, we grab our sherbets and waste no time in heading for the dancefloor. As we're dancing away to some Eminem-Jackson remix, Dirty heads off to the loo.

With my friend otherwise occupied, and Maria Jose and I alone, it is the perfect opportunity to implement my bastard tactics. But before I can put my bastard plans into effect I become aware of Maria Jose's intensive gaze. She has moved up close and is starting to dance very sensually. She looks me straight in the eyes, bold as you like, and slinks her arms around my neck.

'You know what, there is someone in here I am flirting with?' she says.

'Oh good stuff. And, er, who would that be?' That's it, gotta keep cool, I'm a fucking bastard, I can deal with this. This is going to be easier than I thought.

'Well he's very, very close. But I no sure he likey me.'

'Really, oh I'm sure he does, likey you very much, and he'll be back in just a sec,' I say looking in the direction of the toilet, acting coy.

'Hah,' the little minx throws her long silky hair back in laughter, 'I no mean Daveed, I talking about someone else… friend of Daveed.'

I never thought you could hear someone gulp like Daffy Duck, but you can. Why am I feeling like a little boy with a crush on the older girl next door? I'm trying to maintain my bastard composure, but instead I find myself melting.

'Well, I can assure you that I…' I am cut short by what I can only describe as the most mind-blowing, awesome kiss that I have ever had the pleasure of experiencing. Thinking about mind-blowing kisses does make me sound like a whoopsy (and yes, I did have my eyes shut to make things worse) but this was so fucking fantastic.

You think you've snogged some girls that are good, some that are bad, and then you discover a seductress that can have you wrapped around her little finger with nothing more than some fantastic lip work. I swear, this Siren had been practising at the art of kissing since she was old enough to recite the alphabet. I am completely in her control, to the point where momentarily I forget I am in a club, I don't give a monkey's that this Brazilian bombshell is playing me like a fiddle. She is so impressive that everyone else stops dancing to watch, they can see the intensity that I am feeling. Dirty reappears, not that I would know, and stands open mouthed as his boss seduces his old mate. When I think it can't get any better, the voracious jezebel introduces an ice cube into our lip-locking, not in the inept way my Kiwi had done, but with timed skill and expertise. She knows all the places to flick with a tongue, how to hold you on the edge of sheer bliss ready to implode. The ice melts between our hot lips. She works around to my ear, whispering in Portuguese, blowing softly, speeding up becoming more and more impassioned. Bugger me, I really am going to climax. Then with a final deep, long kiss she pulls away, panting. The rest of the room stands staring, the only person who is more like an automaton than any of them, is me.

As I recover, I see Maria Jose smiling, she's enjoying the effect she's having on me. She winks and grabs my hand to pull me over to the bar. Incredibly there is no queue to get a drink, everyone must be on the dancefloor.

'Would you like some water?' I ask her. I know I need some after that.

'Yes please. And hold my breasts.'

'Two glasses of water please. Excuse me?' Did I just hear right, did she ask me to hold her breasts? I look at the barman, confused, and he gives me that face, 'What are you waiting for you dumb fuck, do it quickly or I'll come round there and do it myself.'

By now, I am totally fazed and any bastard exterior I thought I created has all but dissolved. She is completely in control. I stand there agog before cupping a poont in each hand, nearly crying. I grope her like I am checking a couple of very large avocados to see if they are ripe. She groans a little, encouraging me to squeeze some more.

'That's it Max, dahrrling, harder, firmer.' I am like a kid in a candy store. It must look like I am touching a boob for the first time. She kisses me again, I am hers to do with as she pleases. And that's exactly what she does. Looking me straight in the eye and wearing a wry smile she declares, 'Now, the bed in my hotel is way too small. We go to yours.'

Babble is about all I can do.

Half an hour and an unconventional cab journey later, which had caused the driver so much excitement he nearly knocked a woman off her bike by Trafalgar, we arrive at my place. I can hardly get the key in the door with excitement.

Crossing the threshold, I stumble into the lounge and put on some suitably sultry music, the Buena Vista Social Club. Predictably I light up a candle (if he could see me, Dirty would have his head in his hands about now). Throwing my coat on the couch I make my way into the bedroom. Bugger me if my Brazilian hasn't already discarded her dress and, well by the looks of things, all her clothes. The bedsheets are carefully placed just to cover the pleasure spots. It's clichéd, and I thought that it only happens in cheesy American films but I'd be lying if I said it doesn't do the trick. God doesn't she look wonderful. The cream sheets are drizzled over her chocolate brown legs. A single firm thigh lies on top of the covers and her slender shoulders give way to a partially protruding bosom.

Before I know it, we are at it like Catholics. And most notably I am introduced to the delights and benefits of a true *Brazilian strip* – and I ain't talkin' bout no football team neither! So much cleaner, more beautiful, far sexier, much better. Mind-blowing would be selling the rendezvous short. The only thing that ruins this carnal bliss is when Maria Jose starts wailing like an Apache squaw doing a war dance. Now, I know that some women like to be vocal in the bedroom and, for the most part, us chaps like to plough away with the job in hand, but this is ridiculous. She is blatant screaming, I suppose all to my credit, but she's really putting me off. I want to laugh, it's difficult to suppress the urge, but to let a single giggle pas my lips would be fatal. I lie there, under this howling, writhing woman, waiting for my next-door neighbour to come round and tell me to 'shutthefuckup.' Although knowing the dirty little bugger he is probably cracking one off listening to her screams. Not that I'd blame him – I'd be doing the same.

I wake in the morning, make some coffee and lean on my *Juliet* balcony. The street below is busy with the early morning tradesmen and market stall holders who are setting things up. 'This could work,' I think to myself. She is attractive and stylish and foreign. And the best bit is she lives abroad. People always criticise long-distance relationships, quite frankly I can't think of anything better. They provide you with the independence you require. And when you do make the effort to meet up you make the most of the precious little time you have together, making it so much more intense. Essentially, you only see each other when and because you really want to.

As I stand there, lost in my world of pensive bliss, Maria Jose shuffles into my lounge, wearing one of my white shirts. It is a sight to behold, that olive skin and chestnut brown hair, slinking towards me with those big mugs – big mugs of steaming coffee. So we stand there, drinking. It's all good.

'Maxy, I likey you verrry much,' she says suddenly.

'Well, I rather like you too Maria Jose.' It's true, I do like her. I look back out onto the street. The owner of the deli below is unloading crates of mangos, one of the crates has just splintered into several pieces as it was dropped from the back of the van. Various Punjabi expletives can be heard above the murmurings of the market. I laugh to myself, this is why I love London – the grittiness. I enjoy the scene and take another sip of coffee.

'Dahrrling, my parents will be over in London next weekend, I would like it so very much if you would have dinner with us.' Maria Jose shatters my reverie. And yes, that was the sound of my bowels giving way. It's the last thing I was expecting at that moment, revelling in the sun and the post coital bliss. I almost scold myself choking on the blue mountain.

'It was the candle wasn't it?' I mumble despondently.

'Sorrry, what d'you mean?' Poor Maria Jose doesn't know what the hell I am on about.

However, if Dirty was here he'd be agreeing wholeheartedly. But I had played the bastard role hadn't I? Then I realise at that moment that I had done no such thing. She had been in control all evening. Maria Jose had seen through any type of guise I was trying to create. What I didn't realise then that I appreciate now is that some men are bastards, and probably always will be, guys like Dirty. And believe me he would be the first to admit it. Others of us are the romantic types (or at least we make some sort of effort). Most importantly women can spot each type a mile off. They know which flames will burn them and which ones won't. When I looked back I hadn't done anything bastardy all evening, I was just my usual self. Foolishly I was expecting her to say 'thankee very much,' grab a cab and fly back to France – not to be seen until my next trip to Paris when I would undoubtedly give her a call. But I suppose if she had wanted the full bastard treatment she would have chosen Dirty. But she didn't make a play for Dirty because she wanted more, or at least the probability of something more, and so she had chosen me.

From then on I decided to leave the bastard routine to Dirty, who is the master. There is no point pretending to be something I am not, more than anything else it is too bloody difficult. It would just complicate an already complicated situation. Besides, what's the point of hiding in the shadows of bastardom when women have infrared goggles that let them see into your deepest chasms. At the point of intercourse I would always light up a candle, Dirty would always forget their names. That's just how things are.

11

Losing the ability

You know the feeling, you're sitting at a bar in some trendy establishment and some goddess, a veritable Aphrodite, is sitting two stools away, sipping her Cuba libre evocatively. As she sups, her eyes peer up from behind the rim of the cocktail glass, lingering more than long enough for you to register her interest. You know that she is there for the taking but you can't do Jack Shit about it.

You dream of moments like these, where an attractive (or even moderately passable) girl offers herself up on a plate. Of course, in the dream you breeze over brimming with self-confidence, a veritable Lothario. Clutching the Dom Perignon and two flutes, you coolly pull up a pew. You take the gold-tipped Sobranie Black Russian from the cigarette case and, without looking at her, you light up, letting the mild smoke fill your lungs before blowing dollar sign smoke rings. You give her a sideward glance as you crack open the champagne. The cork comes with ease, sighing like a satisfied woman, rather than an exploding bullet that takes out the barman's eye, and gets froth on her frock. You pour the ambrosia with an air of sophistication that comes only with birth. Before you have spoken a word she is delirious with enthusiasm.

But dreams have a habit of pissing on reality. Instead, you look up meekly and give a pathetic smile, chuckling nervously you tip your glass in her direction. Fuckwit. That's it, you've ballsed it up – a serious loss of cool points with absolutely no possibility of recovery. You are now your own worst enemy. You know that you have boo-booed. The more that you think about going for it regardless, the harder the notion becomes. Why can't you just get up from the bar stool and waltz over to where she's sitting? Can you buggery. Even though, for some reason (probably out of pity), she is still giving you the eye, you are glued to that chair. Your arse is made of lead and diving weights have been attached to your ankles. To prise yourself out of that stool would be a feat akin to launching the Wright Brothers' plane from the surface of the Sea of Tranquillity. You are going nowhere.

So why is it I can make a play for women that I have no hope in hell of pulling and yet fail to get anywhere with Miss Congeniality? It would take just 10% of the effort employed in the first instance to succeed in the second. Perhaps it is because I like the chase, after all there's no point in hunting a lame fox. Nope, I would like to believe it is because of such manly reasons, but the reality is much more deprecating. Plain and simple, it's because I am shit scared. An assertive woman, a woman who knows what she wants can be a frightening prospect. I mean, if you never expect to pull, and I don't for the most part, but on one occasion in ten the gods are looking favourably upon me and I should actually score, then wow what a rush. The unexpected success makes the whole experience even more pleasurable. I live for that moment. That's why I carry on going to these godforsaken meat markets. It's precisely because I never expect to pull the girl that makes pulling her so pleasurable. Imagine getting a hoop over the £20 note at the funfair. There's nothing dishonourable in losing because we all know it's fixed. But there is every reason to celebrate if you should actually hit the jackpot. Being half-cut helps. But when I am stone cold sober and a pull is guaranteed, well I'm sorry, that's just unfair. Such a thing can make my bowels dissolve. Knowing that knocking bones is a foregone conclusion puts a hell of a pressure on us men, you know? It's just not right. It's bad enough thinking about foreplay, clitoral stimulation and premature ejaculation at the moment prior to intercourse, but forcing a man to contemplate it before even exchanging forenames is simply sadistic.

Getting women is like becoming a millionaire, the first one is the hardest. When you're desperate, women know it. Nothing will attract other women more than a beautiful girl on your arm.

'It's a popularity competition, women like men that have women. I suppose the knowledge that you don't have to pull also gives you a confidence that women can find very attractive,' says Raj.

'You mean compared to the desperation that I have been undoubtedly displaying over the past few weeks,' says Ed, despondently. He has been in a perpetual trough for the last month or so – ever since 'Britney' realised he wasn't a bastard after all. She wasn't looking for a nice guy.

'I just don't seem to be working the banter as I would normally. I can't even pluck up the courage to go and chat to a girl I like the look of in a bar. I feel doomed before I take the first step.'

'That's your problem, buddy. When you're seeing a girl it's like some kind of pheromone you emit, "*odour d'*I-have-a-woman-already", come get me if you're good enough. It's not arrogance, it's totally subconscious, a kind of self-confidence that you're unaware you possess. And boy, does it make you desirable.'

'I'm sure you're right. If that's the case I must have bathed in the pheromone equivalent of Old Spice.'

'And the worst thing,' I say, not meaning to make things worse, 'is that it's an ever-deteriorating state of affairs. Great, so the only way that I'll score again is if I have a woman already. I think there's a flaw in that plan.'

'Don't worry, mate,' says Raj, more positively, 'a solution has been provided for in the grand scheme of things. After a while, you won't care anymore.'

'That doesn't make me feel any better, how is that a solution Raj?'

'Because not wanting a woman, having that aloofness, can be just as attractive to them as your confidence when you already have a lass.'

'He's right,' I nod in agreement, 'and once you start getting more female attention, you'll start to get interested again.'

12

Losing the desire

No.

It's a simple word, a small word. But it is a word with amazing power and mystifying effect. There's a flipside to the coin that is the upfront woman; the man who doesn't give a rat's arse. As we, at times, are overcome by a woman who is openly keen, so a woman can be bewildered by a man who turns down sex. I mean, why would he? It goes against both natural instinct and social conditioning. And he's not saying no because he is intimidated, or shy. He is simply not interested.

The man just sits there like the dog being pawed by the cat, coaxed into playing but having none of it. Yet, it goes against all the rules of nature. If she shows enough cleavage, pouts to the point of resembling Leslie Ash, brushes her leg against his and slaps his knee as they share a joke, then he's bound to be interested. I mean that's giving him a pretty clear picture, right? That's following all the rules set out by Girlie Nazi magazine, isn't it?

The woman has followed Cosmo's advice to a 't', she has taken heed of all the pearls of wisdom set out in that awful American book *The Rules*. Sure she has, but she could flash her knockers at him all day and it would be as enticing as a Vanessa Feltz centrefold.

It's not that the woman is one of Dirty's cast offs. Far from it. She might be attractive and sexy and witty, she might even tick all the boxes on his anatomical checklist. It's irrelevant.

A man goes through the cold turkey that is 'losing the ability' to attract a person of the opposite sex. It's a low point.

It is the ultimate dip in a man's dating peak and trough cycle. Then he comes out the other end and he gets catapulted to the opposite emotion. He's no longer failing in the hunt, he's not remotely interested in the quarry. And the less interested he becomes in the sport, the more the fox finds him attractive.

Sometimes we're just not interested, not in the mood. But we're never allowed to vocalise our lack of interest, it would be blasphemy. It's the chaos theory to end all imbalances within society.

'Guys, you know the other week we were talking about Ed not getting anywhere with women,' says Raj one morning after the night before.

'Thanks for reminding me. But you were right, I haven't been interested since we spoke about it. I've been feeling quite liberated actually.'

'Well I've been the same, but not liberated, more bored,' Raj admits, 'I met this cute chick in Funky Buddha. I felt pretty indifferent but I *had* to pull her.'

'Oh no, one of those moments,' I say.

'Yep. And she suggested going for a drink at mine. I just wanted to go home and go to bed, but I didn't feel I could say no.'

'Of course not!' I declare.

'So, we get to chez Raj. I'm making chat with her but I really can't be arsed. She starts snogging me and then she makes those come-to-bed eyes. Before I know it, I hear myself asking her to stay the night.'

'We've all been there, mate. You want to kick her out, but you can't.' I think back to the times it has happened to me. I once walked a girl around from one bar to the next just so she'd get tired and bored and want to go home. Her home. I wanted the comfort of my own bed and to wake up alone. The thought of making small talk about bollocks until midday the next morning wasn't a price that I was willing to pay, just so I could sleep with her. In fact, I didn't want to sleep with her at all. But it was hard to say no.

'It's fucking awful,' Raj continues. 'I think of all the foreplay I'm going to have to go through, the sex itself and then the worst bit – remaining affectionate and enthusiastic after having shot my load.'

We all chuckle knowingly.

'I know the feeling,' says Dirty, who had decided to join us on our beers. 'It's when masturbation goes from the obligatory substitute to the preferred alternative.'

Everyone laughs again.

'But I still couldn't say no,' says Raj. 'What if I had asked her to leave?'

'Buddy, it just wouldn't compute, she wouldn't understand, we're men after all and apparently all we ever want is sex,' Ed laughs.

'Can you imagine the look on her face if you said, "Okay, I'm going to bed now, I'll call you a cab".'

'Mate, I wanted to but I couldn't. It's happened the other way round, plenty of times. It's almost like I'm expecting the girls to tell me to sling my hook. But I couldn't ask her to leave, to deny her sex. It would have been such a huge insult.'

'Gentlemen,' Dirty puts his penny's worth in, 'sometimes it's just easier to do it and get it out the way, than not to do it.'

As ever, he's right. In a way. But why should Raj feel like he has to let her stay. If the tables were turned, it would be verging on a criminal act. It's a hang on to the archaic rituals of a society that we are supposed to have left behind long ago. It makes as much sense as offering a woman your seat on a crowded tube train. I do it because I feel the pressure to do so, it is expected of me, but there is no logical reason for me doing so. That is aside from politeness. Raj slept with her just to be polite.

Just as you have some women stare at you contemptuously on crowded trains, while you enjoy the comfort of your seat, or you have looks of indignation at a crowded bar when you get served before them, the greatest insult is to refuse their advances.

'I was chatting to this girl once, in a bar,' I reminisce out loud, 'and I had been going through one of these phases, I think she mistook it for an alluring arrogance. We got on really well, I liked talking to her, then she suggested we went to hers for coffee.'

'Did she actually say coffee?'

'Yeah,' I laugh, 'but she wasn't drunk enough to be blatant or obvious, she was trying to be subtle. Although she did put on a slightly theatrical butter-wouldn't-melt-in-her-mouth look. And then I said, "Ah, I'm okay, thanks though, perhaps another time, I'm kind of tired".'

'What did she say?' Ed asks.

'I don't think she believed what she was hearing, she sort of put her head on one side, like she was on *Ricki Lake*, squinted, looked affronted and said "fine", like a bloody toddler. And then, she got up and walked off.'

'They don't like it,' Dirty explains, 'you see it's the one thing they have over you. The woman is the one who decides whether you'll be having sex tonight or not, not you, she always has the upper hand. When she actually offers it and you say no, you're beating them at their own game.'

'Awesome,' say Raj, 'that's what I should have done.'

'You know the other thing that seems to put them off?' Dirty continues, 'It's a put-off rather than an insult. But it's all tied in together.'

'No what's that?' Ed asks.

'Your confidence.'

'How do you mean?'

'Well, for us it's a numbers game. Try it on with ten women and you're bound to get one. But women aren't used to being refused, whereas we are. Whenever we get knocked down, we take it in our stride, we have to.'

'Yeah, the other week,' says Raj, 'with a different girl, who I did like, she came up to me and we started dancing. Anyway after a while I kissed her...'

'Cute,' I joke.

'Shutthefuckup. Anyhow, we got talking, and I bought her a drink. She suddenly says, "You're quite a bit shorter than the men I normally go for".'

'Shit,' Ed says, unimpressed.

'Yeah, well I would have been offended, but I'd already pulled her and was thinking to myself "Sweetheart it won't mean dick when I've bent you over on all fours and you're screaming my name in about an hour's time".'

Dirty roars with laughter and slaps him on the back, 'That's my boy!'

'But of course, if you'd told her that her arse was larger than the girls *you* usually go for, you'd have been wearing her drink,' I say, smiling.

'It'd have been true as well.'

'It's almost as if she is trying to bring you down a peg or two because your insecurities play on you less. Why else would you be so personal and rude about someone you've only just met and whom you fancy,' says Ed. 'It's as if she's levelling the playing field after having shown her interest.'

'You're right,' says Raj wearily, 'I'm tired of all this. I'm tired of feeling like I'm doing something wrong just because I go up and chat to a girl, I feel like they resent me for it. It's as if I'm committing some sort of misdemeanour, the dating world's equivalent of jaywalking. And if I do get lucky, I feel like they're acquiescing rather than embracing my advances. It's dispassionate. It's more like a submission with consent. I find it so disappointing and draining. I need a holiday!'

13

Offshore

When you have failed to find a nice, normal, sane girl at home, what is a man to do – reach for his keyboard and sign up to Thai-brides-R-Us? Nearly, but not quite. We had hoped that we hadn't reached that stage just yet (granted we weren't far off). I have no prejudice in buying sex, we all buy it in a way, regardless. I don't even have a major problem with purchasing the spouse of your choosing, but out of the three billion women on the planet (and still in my youth) I would like to think that I can form a relationship with *one*, without financial consideration changing hands and still on my terms. Raj and I decide that it's time for a vacation.

We sit in a souk bar in Farringdon called Bed Bar, notebook at the ready to jot down ideas for the perfect holiday destination; we need a break from hunting British quarry.

The waitress brings us our drinks, her glumness is infectious. She's young and pretty, but dressed in a predictably frumpy fashion, some sort of greasy residue has left its mark on her white blouse and her unkempt hair is scraped back, revealing pallid cheeks. Seeing her miserable face just makes me want to get away for a week all the more.

We console ourselves by knocking back the Pimms, like monks on mead at Michaelmas.

'So where shall we go?' I ask Raj.

'Well it has to be somewhere hot'

'Yes, hot,' I scribble it down.

'With great beaches,' Raj carries on listing the essential ingredients.

'Bea-ches.'

'Somewhere historic, steeped in art and beauty; somewhere we can delve into the local cultures, have some great food and intellectual stimulation.'

'California?'

'Perfect!'

To your average hot-blooded male, particularly one who has recently seen less action than a French commando, California possesses all the ingredients to make a fool-proof elixir with which to combat the lack of loving illness. California and its girls conjures an image to us men that could only be equalled in the girl world to a country populated by Robbie Williams clones. *Baywatch, Charlie's Angels, American Pie.* Beautiful blondes with honed physiques and dark bronzed skin that looks like they've been left overnight to marinate in Ronseal, silicone implants that defy the earth's pull as they jaunt on the volleyball court, and yet more dim than a class of blonde special needs girls in Basildon.

California *has* beautiful women. Legend has it that these sun idolising, in-line skating, cheerleading honies are highly susceptible to the British charm. One whiff of our accents and their draws would be dropping to their ankles. If we can't pull in California we won't be able to pull anywhere, ever.

There are times when I should realise that I am undoubtedly a member of the more stupid sex.

We shell out seven hundred quid for our flights, pack enough sun cream to coat a small elephant whale, find the naughtiest beach shorts you've ever seen (turquoise and white jacquard Lycra briefs from Pringle) and buy a bumper pack of American brand condoms called Trojans (we make the obvious jokes at the counter about 'Greeks bearing gifts' and 'wooden horses' but the teller doesn't share in our childish humour. Mind you she is American. Troy probably means nothing to her, other than the wire operated puppet of *Stingray* fame who swam with that sexy Marina lass – you know, the one that all boys fancied).

We had heard only bad reports about LA. An urban sprawl that lacks character and is devoid of charm, but rife with violence. Santa Barbara, however, sounded by all accounts *the* place to be. While it might bring back memories of an appalling *Dallas*-esque 80s soap, Santa Barbara *is* California. Spanish adobe buildings line the streets like large sandwich cakes, painted in Battenberg yellows and pinks. The sidewalks are littered with the tallest palm trees you have ever seen. Invariably at the bottom of the palm there is a hippy playing Bob Dylan on his didgeridoo. The irony is that he is probably way more wealthy than the sun kissed blond guy who drives past in his *Corvette*, hoping to get noticed by the chicas parading up and down the esplanade. The shops are sumptuous, Gucci, Prada, even the Banana Republic looks different to its branches in other cities. Starbucks latte comes automatically 'skinny'.

Sipping our local brand beer from ice cold bottles, we sit outside one of the town's many sports bars (Oakland Athletic are beating Anaheim Angels in the playoffs) we perch on the edge of our stools in silence, agog at the sheer number of top tottie to pass our table. We look at each other and nod approvingly, California was the right choice. These girls are gorgeous but clearly vacuous and bound to fall for our British banter.

That night we prepare for the feast. There is a reason why Santa Barbara is a great city. The place is exclusive, and exclusivity begets frigging expensive hotels. So we decided early on to rent a room in one of the many fine motels on the outskirts of the city. One large double bed (just as well we brought sleeping bags), in a cramped room with complimentary breakfast served from 8.30 to 10.00 – rank coffee that tastes like filtered Irish peat and synthetic muffins that contain a liberal sprinkling of rat droppings for chocolate chips.

Tonight will be our first experience of Santa Barbara's après surf. We break out the double cuff shirts and chinos. After all we want to distinguish ourselves from the local competition, and what better than a bit of Jermyn Street's finest tailoring. Having forgotten the plug adapter for our travel iron, we make a quick run to the 7-Eleven supermarket in search of an American iron. The shirts must be pressed; it may mean the difference between pulling and not pulling. Of course we don't have an ironing board but the bedside table and the complimentary motel bath towel prove an admirable substitute.

We jump in our racing green Pontiac Sunfire. It might only have said 'midsize' on the hire form but it's almost as hot as the top of the range convertible. And, at half the price, it suits us perfectly. Our venue of choice for the evening is Valencia, a new bar on the roof top of a chic hotel in Santa Barbara. We step confidently out of the car, press the beeper to activate its central locking system and saunter towards the club as if we're Crockett and Tubbs (although we haven't rolled up our jacket sleeves, I promise). We get to the front of the very short queue. This is different to London already, it's looking good. In place of the West End hag – a.k.a. the clipboard Nazi – California has hired Conan the Barbarian's slightly less intelligent and slightly less charismatic cousin to be the doorman. At his request (an expressionless upwards nod of his head unaccompanied by words), we show him our passports, which he holds like playing cards in his ham fists. He looks up and down several times, from the Max aged 16 with spots and facial bum fluff in the picture to the Max in front of him. This is tighter than the security at JFK. Any moment now he'll ask me to remove my shoes so he can inspect the frigging soles. The final litmus test, he passes a blue UV light over the inside back cover, which reveals a glowing royal crown. I never knew that happened. I am fairly patriotic at the best of times but seeing that symbol of all that is British, whilst abroad in one of our former colonies that is now *the* world superpower, it has to be said that it made my heart flutter with pride. I feel like the father who sees his son score his first goal for the under-11s team. I make a joke about said colonial history and how great old Liz is. It's not well received. Then I realise that the doorman is probably a Gulf Vet who served first time round with a British platoon and, despite his colossal size, got his *ass kicked* by a short squaddie from Pontypridd.

We leave Dolph Lundgren to grunt at the other punters, as we move on to a much friendlier maitre'd. He's a short but stocky man in his early thirties, his cropped black hair is peppered with grey flecks. Whilst his suit is immaculate and fits like the proverbial glove, one can't help but think *mafioso* when you look at him. He pleasantly informs us that entry is free and that drinks are 25 bucks a pop.

'Fuck,' I exclaim.

'Fuck,' says Raj.

'Gentlemen, watch your mouths, no cursing please,' says the maitre'd.

'Sorry. Twenty-five dollars. Fuck.'

Ignoring his disapproving scowl, we take the lift to up to the roof garden on the ninth floor. There are two other people in the lift, both girls. The taller one has her blonde hair classically curled like a 1950s starlet. She's wearing a halter-neck top in powder pink. The shorter brunette pouts in a fashion that is almost ludicrous. There is no getting away from the fact though that they are beautiful. Beautiful and aloof. They don't talk for fear that any form of movement will send tremors across their face resulting in at least one hair being out of place.

The club is lavish. Spanish hacienda meets New World chic. The music is low and chilled, laced with that Spanish influence you find everywhere in California. Several hundred twenty-somethings are huddled into the main courtyard, a fountain trickles and flaming torches flicker, gasping for breath in the night sky that is like an almighty ebony slab speckled with twinkling quartz crystals. Deep fuchsia bougainvillea reach up to it, sexy and infectious, like the high hum of flirting and laughing. It seems only the beautiful people in Santa Barbara have been allowed into the Valencia.

'Perhaps they're all like this,' I think to myself. The women are all as stunning as the two corkers in the lift, like extras off the *Beverly Hills 90210* set. They are immaculate, high on life and full of self-worth. Raj and I don't need to talk, a look to each other says it all. I know he's thinking the same as me, that I've never seen so many stereotypically fit girls in one club. There's no point in performing the Rating Ritual here, it's a bit academic. It would be like comparing one pearl against a load of others, searching for minor imperfections, rather than finding the one pearl in amongst a bag of marbles, which is what we're used to.

'Right, all we have to do is talk loudly enough and our English accents will do the rest for us, they'll come flocking,' I assure Raj. He nods with excitement.

So, in a fashion akin to Terry-Thomas and Leslie Philips, we talk at three times the normal volume of conversation. After ten minutes we are exhausted. No one is looking. None of the girls have taken the bait, not even a tentative or exploratory nibble. At that moment two girls who are pushing their way through the crowd stop in front of us.

'Hi, howsit going?' one of the girls asks. She is a brunette with Mediterranean features. Her slightly taller friend is clearly of Scandinavian origin. I raise my left eyebrow at Raj, in true Roger Moore fashion.

'One is doing exceptionally well thank you, and your good selves?' I ask.

For the first time the blonde speaks, 'Oh my god. They're Australian. Come on Jules let's go.'

And with that they melt into the throng.

Suddenly a large hand claps on each of our shoulders. The strong grip is like the hold a sheriff might have employed in one of the old Western films having just apprehended the wanted cattle rustler.

'Hiya, howsit goin' fellas?'

We turn our heads to face a large barrel chest. Slowly looking upwards we meet the round face of a friendly looking chap, dressed smartly but not well enough to betray his professional football look. The thing you notice most is his smile. His teeth gleam and sparkle at us like bathroom tiles in a Viakal advert.

'Very good, thank you.'

'You boys aren't from California are ya?' he bellows

'Er no, we're here on holiday,' answers Raj.

'Let me guess. Australia?'

What's with the Australia thing? Can't they tell the difference? Now I know how Canadians feel when they're perpetually mistaken for Yanks. I wonder if all the Aussies that come to the States are asked if they're British. Probably not, they'd be liable to deck anyone who said that. Ah, that explains it, the Americans have probably come across so many irate Aussies who have been mistaken for pommies that they realised it was safer to presume *we* are all from Oz. Conversely, the reserved Brits would be more likely to correct them politely, rather than treat them to a fist sandwich. And so, keeping to form –

'Actually, we're British,' I explain.

'Brits eh, you boys are popular here, allies against the Rag heads!'

'Ye-es quite,' I spot Raj cringe.

I don't think he even noticed that Raj might not be of 100% Anglo-Saxon descent.

'You know you boys need to get out there and work your stuff. Use that accent, man, you gotta head start against us local boys.'

We look at each other despairingly.

'Yes, we have tried that, but it doesn't seem to work.'

He ponders for a moment and then throws his head back in laughter. As his guffaw subsides he leans in close, what he might consider a whisper but to you or I is normal speaking volume.

'Well ya need to grab some ass,' he explains.

'Ass?' we question.

'ASS!' he roars.

And wearing a lunatic-like grin he looks around for a suitable victim. He spots a girl in tight jeans walking past. He draws his hand up high past his shoulder, devilment flashes in his eyes. His hand comes down like a great pendulum. We wince in anticipation and disbelief. As his palm makes contact with her fleshy rump, there's an almighty slap and she lets out an awful yelp. He's holding onto her like a bowling ball. We expect to see her reel round and return the favour across his chops. But instead, incredibly, she's smiling. The rapacious jezebel actually enjoyed it. Then, she winks and blows him a kiss.

'See boys, you listen to old Buck and you can't go wrong.'

'We can't do that,' I say, sounding horrified.

'Sure ya can, these hussies love it. Show 'em who's boss. Anything less and they won't think y'all interested.'

'For God's sake, I'm telling you we can't do it!'

'How come?'

'Because we're British!'

Buck wanders off, somewhat bewildered at our inability to *grab ass*. Doesn't he appreciate that, as Englishmen, it takes hours for us to simply strike up the courage to approach a girl and *talk* to her. Let alone make an intimate introduction between our hand and her derrière. *è*Clearly we are going to need to effect more radical tactics. We need to be more proactive and stop wasting time on the subtleties that are so clearly lost on this breed of prey. We need to actually approach them.

Raj notices two young girls standing by themselves, just next to the fountain. Although they aren't sisters, they could conceivably be related. They both have slight figures, impish, with long brown hair and inviting eyes. Raj expresses his carnal interests in one of them and I offer to make the ice-breaking move. I saunter towards them; outwardly brimming with confidence, inwardly dissolving like an aspirin. As I get within striking distance – a term, which to my American friend with the ceramic teeth, would have quite different and literal connotations – the pair turn to face me. The one on the right, the slightly older looking one, turns her head and makes eye contact. Here we go, looking good. *Locked in captain, move for the kill.* I smile, cheekily. She moves towards me. The fluttering in my stomach increases, but so does the adrenaline, the excitement, the expectation. I open my mouth and extend my hand at the same time, 'Hi I'm…'

Before I can say anything further she blinks those cold eyes and in a flash, before opening them again, turns sharply on her heels.

An SS officer would have been envious of her technique. A snap, a click and a march in the opposite direction. I was astounded. She had looked me straight in the eyes moments before. She knew I was coming over to talk to her. She might at least have politely declined, it was so outrageously rude. I was in such shock that I don't know what came over me, I am in denial. I stare in desperation at the friend, like a pleading beggar with leprosy. I reach out with both hands, imploringly, as if to grasp her before coming out with the immortal line, 'No wait, you don't understand, all I want is...'

She takes a step back, to withdraw from the environs of this madman in front of her. Whatever pestilence he is carrying it might be contagious. And, in as swift a fashion as her friend, she scarpers in the same direction. I am left there, astounded. Feeling like everyone in the club is staring at me, thinking 'Dude, what a loser!'

Raj is as mortified as I am. He's feeling for me, I know he is, and that makes it better.

'Buddy, what the hell was that?' he asks.

'I haven't a clue, you ever seen anything like that? I thought Californians were supposed to be cool and friendly. The Beach Boys had it all wrong!'

It's at this moment, sharing in the hilarity of the situation that Vanessa arrives. I feel a clawing in the nape of my neck. It's quite nice, actually. Like being groped by Flo Jo. It doesn't compute at first and Raj notes the concern on my face. I turn to face the person behind the nails. Standing there is this paragon of beauty. She stands tall and has mischief in her eye. I feel like I know her. Suddenly I realise where I have seen her before, it's the blonde from the lift. She stares me square in the face, her nails still doing their work. Her eyes taking in the look of pleasure on my face, which is the result of her caressing.

'Hi, I wanted to tell you that I like your thang!' she smiles, sweetly.

'My thang?' I'm clueless.

She laughs at my anglicised pronunciation of *thang*. Her smile is kind and alluring.

'Yeah, I like the way you're dressed.' She glances around her at the other men, her eyes registering them all but focusing on no one in particular. She draws in a deep breath and returns to me, 'You're British!'

'Yes, that's right, we, I, am.'

'You're cute. You look like Christian Bale.'

I turn the colour of a sundried tomato. Batman, eh?! I start babbling. My eyes are looking everywhere but into hers.

'Really, I think you're being too kind. I mean...'

'My name's Vanessa, what's yours, *Christian*?'

'Er, Max. You know Vanessa you're...'

Before I can get out my compliment, the phone in her pocket starts to emit a rather annoying ring tone. It's one of those old-school Nokia type rings. The Americans are way behind us in the telecoms world. She reaches out to me with her free hand, in that 'please excuse me' kind of gesture and raises her eyebrows in a somewhat theatrical fashion. She's trying to convey to me to go nowhere and that she won't be long. Then suddenly...

'Yeah Jeanie, listen I've just met this really cute English guy. Uh-huh. He looks just like that actor.' There's a pause. 'Yeah I know!' What does she know? 'Jeanie... Jeanie wait a sec!'

She turns and faces me again, she's not listening to the whiney voice on the end of the phone. Instead she is looking into my eyes, where an intensity has caught fire. She gives a broad smile, a grin like the Cheshire cat. My God, Americans do have lovely teeth.

'Max?'

'Yes Vanessa.'

'Kiss me, Max!'

Well, it's the last thing I'm expecting. It must be the last thing Raj is expecting as well, because I hear him choke slightly on a mouthful of caipirinha. He hadn't succumbed to buying one of the $25 a pop drinks, he had convinced a petite Chinese girl he was chatting with to let him take a sip of hers. Even she couldn't believe her eyes. She had turned to look away from Raj and instead stare at Vanessa, and from Vanessa to me, to see what I would do. Vanessa had clearly said something that was not the *done thing*. The Chinese girl is wearing a look on her face that is something between shock and disgust. A reproachful scowl because Vanessa had let down her sex. Clearly, inviting a man to kiss you is not something any self-respecting Californian girl should ever do.

What am I to do? I feel like everyone is watching me – even Jeanie on the end of the phone. I'm sure I can hear her whine cry out, 'Has he kissed you yet, has he, has he?'

The pressure is ridiculous. It was so out of the blue and so damned unfair. I need a while to psyche myself up to that sort of thing, at least two hours of inane chatter, a quart of brandy, six Stellas and some Barry White before I remotely have the courage. I look at Raj. He's looking at me with that face that says, 'What are you waiting for you friggin' Muppet, snog her now or I'll do it for you!' I look back at Vanessa. Then back to Raj. I do this another two times before I get a grip of myself. I lean in. The spectators draw breath, including Jeanie. We lock lips. My left hand goes to explore her bottom, after a few seconds my right one joins in. She tastes great and smells even better. She gets into it immediately. It might be Hollywood territory, and I don't know if that had an effect on me, but this is the nearest thing to an onscreen kiss I have ever experienced (perhaps apart from the Brazilian). Everyone else around us are *extras*, the camera pans around us. It's the kiss at the end of *Four Weddings* without the rain and the corny line. Then it steps up a notch and becomes a little more erotic, as kisses go.

As an Englishman such a kiss would be the precursor to an invite back to the girl's apartment for more of the same, and some on top – her preferably. But we forget that different countries have different cultures, with different mating rituals. It was unusual that Vanessa had asked me to kiss her in the first place. For me to force the hand and push for me to go back to her place, would be as warmly received there as Buck's arse slapping technique would be received in the UK. The irony is that you get to sleep with the

British girls, but it doesn't matter how many Californian rumps you brand with the palm of your hand, there's no going past first base for at least a month! You think Catholic Europeans have a bad reputation (or good depending on how you look at it) of not putting out, well they have nothing on the Californians.

Although we didn't know it then, that was the most action we would see in the Sunshine State. I left Vanessa in the club, with a large black guy who looked suspiciously like a minder. Vanessa – my one fond memory of Californian women. But at the time we hoped that it was just the start of better things to come. We should have thrown in our chips and left happy. More importantly, we should have known that the bank always wins.

The next fortnight is spent frequenting student bars in places like San Luis Obispo. San Luis has a student population of 30,000 – if anywhere is going to have great parties, teeming with girls, this is going to be it. Our timing is impeccable, we arrive in the town during WOW week. WOW week stands for *Week Of Welcome* – or, in English, Freshers' Week.

Seeing the banners, welcoming the new students, draped high across the streets, sends an excitement through our veins. It's hot, the pavements – sorry sidewalks – are full of students drinking smoothies in their Abercrombie & Fitch baggies. The girls are in hot pants or small gym skirts, finished off with a thoughtful bikini top. This place is like the town in *Back to the Future*. In fact, I'm sure I just saw Marty fly past on his skateboard, holding onto the rear bumper of an SUV. Having driven through the main drag we get directions to the college campus, from a girl who looks distinctly like Buffy. Heading away from the town centre, into the hills on the outskirts, we find the illustrious University of California Polytechnic, otherwise known affectionately to its members as *Cal Poly*.

Raj and I cruise through the main drag of the college. It really is like any American high school that you have seen on TV. I thought they were just clichés; the yank equivalent to undergraduates on bicycles wearing gowns, negotiating narrow, cobbled streets in a city of spires. Nope, it really is like that.

As we slow down, nearing a bend, we let a group of girls jog across the road, in front of us. A group of 20 19-year-olds, who are clearly part of some running club. Every single one of them has a 'right tidy little figure', as a Welsh friend of mine would say. Tanned, lithe and firm bodies. You would never see a group of girls like that at a British university, they'd be swilling pints of Fosters in the Student Union bar. And then, as if to complete the picture, a girl carrying a pair of pom-poms walks past us, on the other side of the road. She is kitted out in the full cheerleader get-up. Raj can't believe his eyes. He winds down the window, and without a care in the world yells out, 'Hey love,' with his usual aplomb. She stops and looks over in our direction, with that 'what me?' look. And as if to answer Raj shouts back, 'Yeah, you. Are you a cheerleader?'

The poor girl looks confused. Possibly because it's a man with brown skin who has what sounds distinctively like a British (or Australian) accent, and why is he asking such an obvious question?

'Well, er, yeah I am. Say, are you guys Australian?'

Instead of correcting her, politely, Raj screams back, 'Wow, I've never seen a real-life cheerleader.'

The poor girl goes the same colour as her pom-poms; being crimson.

In short, San Luis promises great things. It is not long before we have ingratiated ourselves with the undergraduate student body. We have informed them that we are on an exchange from an English university. We aren't here to take classes for a semester, or anything straightforward like that, oh no, we are here to set up an exchange between our two academic institutions. We soon realise that, as two British guys, we are somewhat of a novelty in San Luis. Within the first few hours on campus the frat guys have invited us to a couple of house parties.

You see, the fraternities are in the throws of their pledge week. During this one week period, the new male freshers go through a strenuous selection and initiation process, in order to join one of the coveted Frat houses. Part of this process incorporates some serious private house or keg parties – so called because of the essential ingredient of a keg of your finest West American gnat's piss.

Our first keg party is that night, at the Phi Alpha Gamma frat house. But it's only two in the afternoon, and we have been assured that the party won't be 'kicking' until around eleven. Thankfully we have arranged to meet Sara-Jane at seven.

Sara-Jane, or SJ, as she apparently likes to be called, is a friend of a friend. When we decided to come out to California, Dirty had told us that he has a friend in San Luis, and that if we should stop there, we should call her up. He assured us that she is a great girl, a lot of fun to hang out with, and that she would undoubtedly be happy to show us around. If we are lucky, we will meet all her cracking friends to boot. Well, who could refuse such a thoughtful invitation? So we had called SJ as soon as we knew we were on our way to San Luis. When I spoke to her, from a roadside service station in Big Sur, she had told us to meet her on Friday night at the English pub, called the Frog and Peach.

SJ has that very alluring all-Californian accent. It really does evoke images of *Baywatch* lifeguards. I had Raj putting his ear next to the receiver, straining to hear her voice.

'She sounds like a right fitty,' he deduced, from the snippets he managed to catch. He's right though, she does sound lovely. It sounds stupid, but I already find her attractive, her accent just does it for me. And she has promised to bring one of her friends along, to make it a double date.

It is just before seven and we are sitting at one of the bar-side tables in the Frog and Peach. The pub is empty apart from us, and some old guy with a droopy grey moustache sinking his beer at the bar. It's an English pub but they haven't heard of bitter, or ale for that matter, so we grab a couple of Buds. We can't help but feel excited, this is going to be one of the big nights of our trip, if not *the* big night. We have a date with two Californian girls, and then for the latter part of the night we are heading to a college frat party. How much better can it get?

It's ten past seven. They're running late, we check our watches. We're nervous, but still on a high.

'Man, I wonder if they're both blonde?' Raj moots.

'Yeah, and if they have tanned bodies, like those girls in the jogging group from earlier?'

'Or the cheerleader,' we both gaze like idiots, remembering her exemplary figure.

'Aww, don't!'

At that minute, there is a 'holler' from the entrance to the pub.

'Hey boys! You must be Max and Raj!' I recognise that same alluring voice, which now booms across the empty saloon. The owner of the voice, however, is not, it appears, so alluring. We look up to see a girl the size of Roseanne Barr, with eighties bouffant hair. I don't know how she got through the door. It's clearly the result of too many of those burritos, the ones that are the size of small children, which they are so fond of eating around here. Standing next to her is a girl of equal proportions with white blonde hair, not the nice kind, more the 'death rock' sort of blonde hair. She is pale and wearing black stonewashed jeans. I look at Raj, he has come over very ill looking – worried, disconcerted, pissed off – he seems to be displaying all these traits. We should have guessed that SJ would be one of Dirty's usual swamp donkeys.

'I'm SJ, great to meet you, at last.' We shake hands. 'This is my friend Lou,' she introduces the pale girl, who has a high-pitched, chipmunk-like voice that could, and probably will, grate after a few minutes.

We resume our seats while Raj gets some beers in.

'So David told me all about you boys, old friends from college, right?'

'That's right, and how do you know Dirt...er, Dave again?,' as if I have to ask.

She goes a little red and, like an excitable sow, releases a terrifying giggle. 'Well, I was over in the UK, on a college programme, like, and well we met at some bar in Piccadilly, I think,' she explains.

Chipmunk looks at her friend and they giggle in unison; she has clearly heard the full, gruesome details. In other words, Dirty had picked her up in Tiger Tiger, taken her home to his pad and shagged her senseless. Now I'm glad she's unattractive, the idea of stirring Dirty's porridge makes me nauseous.

Before Raj returns, SJ moves around the table to sit next to me, forcing Raj to take a pew alongside Lou. We've been paired up already, it would seem. It's not a good sign. I don't think I have ever been happier to see Raj. Being left alone with these two, even for a few minutes, was too much. I note the fear in his face, again, as he sees the seating arrangement has been engineered. Divide and conquer.

'Anyway, we were kinda thinking,' says Lou, 'we could go out for some food and then go dancing. You know if you boys haven't got anywhere to stay, we have some couches at our place.'

They smile, sweetly and almost innocently. And I believe they think that we might, actually, be tempted.

All that Californians seem to do is eat. At baseball games, the cinema, shopping in the mall. These past times are all just vehicles to facilitate the mass consumption of vaguely edible shite. You would think that California, the Sunshine State, would have a Mediterranean diet of fresh fruit and lots of salads. You would be forgiven for having such preconceptions, but you would be wrong – it's bubblegum ice cream, smoothies (devoid of any tracings of fruit, yet brimming with colourings and sugar), Tri Tip sandwiches (things the size of a 'Scooby snack' filled with leather-like steak) and coke served in German steins – *don't worry, sir, you get a free refill!*

The thought of more greasy food adds to our general malaise. And then dancing? Those two would clear the floor. The invitation to crash at their apartment is the proverbial straw that breaks this particular camel's back. We have to extricate ourselves from this situation, and as soon as possible.

'That sounds like an excellent idea,' I lie.

Raj looks at me with mortal fear and in utter disbelief. 'But let's go dancing for a bit first, build up an appetite, so to speak,' I suggest.

I give Raj that 'trust me, I know what I'm doing look.'

'Great,' whoops SJ, she is all smiles, 'we'll finish our drinks and head over to The Graduate.'

'How about Mother's Tavern, I heard it has great music,' I say.

The two girls agree. We spend the next ten minutes finishing our beers and chatting about our trip and England and Dirty – the little shit.

'Dude what on Earth are you thinking of?' Raj whispers, with some force, in my ear, as we leave the Frog and Peach.

'Don't worry,' I reassure him, 'just follow my lead, okay?' I can see he doesn't look convinced.

We cross the road and head into Mother's. It's early but, being WOW week, it's heaving with undergrads. They're not first years because, at eighteen, they aren't old enough to have a drink. But these seniors are newly turned legal imbibers. At street level the bar is full of sweaty students, jumping around to house music. We follow the two girls up some stairs to the mezzanine bar. It's also crammed, but these punters are all queuing for drinks, or standing around chatting to their mates. The twosome tell us to wait by the balustrade while they get the beers. We look down at the throng of dancers in the bar below, jumping together.

I'm not proud of what I do next, but I have no choice. There are times to be a gentleman, and times to think of yours truly. This is an occasion for the latter. I see that the girls are almost at the bar. The queue is several people deep so they can't really see Raj and I, even if they do look back for any reason. It has to be now.

'Right mate, follow me!' I yell at Raj, so he can hear me above the music.

'Eh, what are you on about?'

Idiot, he always was slow on the uptake.

'Do you want to be dancing the fandango with Chipmunk over there for the rest of the night?' I ask facetiously. 'An evening of harpooning is certainly not on my agenda!'

'No! Of course not.'

'Then let's get out of here!' I shove my way past some of the revellers, without pausing to apologise. I get to the top of the stairs that lead down into the lower bar. I turn back to make sure Raj is behind me. He is at my heels, but I also see Lou look back from the bar and clock us.

'Shit, hurry up, mate.'

We make a quick descent down the stairs but we are slowed down as we hit the human wall of dancers. We prise our way through. Halfway into the sea of people we look up to see the two girls at the balustrade. They are holding four bottles of beer, and appear highly bemused. Finally, we pass out of sight, underneath the mezzanine floor. The crowd has thinned out and it's easier to move through.

'Where are we going Max?' Raj shouts.

'Well, I noticed earlier that this place has a rear exit. It takes us down Bubblegum Alley and onto Marsh Street.' I can see the incomprehension on Raj's face.

'It's where the car is parked!'

His face lights up, 'So what are we waiting for!'

We burst out of the fire exit and into Bubblegum Alley (as gross as it sounds, it literally is an alley covered with thousands of bits of bubblegum – it looks like some Jackson Pollock creation). We pause to drink in the cool air. Running down the alley, taking care not to brush up against the gum-coated walls, we fall onto Marsh St. There she is, our Pontiac, waiting like a trusty steed.

We speed off, thanking our stars for a lucky escape. We head uptown towards the college and the area known as Foothills, where all the frat houses are based. We get to the Phi Alpha Gamma house. It all looks pretty quiet. We park the car and saunter up to the front door of the frat house, which is guarded by two huge blokes. Jocks. They appear fairly stern, and not as if they are about to let us in. What is it about door men the world over, even if they're only overweight 21-year-olds, who lost their last living brain cell on the football field. Bouncers are supposed to work in the entertainment industry, but they all seem bent on ruining your chances of enjoying yourself.

'Yeah, whaddya want?' the one on the left demands. He looks like a clean-shaven *Desperate Dan*.

'We have been invited to the frat party tonight,' Raj explains.

'Hey, you are the English guys, right?' suddenly he has become as friendly as a cub scout on 'bob-a-job' day who has just been paid a tenner for washing someone's car.

'Yes, that's right, over here on an exchange,' I say, mildly convincingly.

'Well, you boys go right on in, beer glass on the side, hit that keg, man!'

We didn't need to be told twice, not after our near miss with Dirty's castoffs. We thank the two jocks and head inside. The frat house looks like any other suburban American house: single storey building with white wood façade and pitch roof. The only thing that sets it aside are the three-foot high Greek letters above the doorway – Phi Alpha Gamma. The dark hallway leads into a brighter lit lounge, where all the party goers are 'hangin'.' It's far rowdier than a student house party back in Blighty, and that's saying something. Old-school hip hop is playing and already some people are dancing around in the centre of the room.

It's only around nine, we thought we would be a bit early. The party is in full swing. In fact, it soon becomes apparent that they are all pissed. A small group of people are busying themselves in the corner of the room, near to the kitchen, like a small swarm of wasps around an open jar of strawberry jam. Once they have got their hands on their sticky bounty they get out the fray and head back into the room. The open jam jar is the keg; the beating heart of any college party. Collecting clean cups of our own from the sideboard we make our way to join the swarm. It's not long before we catch sight of the tap. The guy in front is filling up his glass, for what looks like the eighth time.

'Hey dudes, tuck in,' he says as he turns around. 'Man, aren't you guys from England or something?'

How he knows I'm not sure, I suppose we stick out like sore thumbs. Check – no one else is wearing shirts and slacks with leather shoes. All the other guys are in polyester sports tops, about three times too big for them, baseball caps, faded jeans of equal disproportion to the sports tops, and trainers... sorry, sneakers. It seems that everyone has heard about our arrival. I don't think they can have many English people passing through this town.

'Er, yes we are,' Raj says, smiling.

'Cool,' is all he says, before wandering off.

'Right Raj, pass us your glass, let's get these jars filled and start to introduce a bit of British into this frat party.'

With beers in hand, we stand in the centre of the sitting room. We are like invisible men, sober spectators to the drunken carnage. The party has only been going for an hour or two, apparently, but they are like schoolkids tasting their first sip of alcohol. For some of them this is not far off the truth. The room is divided between the semi-seasoned seniors and the learner drinkers that are the freshers. But even the seniors seem pretty foxed.

'Hey, Raj, isn't that the cheerleader from earlier?' I point with my glass at some girl who has just walked in with two friends.

'Yeah, I reckon it is, oh shit, she's coming over.'

Sure enough, the girl has spotted us and is whispering to her friends. The three of them bounce over towards us.

'Hi,' she says, in that high-pitched sickly way that only Californian girls know how. Not that it's not attractive, in moderation.

'Er, hello,' says Raj. He's not so confident outside the security of the car.

'So you guys are the English guys on the exchange, right?'

'Yes, that's right, we sure are,' Raj maintains our pretence.

'I'm Mandy,' she introduces herself. 'These are my friends Jo and Kerry-Lee – they're cheerleaders too.' The saucy little minx giggles, the others giggle too. If you could see Raj blush, he'd be blushing.

I change the subject, 'So how many of those keg things do you normally get through at one of these parties?'

They look at each other with incomprehension. Then they look at me, blankly. Have I made a faux pas? It's as if I've asked when we sacrifice the neighbour's dog.

'Well,' Mandy says, 'just the one.'

Just the one? But they're all steaming! There can only be 60 pints of beer in the entire keg – and there must be 40 people in the party. The girls see the shock on my face.

'You know this is a dry campus!' pipes up Kerry-Lee.

'Dry campus?' Raj bemuses.

'Yes, we don't have alcohol on campus, only in the frat houses,' Jo kindly explains.

We decide that it's best not to explain that alcohol is one of the raisons d'être for doing a degree in the UK. Our American cousins get awfully prudish about this sort of thing and, after all, we are looking to impress these girls.

'Oh yes, of course it is,' I say quickly, before Raj says something, which will get us branded AA loser members of the year. Thankfully the girls soon move onto the comfortable topic of our 'adorable' accents. Like dogs doing tricks, we perform to their giggles, whoops and cries for encore. Pronouncing this word, saying that phrase.

'So, you boys are just here for a week or so?' Mandy enquires.

'Yes, afraid so, we have to get back to our own studies in the UK,' Raj lies.

We thought this would be the safest cover. If we had said that we are over at Cal Poly for the whole semester, it would have raised questions on course credits, academic supervisors, accommodation etc. – none of which could answer convincingly. But this is our downfall.

'It's a shame you guys aren't here for longer, you would have girls falling at your feet,' says Mandy, flirtatiously. And I'm smiling at her flattery, when her message hits home. There's a whopping great 'if' in there. *If* we were here for longer.

'Well, we are here for a week or so,' I plead.

They do that annoying thing of looking at each other again, as if they are communicating telepathically. Mandy, clearly the designated spokesperson, sounds as if she is making some moral statement, 'Yes, but no Californian girl will go out with you for a week, what's the point?'

It's my turn to read Raj's mind. It reminds me of a movie tagline – *Inside your head no one can hear you scream!* Apart from your best mate of course, in situations like this. I was screaming too. I don't want to go out with one of them, neither does Raj. We live on the other side of the Atlantic for pity's sake. But we would like to go out on the town and party with some local girls, perhaps be a little crazy and embark on a totally frivolous affair. A romance that is intrinsically carefree, yet not utterly meaningless. Something that you would look back on in future years with a certain fondness. It's one of those things that makes youth what it is. Fun.

The irony dawns on us that the type of women we would want for a holiday fling are the exact women that we left at home. American girls are the types that we could actually date, if we lived in the same place. We should be living in the States and holidaying in Britain. These girls are far from easy.

But it's clear that it isn't to be. There is no convincing these girls. We look around us and notice that there isn't a single couple *making out*. Certainly, some are unconscious, one kid (and he really does just look like a kid) has even fallen asleep underneath the holy keg; which still isn't empty by the way. But not a single student is lip-locking with another. In England there would be a queue for the toilet, and any other small mildly intimate storage space, in which to nail the bird of your choosing. Not here. We soon realise that while our infamy as San Luis's resident English guys has spread like wild fire, so has the news that we are leaving town within the week. As such, we would never be considered as viable mates.

As if to mark this awful truth, sirens strike up outside the front lawn. The boy under the keg moans. Some of the more sober frat guys begin to swear. Already one or two guests have started to collect their jackets and other accoutrements.

'Ah dude, the fuckin' cops,' someone yells.

We soon deduce that the police are on their way to break up the evening's proceedings. Our disbelief can't get any greater. Not only are their parties tame, and to be honest, pretty dull, but the police really do break them up. Sure enough, as we reach the door, up swagger the bluebottles, complete with flashlights, yelling orders here and there. And do you know what? The students all do as they are told. I would love to see any police patrol unit in the UK, not that we really have them, try and break up a house party. They wouldn't dare, they'd be pelted with bottles. Ah, therein lies the problem, the keg doesn't lend itself as ammunition.

We follow the other disheartened guests down the drive. It's only half past nine and our perfectly planned evening, the highlight of our trip, is over. We sit in the car, pause for a moment to reflect in silence, and then *buckle up*.

14

Online

So Thai-brides-R-Us it is! California had been a disaster. As I came through customs I felt like I should have walked through the Something to Declare aisle at Heathrow – 'Yes I'd like to declare my inability to get a woman; for letting down mankind; for being the only British guy to go to the States and not get nookie with an American girl.' As I walked through I should have handed them my penis back for lack of use.

I had thought about it on the plane back to the UK. It seemed that there was only one thing left to try – an online dating agency. What could I do? I've tried everything else. I blame it on the semi-clad dirty blonde in the advert at the back of *GQ*. It's her fault I reached for my laptop and signed up to Dating World.

I wish that was the truth. The reality is that I was scouting through *Loot* for a new sofa and saw their Personals section. Out of curiosity, I clicked on the link and arrived at Dating World. It seems very different to Single Solution – my previous experience with online dating. All the girls place their photos on the site and tell you a little about themselves – age, profession, minimum bank balance preferred and the DNA of their ideal man etc.

But this disclosure works both ways. The fact that there is an initial vetting procedure must make it easier to wean out the bunny boilers. I suppose it's like a box of chocolates; Thornton's Continental. Or perhaps a large packet of Revels is more appropriate. One date might be a coffee cream, not the best in the bag, but you never know if you'll come across a chocolate-coated ball of toffee, the connoisseurs pick of the bunch.

I go through the laborious procedure of entering all my personal details and requirements. I hand over my £30 for three months unlimited membership and waste no time in browsing through the endless catalogue of potential suitors.

I can search against age, locality etc. But what about breast size, length of legs, likelihood to put out on the first date? Actually, the girls have been very helpful in this department. Most of them have posted a photo on their profile when they signed up. This answers so many of my questions – at least the important ones. It will go part of the way in the search for the chocolate-coated toffee Revel.

I spot one girl who looks reasonably attractive. It takes me to her homepage, which tells me all the important trivia about 'Claire'. Having looked at Claire I become like a madman, gorging myself on the profiles of potential dates. These are women I could make contact with, from the safety of my own couch. No awkward approaches in dimly lit bars. I could apply the scattergun approach and if 40% get back to you there's a result. And the thing is, I know that all these women are single and keen. Keen is, perhaps, the wrong word. Desperate. As am I, granted.

I read through the first 20 girls that take my fancy and I wonder if they have thought about what they have written about themselves. They clearly have but they all seem to say the same thing. I don't think they realise what sort of mental picture will be painted by the men who are scanning their profiles. It's certainly not the type of image that a man looking for a 'partner' would be looking to picture. They all go along the lines of:

> Hi, well I've never done this before (**you so have**). How crazy am I! (**not very**) So what can I tell you about me?!? Well my friends say I'm bubbly and outgoing (**read *fat***). I like reading, swimming and

tennis. I also love football, my favourite team is Manchester United (**good try**) and I'm really into cars (**yeah right, and I cross-stitch**). I like going out to party, don't mind the odd drink but sometimes I just want to stay in and crash on the couch with a DVD and a bottle of *vino* (**you have reached the time to find a husband and want to have your social life amputated**). Looking to meet someone for some fun and who knows where it will go! (**Entice the man with the promise of sex and then it's *ding dong*, 'We're going to the chapel...'**).

Despite my cynicism, and self-disbelief at resorting to this medium, I add a few of the women to 'My Favourites'. I tell myself to stop being such a love-scrooge; this might actually work. Surely this will be better than a blind date. From the photo you can tell if she's attractive or not. What's more you get a bit of an idea about what she's like; her profession, figure, education, likes and dislikes etc. And I'm hoping that women will be less likely to lie when they fill out this form. Flagrant, whopping untruths are more the sort of thing that a guy would employ; use photographs that are ten years are out of date, make out they are not married, that kind of stuff. Having completed this pre-date disclosure, surely on any first meeting it will simply be a question of whether you actually hit it off. And that is always an unknown.

I review My Favourites and decide to send a message to the five most attractive women from the 15 that I have selected. Two are lawyers, one's in media, another is a primary school teacher and the last is a history student at UCL. They all seem to be fairly confident and outgoing and have a variety of interests. They are all quite attractive – or I should say that their photos look good. I bang off the same message to all five, taking care not to cut and paste the previous girl's name in the next message. It reads as follows;

Hi

I thought I'd drop you a line because I read your profile and liked what I saw. (**true**) Seems like we're looking for the same thing. Guess I had better tell you a bit about me. (**trying to be laid back**) I work in PR in the City (**yep think 'cash,' go on bite!**) I'm quite a creative person. Outside of work, apart from the usual partying and seeing friends, I like to write and paint (modern oils mostly, some portraits). (**I'm in touch with my feminine side, I'm a nice guy**) I recently started to learn Spanish, and I also speak Italian.

I'm very outgoing and confident but also a good listener. (**yes, mr perfect does exist**)

I'm looking for someone I will have a great time being with, snuggling up sometimes and also going out with and having fun.

I hope you'll get in touch, yours

Max

It takes ages to write that first email. It's almost like filling in one of those annoying graduate recruitment forms. I'm sure it won't be long before the dating agencies have you sitting psychometric tests. Should that be psychometric or psychotic? I'm not sure. Anyhow, I pondered over the words for what seemed to be ever. It's difficult to get it just right. To sell yourself and yet not sound arrogant. To be cool, but not too cool. A splattering of modesty here and there, and yet still make them want you like a nun wants a dildo.

You have to apply a careful strategy. Emails and texts can so often be taken in different ways. You have to measure each word and its meaning, to make sure you create the exact, desired effect. It's like writing the Book of Job or the Declaration of Independence, each word stands out on the page like its own continent. Equally, it can be difficult to understand the true meaning in those written words. Great importance is placed on small, insignificant prose that can give greater or lesser meanings.

I feel excited, making direct contact with all those women who I know are single and who are looking for a man. My carefully drafted message has moved from my out tray and now sits in the inbox of my favourite five. I twiddle my fingers for a minute or two. I turn my attention to the press release of a well-known west London restaurant that I'm supposed to be drafting. The wait is too much, I click on the inbox icon to see if any of the girls have written back to me yet? It's been four minutes. The inbox is empty. I feel dejected. This is ridiculous, it's been a further five minutes. I go and make a cup of tea. I come back and check a second, a third and even a fourth time within the space of twenty minutes. Ping. At the fifth attempt a new message from Victoria1975 arrives in my inbox.

Hi,

What area of PR are you in?

This will sound like an odd question!
But do you mind telling me how tall you are? I am 5'11" so it is kind of relevant!

Look forward to hearing from you,

Victoria x

Relevant. Why is it relevant? Unless I'm wrong, she is, like me, unable to find someone out in the 'open market'. And so she is resorting to the help of an online dating forum – namely *Loot*. It's not even the most glamorous of online dating channels. It's the place where you search for pee-stained old furniture and spares for a Ford Capri. Yes, I know, I'm there as well. But I'm approaching it with a slightly more open mind. And I'm desperate.

She's 5'11 which is pretty tall for a girl. In heels that will boost her up to a potential 6'2. When I'm in shoes it means she would be a conceivable two inches taller than me – two inches. I appreciate the fact that women like to feel secure and that part of that feeling is created by the man's physical stature. But surely women are supposed to have a new found security, independence and confidence. Height, like a man's personal property, should no longer be prerequisite for a perfect match. Being an inch or two taller than their other half – or in this case the same height in your socks – shouldn't create an insurmountable boundary to being with someone.

How can you be that picky, how can you disregard another human being, their life and all their qualities over two inches – and not even in the area where it counts. I mean, ideally any woman I date should be slimmer than me, have a firmer bottom and have boobs that are at least three times the size of mine. But if I told a slightly porky lass with B cup breasts to sling her hook, well that would be downright unacceptable. And yet I'd be more than willing to give Bridget Jones a try the way I'm feeling at the moment.

Perhaps this online dating forum was not such a good idea after all. Perhaps the women weren't going to be as amenable as I first thought. I feel really down. The last thing I was expecting is that these women would be highly picky – but then again why shouldn't they? Just because they have subscribed to an online dating society, they haven't forfeited their right to be selective. (Or have they?)

I think to myself 'what the heck' and reply to Victoria, enclosing my exact height. An hour later still nothing. The site sends me an email alert when she's read my message. Still no reply. I don't hear from her again. This is horrendous, I want her to write back, even if it's a 'Thanks, but no thanks.' It's like a little seed in my mind, I can't help but think about her. Its roots sprout out, niggling as they spread their tendrils. The rejection is too much. I write to her again, with a chatty email. Nothing.

But, as I go into my inbox for the fifteenth time that hour, I have two new messages – neither of which are from Victoria. One is from Amber, an American girl in her late twenties. The second is from the student, Jayne. My spirits instantly lift. I'm back in the picture. Life is good again. Victoria… Victoria, who? As quickly as she had entered my life as a potential partner, Victoria walked out of my life.

Jayne is in her final year at UCL, reading ancient history. Apparently she is looking for a man to make her laugh. She describes herself as '*very* attractive'. *He* will be good looking and laidback. She is fed up of men looking for one night stands. He also has to have his own teeth, apparently. She sounds pretty cool and chatty in her email. And she asks if I would like to meet for a drink after work in the next couple of days. Is that it, is that all it takes? The exchange of an email, or two. She doesn't know who I am, I could be a mad serial killer – or even a desperate failure in love!

Oxford Street is heaving. The air is hot and dry, I have to squint as I exit from Bond Street tube. A torrent of shoppers pass the exit, and some branch off, flowing down the steps into the depths of the underground station. A constant stream of double-deckers push their way up and down the main street. The buses glisten in the sun's glare. Their beetle-like red shells shine magnificently. People are busy shopping for their holidays. Couples can be heard arguing which factor sunscreen they should buy, the women protesting that they still want a tan, 'Why else are we going on holiday, put the Factor 2 in the basket.' The men are being dragged from one shop to another in search of the Holy Grail that is the perfect bikini (in the right size). I hate Oxford Street at this time of year. You can get knocked about so much that it verges on an assault.

I have arranged to meet Jayne at a place just off Oxford Street. Amidst this consumer frenzy there is a little-known gem, hidden behind the main drag. It's like Diagon Alley, a narrow passage just before Selfridges leads you to a continental square. An abundance of bistros and bars surround a beautiful fountain. In the summer, live music serenades you while you gorge yourself on olive tapenade and a good chianti. St Christopher's Place is *the* perfect location for a first date.

Even at this ridiculously busy time of year, there will be a table at Carluccio's, if you are willing to wait long enough. Intimate yet public, exclusive but inexpensive. Perfect.

I stand outside the restaurant, just by the glass doorway. I have arranged to meet Jayne outside, she's five minutes late. I look back towards the direction I have just come. My eyes flit from one mad shopper to the next, as I try and spot Jayne. I'm trying to remember what she looks like, picturing her photo on the site. But the images of the different girls begin to mix in my mind. Is she the blonde one, or the redhead? I can't remember.

My phone begins to vibrate, a text from Jayne tells me that she is running ten minutes late. She says I will recognise her because she is wearing a turquoise corsage.

The mist in my mind clears and I start to remember her basic features. She has mid-length blonde hair and has that girl next-door look about her. She describes herself as 'very attractive'. She has a cheeky look about her in the photo, sort of vivacious looking.

I clap my eyes on a girl walking out of the alley into the square. She sort of fits the image in my mind, except her hair is shorter. Perhaps she's had it cut. She's smiling and walking in my direction. I start smiling, coy like, back at her. She steps up and right past me. She ignores the hand I have just reached out to greet her. I feign as if checking the time on my wristwatch. I turn around, subtly, and see her embracing a guy standing behind me. Sure enough, no blue flower.

As I turn back to face the alley way, in that brief instance, someone has appeared at my elbow. A plump girl with pale skin and mousey, shoulder-length hair – the highlights have grown out.

'Hi, Max?'

She must have noticed the pained expression on my face, wearing that 'and-you-are?' look, as I squint at her vacantly. As if to reply to the unspoken question, she volunteers, 'Hi, I'm Jayne!'

I make a double take. Sure enough, there it is, the damning evidence. The turquoise corsage.

'I thought you were blonde?'

Did I just say that out loud? Shit. I couldn't help it, it just, sort of, slipped out. And a confused look overcomes her face, as if she's saying to herself, 'Er, yes, and your point is?!'

But the deception is out in the open. I know she put up a photo of herself that quite obviously shows her in a good light. It's not often that you come across someone who looks that much better in their picture than they do in real life. In the magazine world, we'd call it a great touch up. She's not going to get one of those tonight.

And now she knows that I know.

It would be okay if she had undersold herself. But instead of a date with an attractive blonde, I am about to make small talk with the human equivalent of a slurry pit – loose, chunky and grey. Like so many women, she's opted for all-over black – black trousers, wedges that make her look like a trainee tranny and strappy top (reigning in at least four sets of flabby boobs). She's not really overweight, she's just frumpy – bland and devoid of any style. If she was a type of house, it'd be a Barrett home.

Deception aside, you may say I'm being harsh. But let's not kid ourselves. It's important I fancy this person. And she is utterly sexless. I would sooner have dinner with a size 18 with vigour, sparkle and self-assurance than this poor excuse for a woman. It's not that there's anything profoundly wrong with her, but that's not the point; it's the overwhelming lack of effort.

As we walk into Carluccio's, my phone vibrates again, and then again. The first text is from Amber, asking me to suggest a place for our first date. It had been a choice between Jayne and Amber; which one to date first. I had plumped for Jayne. I knew I should have gone with Amber.

The second text is from Sarah, the primary school teacher. I had emailed her earlier that day with my mobile number. Her message was quite flirty and cheeky for an initial icebreaker. She makes herself sound easy. I have heard that about primary school teachers. I wing off an appropriate response to each, and put my phone on silent.

We ensconce ourselves at the table. I had pre-booked the romantic one by the window. The Montepulciano looks tempting, so I order a bottle from the gregarious and slightly over-enthusiastic waiter. I decline to sample it, I'll let him know if it's corked. I need alcohol.

I should have remembered 'bubbly' meant 'frumpy'.

I start quaffing the wine, anything that will act as an anaesthetic. I have been talking for ten minutes and she hasn't really spoken. It's clearly not nerves, I'm sure she would be like this after knowing her for years, she's just dull. And rude. Apparently, she can't talk to waiters, just gesticulate. She won't even look me in the eye, is she wanted throughout the Carluccio's chain? Theft of bread tins? Eating and running on a Caesar and Diet Coke? I'm not sure if she's been plugged in yet. Frankly, I feel more inclined to shout for the nurse than the waiter. Eventually, we start talking about dating, and why I had found it necessary to resort to Dating World. Dear God, if only my ex could see me now. She would definitely be having the last laugh, as she always did. I make up some sort of answer that sounds credible, without belying my desperation. But how do you tell a girl that you're looking for a woman on your terms, not theirs? And all I know is that this woman would be the antithesis of Jayne and all those like her. That I want someone special, but who doesn't know it, not someone who's boring and thinks their God's gift. Why are there so many girls who are able to drink in all the style tips of fashion magazines, but however much they model themselves on Kate Moss, they can never become her. *Reading Grazia does not maketh the woman.* Next stop the monastic fraternity.

I realise that the question was just a launchpad for her to bore me with her retort. The entire history of her previous relationships and why all men are useless and beneath her (and her wedges). If you were on the table next to us, you'd be forgiven for thinking that I was actually having a drink *with* Kate Moss, rather than Kerry Katona. Self-awareness is not a virtue that Jayne possesses.

After 30 minutes of unintelligent babble on Jayne's personal Pilates trainer, Jermaine, and love of American scenes of crime dramas – 'I can never choose between the bloke off *CSI* with the beard and the son on *Diagnosis Murder*' – I'm almost D.O.A.!

I'm trying to finish the wine as quickly as possible. I ask the waiter for a straw.

After a further hour of lending my ear to her whines, *my* wine is finished. I feel it is socially acceptable to make my excuses and leave while I still can, before she begins to cover *'Boyfriends – the early years.'* The waiter brings the bill, I don't think I've scrawled my signature so quickly. In a flash, the tip is sorted, we have our coats and are standing, once again, on the other side of the glass door to the restaurant.

'So, thanks for the drink. Was great to meet you,' says Jayne, struggling with her fucking annoying corsage.

'Yes, likewise,' I lie.

'I feel like I bored you about my previous relationships,' she says, chuckling. Why is she laughing? It's not amusing. I restrain myself from force-feeding her the triffid pinned to her top.

'Not at all, it was… interesting,' I smile nonchalantly. Well done Max, that sounded sincere.

'We should do it again, soon,' she suggests. I smile, and nod. Why can't I just tell her, here and now, that it's a no-go? I'm probably too much of a coward, if the truth be told.

We make the usual, somewhat awkward, parting graces of two people who know they will never meet again. We kiss each other on the cheek, and bumble some more. In an uncomfortable silence we make a final parting gesture. Jayne walks off in the direction of Selfridges, to the right of the restaurant, and I head back up to Oxford Street.

As soon as I am out of sight, I reach for my mobile phone. I cancel the silent mode. I have five messages while I was in the restaurant. Two from Sarah, more teasing than the last and suggesting that we meet up. One from Amber, confirming the details of the date tomorrow. And a text each from the other two girls I had made contact with. I reply to all of them, with suitably flirty responses to Sarah in particular. I also find myself replying to Amber in a vain that delivers an air of promise for the following night's meeting. I can't help it, even though I've never met the girl. But because it's at a distance, I find myself saying things I probably wouldn't say face to face with her, or even if we were talking over the phone. This is exaggerated in my replies to Sarah. I'm being outright, blatantly obvious and as yet we haven't even exchanged a spoken word.

My messages are, in turn, replied to by Amber, then Sarah. Everything is on track with Amber, we're meeting at Carluccio's tomorrow at 7pm. Well, why not, it's a great table. I like the tiramisu.

Sarah asks me to tell her something unusual about me. I tell her I have a curios birthmark on my bottom. And then she informs me she is about to have 'a good long soak in the bath'. It has its desired effect, I'm picturing her doing just that, with me sitting behind her, rubbing her back. Another text arrives from Suzanne, one of the lawyers. She's telling me about the area of law she practises in, and wants to know who I work for.

This is getting ridiculous. There is a constant relay of messages. But it is slightly intoxicating. As soon as I send one message, I grow agitated, waiting for the reply. I'm losing the sense of feeling in my right thumb. I'm starting to forget what I have told to whom.

I emerge from Angel tube station. The evening has grown balmy. My phone beeps at me, alerting me to the fact that I have more messages waiting for my attention. The girls have all texted me again, when I was out of signal. The *conversations* have stepped up a notch. I feel as if I'm really starting to know them, I'm attributing facial expressions, voices and accents to their photos from the site. This is ludicrous – I'm starting flings with virtual women. Is this what it has come to – a virtual relationship with binary information. And yet I find myself getting annoyed if they don't text me back immediately. It's like they have stood me up for a date. But when I do receive a message there's an immediate emotional pick me up. I'm dipping in and out, as and when I need someone to make me feel good. My God, is this the future of dating in this town, this country? I have to check myself into the text-obsessed clinic and end this now before I get indefinitely hooked on this instant digital loving.

I promise myself that I will meet up with Amber, I don't want to let her down, having gone this far. And she seems cool. But I clear all the other girls' names from my phone, and then I turn it off. No beeping, no vibrating. No more virtual two-timing. It's hard at first, it's like cold turkey for text addicts. I'm missing the attention, the potential of meeting these keen women.

I make it through the night, although I can't say I wasn't tempted to turn my phone on at some point and text someone, anyone. The next day I feel better, I'm back in control. I'm looking forward to meeting up with Amber. I turn my phone on for the first time, and, without reading them, delete the messages I have received over the night, from the now unknown numbers.

There I am, for the second night on the trot, standing outside that glass door of Carluccio's restaurant in St Christopher's Place . It's even warmer this evening. The dry heat has been replaced by a mugginess that could grow uncomfortable. However, the heat hasn't deterred the ubiquitous weekend shopper, not in the slightest.

An East Coast American twang brings me back to reality.

'Hey, Max Hunter, I presume?' The American accent has always made me melt. My eyes focus on the girl in front of me.

I snap out of the dream and remember why I am here. It's Amber. It's definitely her, I mean she actually looks like her photo. No, wait, she looks better than her photo. Her long, light blonde hair hangs straight, down to the middle of her back. She's wearing a deep red, slightly see-through, chiffon top that matches her juicy vermilion lips. The hipster cords show off a great pair of firm thighs. She looks fantastic, and has a really warm smile.

'Hi Amber, it's great to meet you at last.' We exchange kisses. 'What a lovely evening!'

Some people you meet, you immediately feel very comfortable in their company. As well as clicking with someone romantically, you can simply feel very at ease with them. That's exactly how I feel with Amber. I think that this is going to be a really great date. And to think I nearly didn't turn up.

We ensconce ourselves at Max's table by the window, overlooking the bustling square. Yes, the table does have my name written on it, at least it should do after all the dates I've had there over the past year. Outside, a young woman has just dropped one of her expensive-looking shopping bags, and what I presume to be a new summer wardrobe now lies strewn on the York stone. A young man has come to her aid, he's on his haunches, helping her gather up the garments. I wonder whether that chance meeting will be anything more than an act of a Good Samaritan, the beginning of a romance, an affair or a fling. I return my gaze to Amber, who has just finished rearranging her jumper. She fidgets a little more, readjusting the strap of her watch, and she gives a sigh of finality that means all her attention is with me.

Amber has great chat. She's better than I could have hoped for. In addition to her great looks, she's incredibly engaging, and she laughs so easily. We cover a wealth of subjects, like why she came to the UK, how she's liking it, what it's like back home, college, American foreign policy. Anything and everything. She's so enthusiastic, this has to be my best date in ages. Why on earth did this girl have to resort to an online dating site? I put it down to the fact she doesn't know anyone here.

Unfortunately I have another dinner engagement later that night, a friend's birthday bash. When we originally arranged to meet up, I had told Amber that I would have to go to this, and she said that was fine. She preferred meeting up sooner rather than later. The two hours seemed to go as if it were a matter of minutes since we first sat down. We had polished off a second bottle of the red wine, and we ordered coffees to give us a bit of a kickstart.

'Amber, I've had such a great time.'

'Me too, it's been really good.' Her smile is infectious. Two small dimples appear in her cheeks when she beams like that. She nods slowly, to show her sincerity.

'I'm just sorry I have to dash off, I wish I could stay so we could grab some dinner together.' And, for a change, I don't find myself saying it just to be polite.

'Well, let's do that next time.'

Next time? Awesome. 'Great, how about Monday, or even Tuesday, after work?'

I really like this girl, she's a pleasant surprise. Who would have thought you could meet someone so in tune with your own wavelength off a dating site, and one that is so, well, fit. Genuinely, I wish I didn't have to go off to this party. We make plans to see each other early next week. She insists on paying, saying it would be an insult if I didn't let her, and that I can get the 'cheque' when we have dinner next week. This is a novelty too – she's just written herself in my list of top ten birds, ever.

I leave that night with an unsuspected spring in my stride. The birthday party is a washout, but I don't care. Other than the fact I wish I had stayed with Amber for that meal. I text her later that night, on my way home in the cab. I'm not texting her in the same vain as my recent spate of messaging, but as a non-addicted 'safe' user. In other words, like a normal person. I tell her, again, what a lovely evening I had. And that I am looking forward to seeing her in a couple of days for dinner, when there'll be no time constraint. In an instance she responds, saying the she too is looking forward to it, and that she had had a wonderful time.

Monday comes round, and out the blue I get a call from my cousin. He's in town from New York, on business. It's not often we get to meet up, but luckily he'll be around for the next couple of days. I suggest we meet up that night for a well-deserved catch up. As soon as we finish chatting on the blower, I send a text to Amber, explaining that tonight is taken up with my cousin, but that tomorrow is free and clear, if that is good for her.

Her reply is the last thing I would ever have expected. I can't quite believe it, as I read it a second time. Perhaps she meant to send it to someone else? But the sign off at the end of the text removes that as a possibility. I'm astounded. The text reads as follows;

> Tomorrow is fine. I just have to ask r u seeing anyone
> at the moment – that might or might not be an
> obvious question. And what stage are we at? Have
> a good night with your cousin. A x

Is this for real? This is a bit out of left field. What stage are we at? We're at the stage where I'm still remembering her first name, that and making a note not to fart in her presence. We've only just met for God's sake. We've had a few glasses of wine and spent two hours in each other's company. I'll grant you, things went exceptionally well. But we've still only known each other for two hours. One hundred and twenty minutes. This is not crunch point after months of dating, the point where we decide whether we're going steady. I read the message for a third time. I laugh. It turns from a normal laugh, to one of disbelief, into a slightly psychotic one. My right eye begins to twitch, like Herbert Lom's when Inspector Clouseau accidentally kicks him in the nuts. I thought she was so, normal.

I should have left it there and never written back, but I can't help myself. I don't want it to be true. Surely Amber's not a *BB* as well. I have to give her the benefit of the doubt. Perhaps the meaning has been lost in writing the text, perhaps her predictive text messed it up. God I'm starting to become like a girl, making excuses to account for the awful and obvious truth. Perhaps she works for the government and a rogue agent has intercepted her text messages, ruining her love life to get back at her for some deed done in the field. Bollocks, she's stark raving mad and insecure, just like all the other's I've dated before her.

I write back regardless;

Of course I'm single, otherwise I wouldn't date u – don't know y it would be an obvious or not obvious question – confused. What stage are we at – well we just met, we r getting 2 know each other. But I am looking forward 2 c u tomorrow night 4 dinner.

There was a 'x' at the end of that text too, for extra enthusiasm and comfort. Within seconds this arrives at my phone;

M, I'm not feeling interest from u. I don't want 2 just wait & see w/o any idea what is going on. Makes me very uncomfortable not knowing where our relationship is going. It's too ambiguous & bears a risk I am unwilling 2 take w/o reassurance from u.

What fucking relationship? I'm growing hysterical. I start to shout at my mobile, as if it can understand. Why did she have to ruin it? I plead with my mobile, looking for sympathy. Why did she have to ruin it and be like all the others? My tears of anguish, frustration and incomprehension are lost on the phone. Fuck, I have to see a shrink. At least Tom Hanks had an excuse for talking to that football with the smiley face. What was he called? Mr Wilson, that's right.

'Dude, that's mental. What stage are we at? Relationship?' Raj proved to be of greater comfort than my trusty mobile.

We have congregated at my flat after work for a beer and a rather formidable jalfrezi, from the Risaldar General down the road. Ed has joined us, himself fresh from a failed date with one of the girls from his gym.

'Where did you say you met this girl?' Ed chipped in.

Oh great, that's the question I was hoping they wouldn't ask.

'Dating World,' I disclose reluctantly. 'It's an online dating service,' I feel the need to expand on the self-explanatory name.

Raj has clutched his stomach in what, at first, seems like pain induced by gorging on his peshwari naan, but it is clear to see that it is hilarity. 'That's fucking desperate!' He claps his hand on my shoulder, he is filled to the brim with mirth.

'Hey,' I shout, 'if you don't pack it in I'll go get an ear bud and we can relive your trip to the clinic.'

'Alright, chill, no need to hit where it hurts, literally.'

15

Spent

But that night, I learned some girls try too hard
Some girls try too hard to impress with the way that they dress
With those things on their chests and the things they suggest to me

Now, I'd rather go dateless than stay here and hate this
Her volume of makeup, her fake tits were tasteless
So I said I'd call her, but never would bother
Until I got turned down by another girl at a party

The Blink 182 song rings out as we sit in Bar Local in Clapham. The irony seeps through my skin as I listen to the lyrics. We relax in our own company. The beers are going down smoothly. There are several attractive girls amidst small groups of revellers, warming up before venturing on for a night of cheese at somewhere like Infernos. They are the kind of girls that we would ordinarily go over and chat with, but we have lost all enthusiasm. Blink aren't helping.

I'm staring at one girl in particular, she's seated at the table across from us, with her back to the window. She has blonde hair tied back, and green eyes that display an eagerness as she chatters. Thoughts begin to run through my mind as I look at this attractive 20-something, although I'm not really focusing on her any more.

'Guys, our position is futile. That's the only thing that I have learnt from this past year.' The stream of consciousness pours out of my mouth. 'We have been deceived. We have been forced to accept the new woman in society, to respect the professional woman and all that she has achieved, to accept the fact that there is no difference between the lifestyles of the sexes and their respective ambitions.'

'The cool, relaxed, independent and SINGLE woman does not exist,' Ed adds.

'No they're all SINBADs,' says Raj, as if it's obvious.

'Arabian pirates?' says Ed.

'No,' he says, as if we're being stupid, 'S.I.N.B.A.D. – Single Income, No Boyfriend, Absolutely Desperate.'

There's a moment of quiet as we mull it all over. Raj breaks our silent pondering.

'I want a refund,' he says.

Of course, there *are* some eligible, wonderful women out there, should you want to enter into a serious relationship. But for those of us who want something between friendship and serious commitment there's nothing, zip, *nada. Capisce?* And yet this is supposed to be the norm in the fast-moving world of the City. Where is this self-confident professional woman who barely has time for a man in her life, the woman with the 'go get 'em' attitude. I have never met one let alone gone on a date with one.

Before I arrived in London, I had been led to believe that, put simply, there are three phases in the dating game that lead to marriage. The first are the young, naïve relationships that you have at school and college during your teenage years, which, thanks to the hormones pumping through your veins, are generally fuelled by an unquenchable thirst for sex. Driving around in your car, making out at college parties, getting to first base for a slice of warm apple pie and the most perfect of unions lasting an average of two weeks.

The last is the serious relationship, probably in the twilight of your twenties and in the dawn of your thirties, which progresses to cohabiting and finally marriage. You'll know when you reach this stage because, if nothing else, you'll find yourself spending long weekends away at golfing hotels in Harrogate with your other 'couple friends.'

I am in the interim phase; looking for a little more than the high school romance and something short of the commitment that requires a trip to Hatton Gardens.

'Perhaps the adage that the perfect relationship is either three weeks or a lifetime is true,' Ed pipes up after a couple more minutes of us pensively sipping our Coronas.

There certainly seems to be nothing in between. Yet, shouldn't your twenties be a time of fun and independence, a time to make mistakes. What will happen if we forgo the 'training' that comes with dating adults in your twenties. Perhaps people today are making the mistakes in their first marriage that ordinarily they would have resolved during the dating age.

'It's possible,' says Ed. 'Sometimes, I think that girls are bumbling along, dabbling in a necessary evil when all the time they just want to settle down. The amount of my female friends who have got married recently and admitted afterwards, "My God, I'm so glad I am out of the dating scene, all those difficult first dates, I couldn't bear it". The truth is they haven't ever really dated. They've had random snogs in clubs, woken up in the morning embarrassingly next to some guy they don't remember and awkwardly left after breakfast.'

'Guys,' Raj starts, a little reticently, like he's about to share some epiphany, with which we might not agree, 'do you ever think that we talk about sex too much?'

'Definitely,' says Ed immediately. Raj looks surprised but thankful to be put at ease, once again.

'That it is deliberated, cogitated and digested to the point of staleness,' Raj continues, spurred on by our empathy. 'It's become something to be constricted by social convention and political movements. Sex is sex – it should be enjoyed as it was intended to be, something natural and simple, powerful and emotional. You cannot learn about it or understand it from some columnist in a super-opinionated glossy… "You can do this but it's wrong to do that… we can only make love if you do this… it's only right to have sex if you have promised this…".'

I have become so exhausted by the conventions, rules and regulations; the do's and don'ts that surround sex in relationships. It has robbed sex of that spark, the excitement from the union that I remember experiencing when I was 18. We think that the first time we have sex will be the worst but, the bumbling and embarrassing fumbling aside, it was pretty amazing. In fact, because of this regulatory approach to love making, I just can't be arsed. Well, at least until I get so horny that I start humping the leg of the sofa.

I'm full of mixed emotions; anger, lust, disappointment, desperation, the need to be loved, the desire to be independent. This cocktail of opposites means that I'm not ready for a relationship. And there's nothing wrong with that. It's important that I can recognise this fact, and that I don't allow myself to be immersed in coupledom, just because every other bugger is doing it.

The truth is that you can only perpetuate this life of a dating failure for so long. It drives you mad. I have become so frustrated and disappointed and drained. I am emotionally drained from all the dates. It takes tremendous effort to be nice. Selling yourself, whoever you are, is a difficult thing. You're so worried that the other person is actually attracted to you. But the most draining thing of all is when the meetings with these women inevitably come to a swift conclusion and you have to move on to the next.

There comes a point where you have to recognise the fact that you are at odds with the other person. I had been ignorant when I came to London, but my experiences have given me the foresight that I was previously lacking. I can't continue to blame my naivety for the consequences. I have to either accept the girls for who they are, for what they want, or leave them to it. At the same time, they have no right to demand the opposite from me. I will have to wait.

I feel disappointed because of the false picture that has been painted of the modern independent woman. The image that scorns the role of women of previous generations – all *they* were after was a husband.

'And that's not the case anymore boys!' Isn't it?

'Guys, it's like they have this ideal,' I say, 'that all roads lead to marriage and kids. This desire has laid dormant but then suddenly it's activated upon graduation. "Congratulations Miss Smith, an upper second-class degree in Psychology with honours, now will you please bend over for your oestrogen boost".'

'I know what you mean,' says Ed. 'It's as if a hormone is released, the "husband-seeking" hormone. They work back from date X, the date of the birth of their first child, which is around their 29th birthday. They have had this date stamped indelibly on their brain since birth. Before this date they need to have completed two years of marriage, a one year engagement to plan an inordinately massive wedding and select a rock the size of Montana, and had at least a two year courtship with the intended victim, a substantial period of which is spent living together. This five year period means they need to find the "one" around 23 or 24.'

'You mean last year,' Raj quips.

'Precisely.'

People always talk about the biological clock, but it's more than that. It's about society and its demands. This pressure seems to come at women from all angles, it's pretty tough really. The modern working woman in the City has such high expectations to meet; a pressure to gain respect from her peers, the perfect job, perfect love life, perfect figure and finally the perfect marriage with perfect house and perfect kids. Men don't care, I'm not sure that we ever have. We never feel as if we *have* to be ambitious. If we find the perfect woman, then great.

I have my own ideals, my own terms. I don't feel that I should renege on those terms; I also don't feel that I should be able to force them on someone else. Accept me or don't accept me. But don't give me a hard time for sticking to my beliefs.

'Guys, what has this, have we, come to?' Ed vocalises what all of us have been thinking for some time. He puts his beer down.

'Rikshaws. Toothbrushes.'

'Clap clinics,' Raj winces.

'Wailing Brazilians,' I laugh.

'Blind dates and tweed jackets.'

There's a pause as we all contemplate our miserable luck. Reliving each individual horror. How the past 12 months have been a test of our sanity and self-belief. We have gone from measured dating tactics to downright desperate ploys.

'Guys,' says Raj, suddenly, 'we should be proud of ourselves!'

'How do you mean?' I ask, not understanding how we can possibly glean anything good from these dating experiences.

'The only thing that we can say, is that we haven't compromised our strongest sentiment.'

'Eh?' asks Ed, clearly equally bemused.

'That having left one serious relationship, we didn't get trapped in another, just for the sake of having *a* girl and for regular sex!'

Raj is right. Not only would it have been a huge deception to the woman, but an even greater deception to ourselves.

'Don't settle,' Raj raises his beer. We clink bottles. 'DON'T SETTLE.'

There is nothing more terrible than being in a *serious* monogamous relationship that is devoid of the prerequisite emotion. Love. Not even the sum of all our horrors over the past year could hold a candle to that entrapment and misery. It's not a phobia of commitment. It's the unacceptability of the restrictions created by a partner that you have no real feeling for, all for the sake of having a partner. And shags on tap.

It is time to throw in the dating towel. Call it a night, go to bed, and resume the starfish sleeping position. Well, look on the bright side, it's back to seeing films that *I* want to watch at the cinema, guiltlessly catching the ten minutes Freeview of Channel X every night and stubble rash is something I will never have to think about again.

I hold aloft my bottle of Corona for a second time, 'Well my friends. That's it. We've come (or not), seen and been conquered.'

16

Succubae

It's August. I step out of my apartment and am dazzled by the sun, bombarding me with vitamin B. Life is good. Complication free. Three months have passed since our chat, and no dates. Not a single one. The odd smile or wink from a cute girl on the underground, intent on breaking the strict code imposed by London Transport of no smiling, talking or flirting on any of its routes, has kept me going since that day. The capital is in its first hot spell of the year. That essential three week period that manifests just after Easter each year. It's as hot as the height of summer and preludes a month and a half of downpour, without fail. London has imported its usual quota of stunning fair-weather women. You know the ones, they only come out when it's sunny. They appear from nowhere. Perhaps the druids conjure them up at the summer solstice. I always knew those cards with their long beards, who get naked and whip each other with lavender, had something good to answer for. Strappy tops and short skirts, tottering on dainty shoes. Alluring smiles, inviting pins and bouncers to die for. Who knows whence they come, or to where they return on the vernal equinox.

I'm off to meet Ed for lunch at Bluebird, Conran's place just off the King's Road. No flirtatious exchanges on the District line today. But Sloane Square is rammed, scores of *heatwave honeys* are infiltrating the crowds of regular shoppers, townies and peacock types, who strut their stuff in West London. Apparently Ed has some interesting news for me. I haven't seen him for the last week or so, he's got a new girlfriend and they've been going through that honeymoon period – where you don't leave the bed that first weekend, save for gathering fresh croissants and the Sunday papers. I find her mildly annoying. They met at Blackfriars Crown Court, he was prosecuting her client for fraud. Ed had decided the dating scene was too much to take. He had succumbed to the philosophy of 'if you can't beat 'em, marry 'em.' And he seems happy. But there are moments, usually when he is reminded of his previous single life, when you catch a glimpse in his eye or a wavering in his voice, and you notice the pangs of regret. This is usually when he explains that he is unable to meet us on a Friday evening for a drink. Because he is otherwise engaged, assisting in the consumption of a bottle of Lambrini and watching the omnibus episode of *Hollyoaks*, recorded the weekend before.

There he is, sitting in the window, checking his watch. Yes, I am a couple of minutes late, I chuckle to myself. Good old Ed. Mr Punctuality. I push my way past the yummy mummies, buying pastrami for their adulterous husbands, a gaggle of snotty children, kitted out in Burberrys, scream for the sort of attention they crave and never receive. Past the deli is the coffee shop.

'Hey, loser!' I yell, somewhat uncouthly from the door way.

Ed looks up, and his characteristic smile breaks across his stern face. He stands up and holds out his right hand. I grip his hand and he pulls me in for one of those manly hugs, that we've always done. Our group of friends have always hugged each other. Not sure why.

'It's good to see you buddy. Been too long.'

'Yeah, it has,' he says.

There's one of those pangs of regret I was talking about, this time both audible and visible.

'So how's Kate?'

I move onto the subject of that regret, knowing that it will make him happy talking about her, and not thinking of the fun he's missing out on.

'Yeah, she's great, thanks. She sends her love.'

Like fuck she does. She can't stand me, or Raj for that matter. In fact she despises Raj more than me. I think she sees us as a bad influence on Ed. She says it's bad, we would say it is a healthy influence. And one that it is our duty to exercise. Raj and I both think that Ed can do better, he's gone for Kate because of timing, nothing else. Kate happened to be there when Ed caved in, and decided he wanted another monogamous relationship.

'So what you been up to?' Ed enquires.

His voice is empty, the question is hollow. There's something else on his mind. Not that he doesn't care what I've been up to, you understand, just that Ed can't think of two things at once. Multitasking is not a skill that Ed is endowed with.

'Well, work aside, I started kayaking a week ago. It's something I always wanted to do, and it's a good way of getting some exercise. And I have been getting some paintings together for an exhibition in an East End gallery that's just opened up.'

I don't think Ed is really listening.

'Cappuccino please, cinnamon not chocolate, thank you,' I place my order with the waitress who has been hovering at my elbow since the moment I started to give Ed the update on my life.

'Love life?' he asks.

I had purposefully omitted that from my summary. It's not so easy to discuss this subject, one on one, where one is a happy singleton, and the other a smug almost-married.

'Nothing, not a sausage. But it's better like that at the moment, I just don't have the time for a girl.'

'Perhaps you would make the time, if you found the right girl.'

'Yes, that's true, I'm just not prepared to do that yet.'

There's a pause. The great combustion engine that is Ed's mind is ticking over at full pelt. You can hear the fires being stoked between his ears.

'Max, we were thinking, Kate has this friend…'

'Ah, Christ Ed. "We"?,' I snap back at him.

I instantly feel guilty, I know I've just kicked him in the emotional equivalent of the nut sack.

'I'm sorry. It's just that, I can take my other friends playing cupid, but not you. It's one thing turning up to a work colleague's house for dinner, where it's all couples, bar one girl in her late twenties, who keeps cats.'

I pause for a second, he's staring at his empty espresso cup.

'But I can't take being set up by my best mate and his new girlfriend. I don't need your sympathy, you know how I feel about this. Before this year, I spent my entire adult life in a serious relationship.'

'I know she hurt you,' he says sympathetically.

'Mate, it's not about Jessica, it's about *me*. It's a life choice.'

A fresh espresso arrives at the table, together with my cappuccino. It's got chocolate on top.

'Max, you can't just give up.'

'Huh,' I laugh ironically. Ed knows I'm having a dig, again, at him doing exactly that.

'Hear me out. You will really click with this girl,' he pleads.

'But suppose I don't want to click with her. I'm tired of making the effort. I can't do any more of the initial chat, repeating the same boring stuff about me, who I am etc just to find out we're not compatible.'

'But you can't let that possibility stop you from ever seeing a girl again.'

'Not ever, just now.'

And that's how the banter continued for a while, to and fro. Neither willing to see the other's side of the debate, probably out of fear of acknowledging that part of each argument is true. We are convincing ourselves, as well the other person, that our own position, is truly the position that we want to occupy. And that each of us slightly envies the situation of the other, a case of wanting our black forest gateau and eating it.

'So what's so special about this girl, anyway?'

I'm starting to sound like a bolshie bastard. Good old Ed, a true friend, I know he would never hold these moments of self-absorbed crap against me in future exchanges.

Instantly his mood swings, that grin breaks across his face. He knows he's won already, and so do I, if I'm being honest, it's the bloody barrister in him.

'Well, she's half Swedish to start with,' he sounds more optimistic.

Git, he knows how much I like foreign girls, he's thought about this.

'She is studying for her PhD in International Law. She's a friend of Kate's. Her name is Jennifer, she wants to become a lecturer, at UCL most likely.'

'Ok, so get me onto the important stuff. Is she a BB, what's her chat like and is she attractive?'

He's getting positively excited now, like he's describing a particularly well performing stock that no one else in the market has spotted.

'She's definitely not a BB, she's out of a serious relationship, so she's pretty laidback. She has great chat, very funny but not in your face, and intelligent, goes without saying. And she is a fitty!'

Smiling mischievously he starts making circular movements in front of his chest, he's trying to convey that she has large breasts, I think. The mature woman in the fox fur stole, on the table next to us, gives Ed a disapproving scowl.

'Kate and I are throwing a dinner party for a few lawyer friends this Friday. Jennifer will be there. It will be great to see you. And if you guys hit it off, well that's a bonus.'

It's incredible how the love of a woman can change a man. A man you know so well, and how quickly that change comes about. One minute you're downing beers together in a *boat race* chanting 'drink it down you Zulu warrior,' and next time you see him, he's near teetotal and has bought a monthly subscription to *Country Living*. What's worse, is that he then tries to convert you to his way of life. These couples begin to lead their lives vicariously through their singleton friends. It's like the frigging Moonies. Because they no longer have the freedom to date, they feed off the excitement of dating by setting their friends up with each other. And now, because they're together, everyone else has to be together, to share in this matrimonial bliss.

I'm standing in front of Ed's front door. The week passed in a flash. I had asked myself a hundred times, 'Why am I doing this?' It's not the right time, for me. I have been happy for the last few months. Everything is going my way. Life's not complicated. I don't have to compromise. I have my independence. Even if I like this girl, it's just going to get in my way. I don't have the time. I shouldn't be here. I'm going to go. Ed will understand.

As I turn to leave, the front door opens, it's Kate. I smile, trying to make it look convincing. God she's annoying me already. I can't understand how Ed likes the prospect of being tied to this girl for life, the type who would come down at breakfast and put her hands over his eyes and say 'Guess who?'.

'Hi Max, we're glad you can make it,' she says.

There's that 'we' again. I'm here to see the friend I've known since when *we* played conkers at school, I think to myself. She leans in to kiss me on each cheek. I kiss her back.

'Thanks for inviting me,' I say, trying to sound genuine.

I take off my coat and head into the hall. Ed suddenly appears from the kitchen with two glasses in his hand.

'Max, excellent!' he declares. 'Give me a sec, just hand these glasses out and I'll be back.'

He disappears into, what I presume is, the living-room-cum-dining-room, for tonight. The apartment is in a nice, fairly bog-standard townhouse in Clapham. It's unusual to have a second reception room, it's usually been converted into another bedroom. Kate's extra room is a study, full of law books, and briefs tied together with legal purple ribbon are piled up like termite mounds on the wood floor. The walls are covered with numerous photos of her at various academic functions, she's wearing her lawyer's gown at this degree graduation or that admission's ceremony. There's even an enamelled shield above her desk with a Pegasus on it, I think it's the Barrister's Inn that she's a member of, I've seen Ed wear a pair of cufflinks that have the same emblem. There's a framed photo on the desk of Ed and Kate, in embrace. Ed is wearing that annoying face. Whenever he looks at Kate, he has this meekness, like a King Charles spaniel rebuked for bringing a half-chewed bone into the kitchen. I lie my coat on top of the others, which are draped over the back of the antique chair at her desk, and return to where all the chatter is emanating from.

This is the moment I'm fearing. Where you walk into the dining room (slash lounge) and there are two clear couples, and two clear single people; you and the girl. And whatever pretence is maintained, the two couples, you and the girl, all know that the two of you are being set up; and everyone knows the others know. But, of course, you have to act like it's a regular group of friends meeting up, to chat American foreign policy, or worse, the latest series of house renovating, over carbonara that the hostess has probably ordered in from Deliverance. Cautiously, like some small woodland creature, I creep into the room, as quietly as I can. I'm trying to draw as little attention to myself as possible, and at the same time figure out which one of the girls is a fellow victim of her matchmaking friends.

'Max, there you are.' Ed is onto me before I'm two steps over the threshold. 'Let me introduce you to James and Rebecca.'

A slightly studious looking couple, who look like they started dating at college. One of those small Oxford colleges that discourages sport and expects all its students to hibernate in their rooms, cuddling up with their books on Virgil.

'Oh and this is Kate's friend. Jennifer.'

Ed pops it in there, casual like. As if none of us know the reason Jennifer and I are here, least of all, us ourselves. Ed moves out of the way, he has been standing to my right-hand side, between myself and the other single person in the room. I can feel Mr and Mrs Studious, staring at us with expectation. The all-important moment of meeting. That first look. Chemistry or no chemistry. Boss eyed and buck teeth, or stunning beauty. I don't think I could have been more surprised.

I'm not sure if I believe in love at first sight. That is to say, not true, full, deep and proper love. However, I do think that the Greek classicists had it right, when they identified two types of love. There is the initial falling, which is when you feel that spark. An inexplicable flutter in your stomach that can be experienced, like now, within moments of meeting. This can, sometimes, lead to a second falling. And this is true love, in all its incantations. That deep, long lasting love that you see between couples celebrating their Ruby wedding anniversaries in village halls.

Now when I first clapped eyes on Jennifer, seconds ago, kissed her and gazed into those azure eyes, my stomach did a small summersault. Jennifer has dark blonde hair tied back in a pony tail. Her eyes sparkle and she has teeth like pearls. They may be two a penny in California but nice teeth are a rarity in Britain. My own are far from perfect. While she is blonde, and part Swedish, she is not pale, as one might expect. She has a deep, rich tanned skin. You could say she has a sort of glow. Not the pregnant kind. She's wearing white trousers that sit low on her hips. They fit snugly round the bottom and flare out a little as they pass her thigh. At the bottom pointy Italian shoes show their little snouts. Her powder pink top is tight and classical, with a revealing plunging neck line. She is delectable. The more we talk, the more I can tell we are going to get along, *really* well. And I can see that the same thing is running through her mind. There are glances, lingering too long, and smiles revealing more than is intended.

We chat in a circle for a while, Ed refills our glasses with a rather good Chablis. Kate pops her head round the door, she tells us to get up to the table as dinner is almost ready. By that I presume she means she has managed to get the plastic packaging off the deli boxes that were couriered round earlier. We start to drift towards the table in the corner of the room. It's one of those glass and steel type affairs. Everyone even has little card place names, standing proudly in one of a variety of silver place name holders. Each one is a different geometric shape, cube, sphere etc. Mine is conical. I wonder if there's a reason for it, Kate does everything for a reason. Dunce? Phallus? Who knows. Surprise, surprise, I am one end of the oval table and next to me and sort of opposite as well, to my right, is Jennifer. But all feelings of malice towards my old mate and his missus are long gone. I'm actually enjoying Jennifer's company and am chuffed she's sitting next to me. Ed knows this as well, I catch the odd smug grin from his end of the table. Happy with himself that, at the moment, everything seems to be going to plan. Kate is sitting on my other side, presumably so she can make surreptitious 'faces' at Jennifer, without me seeing. Then continuing round the table, James, Rebecca and lastly Ed.

Ed lights the candles on the table and changes the music over to some Rat Pack compilation. There's a good, relaxed atmosphere in the room, everyone's chatting. I think I misjudged the studious couple. They might look like Harry Potter's parents, but they're pretty cool. At the moment the conversation is in full swing, we're talking about the idea of buying a small property abroad. A pied-à-terre in Tuscany or, I suggest, somewhere on the Dalmatia coast. I hear it's the place to buy at the moment. Frank Sinatra is singing about how he did it his way.

We're getting stuck into the delicious meal, and our third bottle of red wine. Occasionally Jennifer and I go off on a tangent and become embroiled in our own little conversation, while we leave the others to chat about the original topic. Her voice is deliciously silky, it's like syrup being poured out of a jug. Our conversation seems to have its own agenda, taking a personal tangent here and there, which lets us find out something new and interesting about each other. Our likes, dislikes, interests, family etc. I hear about her parents, what it was like growing up in Sweden and how she is doing a PhD, which may involve a period of study in her homeland. The more I hear about this girl, the more I like her. I'm hooked.

Our conversation returns to a group discussion. Ed is telling everyone, probably for the umpteenth time, it certainly isn't the first time for me, how he and Kate met. Ed then thinks it is a good idea to bring up some of the hilarity we shared in the year before he met Kate. Ed is a very bright chap, but there are moments when all common sense fails the man. He embarks upon a lengthy description of our failings and shortcomings in the dating arena, drawing heavily upon my own miserable experiences. Muppet. And of course he wasn't sitting next to Kate, to receive the elbow in the ribs trick. But to everyone's surprise, after I try to extricate myself from the tortuous embarrassment, Jennifer pipes up with an astounding statement.

'Maybe you will meet your perfect woman before she dashes off to Sweden to study,' she smiles, cheekily.

There's silence. I sit there open-mouthed. Someone, I don't see who, chokes on their pasta. Ed nearly spits out his gulp of wine. Kate instinctively kicks me under the table. Jennifer, who is still smiling, looks coyly into her wine glass, as she takes an elegant sip. I turn, slowly, and face the rest of the dinner party. It seems as if they have all gathered around at the other end of the table, bunched together, looking upon their creation. The new couple. This is better than they could have ever hoped. Without speaking, I turn back to stare at Jennifer.

'Mmm, lovely dinner by the way, Kate,' she says.

'Oh er, thank you,' Kate automatically retorts, but she is, clearly, taken aback by what Jennifer just said. And then everyone gets a hold of themselves, and the moment passes.

I give Ed a smile, he throws me a look of sheer surprise. Already the conversation has moved on. I am left behind, loitering on her comment. When you feel that spark, that special ingredient, all previous emotions and best laid plans fly out the window. Rationality disappears. My strong belief that I don't want another serious relationship is like a dim and distant memory. No, in fact, it is someone else's memory. Who wouldn't want to be serious with this amazing girl. I start imagining what she would look like pregnant, what my kids would look like as a product of me and her. My eyes, her nose, definitely her lips and those cute little dimples. The fact they could grow up bilingual, we could spend winters in Sweden and summers in England. We could have our honeymoon in a log cabin by a Fjord. I've always wanted to learn a Scandinavian language. I shop at Ikea, hell I even like Dime bars.

All this runs through my mind in seconds. Fuck, this is crazy. I have to get a grip of myself. That's on a bunny boiling par with the things I have encountered myself, and criticised. Although I suppose I haven't vocalised those thoughts, or put them into action. Yet. I shake the feelings away.

We finish the post-dinner cocktails, sup the final drop of bitter coffee and devour the last of the Godiva chocolates. James keeps nodding off, I'm not sure if it's the drink, that it's late or a combination of both. Rebecca looks indignantly at her betrothed. She returns to the dregs of the conversation, she has come out of her shell a great deal as the evening has gone on, and as more has been imbibed. She rouses James from his slumber for the last time, and informs him it's time to leave. Ed moves towards the study, dragging his feet as he goes. He returns moments later with two light coats draped over his right arm. He throws one at James and holds the other one up for Rebecca to slip her arms into. We all kiss them good night.

'I really should be going as well,' says Jennifer.

I really don't want her to. I want her to stay. I want her to stay all night, with me. Ed, helpfully, produces a third jacket from the study. She slips into the elegant leather number. She says good night to her hosts. And then there is a little awkwardness as they move aside, to let me say my 'Night, night now pucker up.' As I go to kiss her on the cheeks, she doesn't let our eyes lose contact until the last second. God, she smells so good. Then, quickly, she pulls away, says a final thank you, and disappears outside into the awaiting cab.

'So you like her then?!' Ed says, smirking.

The know-all git. Of course I like her, but I'm not going to give him the satisfaction of knowing that, just yet. Although it's damned obvious anyway.

'Yeah she's a nice girl,' I say, trying to sound coy about it.

'*Nice girl*, she's gorgeous and she likes you!' chips in Kate with her penny's worth.

I can't help but smile. Kate chucks one of the suede cushions from the couch at me.

'Okay, okay. You're right, I like her,' I laugh. 'She's wonderful, I do really like her.'

Kate looks over at Ed, I see him wink.

'Charming, beautiful, intelligent, funny, great banter and bags of confidence. Thanks guys. I'd love to see her again.'

'Well she has just broken up with a long-term boyfriend. So perhaps best to play it cool.' Ed kindly informs me after all that.

'Is she ok about it?' I ask, nervously, my stomach rising into my gullet. Fears of déjà vu rush through my mind. It all starts well, so much promise and they go nuts on me. Please don't let this pan out like all the others.

'Yes, I think so, but perhaps best not to rush it,' Ed says.

'We could all go out to the theatre as a group, give you two the chance to chat some more, without it being a full-on date.' Kate suggests.

I'm starting to like Kate. Where the hell is all this humanity and compassion coming from?

The next day I get into work as usual. Well I say as usual, that unfamiliar bounce in my stride is still there, from the night before. I can't see myself, obviously, but I probably have some inane grin on my face. I must do, several of the secretaries have already commented on it. They're always the first to know, anything. I go get a mug of coffee from the small kitchen area down the corridor. Someone has put a poster up asking us not to leave sugar on the worktops, as mice have been seen skulking around recently. Delightful. What is it about London offices and rodents?

Ensconcing myself at my desk, coffee within easy reach, I boot up my PC. It's an open plan office, most media type places are these days, I guess. Apart from the seccies, I'm the only one in the office so far. The lift signals that someone is about to arrive. In strides Rosie, my boss.

'Hey Rosie how are you?' I ask.

'Fine. Thank you, Max. And how are you?' She seems unnerved.

I always ask her how she is, don't I? May be not. The secretaries giggle.

My computer scares itself into life, then calms down to a gentle hum. My inbox pops up automatically. The first thing I see is an email from Ed. I thought I was in early, not sure how he made it in before me, after such a big one. Good effort. The first line makes me feel ecstatic:

Max forget what I know about women, I had an email from Jenn, thanking me for last night, and she said she would be really happy for you to get in touch, and ask her out.

I waste no time in sending her an email. I love email, it's so instantaneous. Do you think that companies realise that their employees only use email for proper purposes about 10% of the time? The remaining 90% of the time it acts as your party planner, social life organiser and as a distraction to the humdrum of the working day. Within minutes we arrange a date for that night. A drink after work in Farringdon.

Jennifer arrives on time. I have been there for a few minutes already. Partly to secure a table at the ever-popular Smiths. But also to psych myself up for seeing her again. I can't quite get over the fact that less than twenty-four hours ago I was a happy singleton. Leading an uncomplicated life. And now all the decisions I have made over the last few months have gone out of the window. All the emotions I have had to understand, accept and lay to rest have flared up, uncontrollably. I suppose you could say I'm sort of, well, nervous. She is looking very elegant in a camel skirt and cream top, finished off with another pair of Italian shoes and clutching, what appears to be, a hideously expensive handbag. She is preened and manicured. I like her, not just because of how she looks, but because of how she makes me feel.

We settle into our seats by the window overlooking Smithfield and start knocking back the red wine. There's no awkwardness at all, not like there is on so many first dates. We chat about all kinds of things. No subject is a taboo, and there is a very relaxed feeling between us. Neither of us is holding anything back. I can't believe how well it's going. I haven't felt like this, with a girl, in years. At least not since I started dating Jessica (before it all went wrong). In fact it's even better than that. I am fascinated by her, we have so much in common.

'No way I can't believe you know the Jenkins in St Kitts, they're my parents' oldest friends.'

'My mum is a teacher too… French, no way that's my mother's subject…Oh my God, carbonara is my favourite – you'd cook it for me? I'd love that [pats my knee]… I always light up a candle too.'

Okay, so you get the picture. If one of Trisha's TV psychologists had been sitting next to us on that first date, analysing our every move, he could have reached only one conclusion. He would have noted the positive body language, moving closer together, lots of gratuitous touching, smiling and laughing, shy glances etc. Then there's the fact that we seem so similar; our philosophies on life, our interests, we make each other laugh. He would have the audience screaming in delight at, in his opinion, the perfect match.

I don't think I could ever have expected things to go this well. We decide to move from the crowded bar, in favour of some dinner. The second-floor restaurant is full, but the maitre d' assures us there is an excellent table on the third floor. I have eaten here before, on a work lunch, but then the client was paying. The top floor restaurant at Smiths specialises in rare meats and the food is exquisite.

Pigeon breast salad. Half a dozen fresh Cley oysters. Pheasant, shot that day, finished with foie gras. Wild boar and red currant sausages with creamed mash. And two bottles of Tinto di Viejo. On top of everything else, we are full to the brim and decidedly tipsy. The meal has been full of laughter and incessant chatter. I have even learnt a few words of Swedish. Knulle. Pulle. Øl. Skål. Which, in English, means fuck, shag, beer and cheers. In that order, I think. We keep reaching through the various glasses on the table, which look like oversized chess pieces standing on designated squares, to find the other one's hand. It's the sort of scene that a few days ago would have made me feel nauseous. I would have asked myself, does that guy really know what he is doing? Some time soon, he will be getting bored of her, no matter how he feels right now. Now I would shout out, bah humbug, this feeling will never end. How can you have these feelings, so strong, yet poles apart and experience the shift from one to the other, in a matter of days, hours even?

It is because it feels so right that going back to her place seems natural. The proper end to a perfect evening. As we slump into the hackney cab's leather seat, having mustered adequate sobriety to give accurate directions, we huddle up together. For the first time in a long time, I notice the difference between this cab journey and all other similar ones I had taken over the past year. That cab journey to fornication (sometimes). Back then it's what I had worked all night for. The endless, mind-numbing conversations. The feigned interest in the new Karen Millen stall that's opened here or had a sale on there. The inane banter I would make with her annoying friend, while she has gone to the loo. The ridiculous amounts of cash I spent buying her, and aforementioned friend, copious amounts of alcopops. Then you manage to persuade them to go to hers. Hers is always better, that way you can leave when *you* want in the morning. And when you get to hers it's time to reap the fruits of your labours. But no matter how good they are, you always leave unfulfilled.

However, this cab journey is not the same. It doesn't feel sleazy. Sure the good old Rioja has broken down those English barriers, well on my part at any rate. But it hasn't been used as a device, as a means to a carnal end. We've just had a great night. And now we are going home. As a couple.

We arrive at her house in Chelsea. It is so tastefully done inside. There are trinkets on the walls and displayed artistically in Heal's dark wood cabinets. Objects that's she has collected on her travels. An Indonesian doorway, large vases, great silks and an exquisite piece of modern art that nearly fills one expanse of wall. There is a femininity in the walls, yet it is strong at the same time.

'Why don't you get the bottle in the fridge, glasses are in the cupboard next to it. I'm going to put some music on, and tidy the bedroom,' she giggles as she finishes off the instruction. For it is an in instruction.

I watch her slink out of the lounge, her bare feet patting, feline-like, on the Maplewood floor. I trundle off into the kitchen. There is steel everywhere. Pots and pans. An array of implements and utensils. An American-style fridge, the type that puts ice in your drinks – crushed or cubed. I tug at the door. It doesn't move. I try again and nearly go flying backwards. In the door is an already opened bottle of Chablis, must be the one. The wet coolness of the bottle in my hand is soothing. With my free hand I pick up two large glasses. I try and kick the fridge door shut with the side of my foot, as I spin round to leave the kitchen. I miss. I hear that giggle.

Standing there in the doorway is Jennifer. She has discarded her camel skirt and accompaniments. She is wearing a small pair of briefs, the kind girls wear in American teen movies. The ones that look like they should be illegal. She has let down her blonde hair. A little cotton top, white with thin straps, hangs from her dainty shoulders and finishes somewhere above her tummy button. I'm stunned into silence. She can see this. Jennifer walks over, placing a hand flat on each of my cheeks, she places her lips over mine. Her tongue slides into my mouth. It's the first time we have kissed. It's right.

I could say it was mind-blowing, or sweet, or erotic, or phenomenal, or hot. And it is all of those things, and none of them. The best thing I can say is that it was right. You might not know what I mean, but I do. And it is better than all those things put together.

She takes the glasses from my left hand, and slips her own hand into mine. She leads me through into the bedroom, without saying a word. She pauses only to turn out the lounge and hall lights. A faint golden glow emits from the jar in the bedroom door. The pine door that leads from the hall, swings open into her room. There are candles, church candles by their dozen. All shapes and all sizes. A congregation of illumination. The glasses go on the side, together with the dripping bottle. Jennifer stares into me as she unbuttons my shirt. Pulling it back and down over my shoulders, past my arms, she lets it drop to the floor. Before I know it I am naked. She slips the straps off those perfect little shoulders, it slides down past her waist and joins my shirt on the floorboards. I slide my hands down her midriff and under the sides of her briefs.

Have you ever seen a body so perfect that you have to touch it? That first with your eyes, then with your fingers and lastly with your lips you have to map every square inch. To appreciate every slight undulation, to explore each dainty little crease, from peak to fallow. Her skin is silky, a shimmering golden brown as delicious as caramel. If ever there was an Eve she is it, and yet beautiful, most beautifully of all she is totally unaware. That innocent naivety coats her with a finishing gloss of total and utter perfection. To avert your eyes for one moment would be to punish them and insult her.

Someone once said that there are some things about which you cannot speak. They are so fragile, so perfect, that to utter it will cause it to splinter into a million pieces. And so it is.

The morning sun shines like an epiphany through the muslin drapes that cover the renovated sash windows. The golden weft from the sky strays over the face of the girl lying next to me. I lean on one side and gaze at her for a while, as she sleeps. Panda eyes, the odd snuffly snore and a wee damp patch by her lips on the pillow. She looks lovely. I can't help but smile, for the first time I can think of, I feel totally content. I'm not begrudging being here, the morning after. There is no other place I would sooner be. Extricating myself carefully from the white cotton sheets, so as not to wake her, I tiptoe through the beams of sunlight. I pause at the bedroom door to give a glance back at her. I head into the kitchen and put the coffee can on the hob. An image of Dirty Dave's disapproving scowl pops into my head. Knowing he'd be thinking less of me, if he could see me now. Well, screw you Dirty! You can have your Friday night shags. You can keep your endless amounts of nightclub mingers, in fact you can have my quota too. I know what I want, and it's back in that bedroom. And I'm buggered if I can't make her coffee. Now and every other day.

While it's brewing I throw on my jeans and shirt. I unlock the front door and put the keys in my pocket. The silly key fob, in the shape of a Scottie dog, agonisingly digs into my nuts as I take my first few steps down the stairs. I suppose girls don't have to worry about such impracticalities with their key rings. They have those Mary Poppins bottomless handbags, which can take a key fob that the chief screw of the Tower of London would envy. I think to myself, 'There must be a delicatessen or coffee shop round here somewhere.' Luckily, as I emerge from the front door, into the hot morning sun, there is a Greek deli just under the flat. I buy some Danishes, the *Sunday Times* and a copy of this month's *Heat* magazine.

I return to the flat, just in time to find the coffee pot blowing off steam. It doesn't sound happy. There's a stir from the bedroom, followed by a slight groan. I remove the coffee pot from the hob. Instantly its aggression subsides. I find a large plate in one of the cupboards. No one has trays these days – God, I'm sounding like my mother. I place the pastries on the plate, along with a knob of hard unsalted butter and a knife. I wedge the two mugs of coffee in between the Danishes. Impatiently I pull off my shirt like it's a sweater and tug my jeans free of my feet. Holding the plate in one hand and the reading material in the other I wander through the hall back into the boudoir.

17

Kismet

I want to tell you about this bit separately. You see, it was all perfect. Walking back into the bedroom, that morning. It was the perfect morning; unaccustomedly warm. You would have been forgiven for thinking you had awoken in a small Tuscan town. Wandering into the village to pick up some fresh breakfast delicacies. That civilised continental breakfast, prepared for your loved one, your beautiful little *angelita*. That morning we ate breakfast together, in bed. Snuggled up. Laying on top, then under the covers. Ignoring the day outside, in favour of basking in our own happiness and the ability to explore all those great new things together. We didn't leave the room until it was almost dark.

Jennifer and I saw each other several times that week, and the following week. We would meet during the day for lunch, and then arrange to go out the next night. We had often spent the previous night together as well. Normally, if a girl suggests seeing me more than twice in a week I would be running for the door. But I didn't mind. Actually, it was the total opposite. I wanted to see her every evening – okay perhaps not every evening, but most nights.

Then out of the blue, last week, at work, I received this email.

Dearest Max,

I don't know how to tell you this. I will understand if you never speak to me again. I can't see you any more. Not for the moment. I want to be totally honest with you, and I hope that, for this at least, you will forgive me.

Last night, something happened that I could never have predicted. As you know, I think, I recently separated from my boyfriend. We had been together for three years. I was at that friend's birthday. I wasn't expecting to see him there. Someone had told him I had started to see someone new. We had a long chat, all night. He realised he had made a mistake, and said that he loved me. I can't just throw those three years away.

Also I will be leaving for Sweden soon, to complete my Masters. It seems silly to start something serious at this stage now.

I never meant to mislead you. There was definitely something special between us. But how do I know if this will last, I'm confused. I know what I had with John was incredible as well, even if it did have its ups and downs. Please don't be angry, particularly with yourself, it's my fault, and I feel terrible.

Please forgive me.

With love,

Jenn

As I read the first paragraph, before I even get to the second or third ones, I start to feel nauseous. It's awful. But I can't help my eyes falling from the precipice of one word to the emotional crater of the next. I can't quite believe it. This really is the last thing that I could ever have expected. I read on. My surprise, and propensity to vomiting at any second, passes to a feeling of utter anger.

'John' – I don't want to know his fucking name! Of course he's going to say he loves her. He wants her back, and will say anything he thinks that she will want to hear. He's probably had a few weeks in London's dating world and realised how terrible it is, now he wants to get back in her knickers. He wouldn't have nobbled the other girl at the office party if he *loved* her.

But the anger passes as quickly as it flared up. Disappointment followed by frustration. Frustration that I can't make her be with me. Then the anger returns. I don't feel angry *at* her, I am just angry. I don't think anything bad of her, I can't. She's not a cow, or a bitch or any other female equivalent of a bastard. Telling myself such untruths won't make me feel any better, besides I could never believe it. She is everything that I ever wanted. I realise that I love her.

Before I know it I'm laughing, quietly and slightly psychotically. The irony has dawned on me. All this time, I have been looking for a woman on my terms. The fact that I have dated this many women over the past year. It flashes before me, little snippets of each of them. It's like witnessing an outer body experience of my love life over the past year – all culminating with Jennifer. I hadn't had Jennifer on my terms. But with her it didn't matter. She was someone that I wanted more than my completely independent life. My terms went out the window within minutes of meeting her. I suppose that I had reverted to doing what comes naturally. The bloody irony that the one girl that *I* want to have a relationship with, something I told myself I didn't want, is the one girl who doesn't want me. Why couldn't she have been the one pestering me with poems, scrawling her forename and my surname down on her telephone directory or discussing the names of our future babies?

You fucking bastard Ed. I wish you hadn't introduced me to this girl. I was happy. I had got my life on track. No women, no complications. My job was going well. Life was perfect. I was over Jessica. My mind wanders back to the dinner party and to the moment when I first met Jennifer. And then I can't help but smile. Thinking of her asleep, that first morning. Her smudged mascara. Her quivering lips, which she licked while she slept. She kissed me like we were in a Roy Liechtenstein painting. But, if I'm honest, life had actually been better then, with her in it, than previously. I can't be angry with Ed. It's not his fault, in fact far from it. I am looking for someone to blame. I'm glad he introduced us. Even being with her for that brief moment. Even if it is not supposed to be. I don't regret it.

'I can't believe it,' says Ed, as we sit in our usual coffee shop on the King's Road. 'She seemed so into you, you were both so "couapley".'

'Well, shit happens,' Raj helpfully points out. I look at him in a way that shows his helpful observation isn't actually that helpful at all.

'It is just so bloody ironic. I was happy carrying on on my own before Jennifer messed all that up.'

'Are you going to contact her again?' Ed asks.

'No, there's no point.'

'She might have changed her mind,' Raj says, now trying to be genuinely optimistic.

'I don't think so. We chatted about things a bit, she's made up her mind. But it was great.'

'You're nuts,' Ed says. 'If Kate told me that, I'd do everything possible to get her back.'

'I know you would buddy. And that's great. But I've thought about it a great deal over the last week.'

'And?' Raj prompts.

'Well, sometimes you're just not meant to be with someone. But I'm glad I had what I had with her, even though it did only last a fortnight,' I laugh.

I can see that they're looking at me as if I have lost the plot. I try to explain myself.

'For the first time in a long while I felt good about a relationship. The last time I remember feeling like that was when everything had been good between Jessica and I. That's two years ago. Since that went sour and I started dating over the last year, I just felt crap about the whole thing.'

'What are you trying to say,' Ed asks.

I pause for a minute, trying to find the right words.

'That Jennifer restored my faith in relationships, it was as if she awoke some deep emotion inside me, something I had forgotten existed. It was something I hadn't recognised in a long time.'

'That's cool,' says Raj, earnestly.

'And now, when that happens again, I'll be able to recognise it immediately,' I smile at the thought.

'You seem pretty fine about out,' says Ed.

'I wasn't at first bud, but now I really am, more than fine, in fact, I feel great.'

The two of them just watch me as I sit there, staring into space, smiling to myself and feeling very satisfied, very calm.

'How about you, Ed?' I ask, bringing myself out of my own reverie.

'Yeah, everything's good with Kate, she says hi to you guys.'

'That's good,' I say, nodding.

He and I look towards Raj.

'Nineteen. Argentinean. We used her in our last ad. Sweet arse.'

Ed and I laugh. It subsides to silence. The coffee shop is quite busy, but it still has that Sunday-papers-and-coffee feel about it. We all share the moment, together. I sip my cappuccino, this time it has come with the requested sprinkling of nutmeg. Ed finishes his espresso. Raj sucks at his straw, there's a piece of biscuit stuck in it from his strawberries 'n' cream Frappuccino.

'Oh,' exclaims Ed, putting down his miniature coffee cup. 'Did I tell you?'

We look at him inquisitively.

'Kate's having a dinner party tomorrow night. She has two cousins over from Canada. You're both invited.'